within reach

PRAISE FOR *WITHIN REACH*

"A powerful love story, *Within Reach* grips the reader from page one as two soul mates fight against all odds to rediscover each other and prove that death is only temporary."

—JAMES MARSDEN, actor of *The Notebook, Enchanted,* and more

"Ms. Stevens's first novel is so intriguing . . . a romantic fantasy between two separate worlds. Full of imagination, mystery, and possibility, it leaves you with a sense of danger, fear, and hope all at the same time—and keeps you thinking, 'what if . . .'"

—RENE STEVEN, primary school librarian, Brookfield Academy

"*Within Reach* is an elegant and sometimes painful story of teenagers struggling with love, loss, and redemption. Jessica Stevens's unique portrayal of misguided souls finding their way through darkness dances confidently off the page. The story's ending lingers reflectively long after the music stops."

—BRADY G. STEFANI, author of *The Alienation of Courtney Hoffman*

"Jessica Stevens has written a gem of a first novel. With relatable, believable characters, carefully crafted dialogue, and a compelling story, this novel is truly a work of art. All at once it is a ghost story, a mystery, and most of all, a love story—a love story spanning lifetimes. If this book is any indication, I'd say that Ms. Stevens has found her calling, and I can't wait to see what comes next."

—ABIGAIL JENSEN WAUGH, librarian

"Don't pick up Jessica's debut novel unless you have cleared your schedule because you aren't going to be able to put *Within Reach* down. It has something for everyone: A phantom boyfriend with something to prove, a beautifully broken ex-ballerina, and a sexy All-American with a dark secret."

—EMILY NORRIS, blogger at www.godsknot.com

"*Within Reach* is an intoxicating, heart-pounding tale of love, loss, and two souls forever bound by their choices. Xan and Lila are the modern-day Romeo and Juliet—proving that nothing will keep true love apart."

—KRISTEN HUNT, author of *Blonde Eskimo*

a novel

JESSICA STEVENS

Published by SparkPress, a BookSparks imprint,
A division of SparkPoint Studio, LLC
Tempe, Arizona, USA, 85281
www.gosparkpress.com

Published 2016
Printed in the United States of America
ISBN: 978-1-940716-69-5 (pbk)
ISBN: 978-1-940716-68-8 (e-bk)

Library of Congress Control Number: 2015954333

Cover design © Julie Metz, Ltd./metzdesign.com
Author photo © Cheeky Monkey Studios
Formatting by Leah Lococo

Dedication

MATTHEW, KEEGAN, AND CADENCE

My greatest wish for you is that you find that someone who makes your soul vibrate.

SHAWN

Thank you for being that someone.

THIRTY DAYS LEFT

Which is worse: to die or to be the one left alive?

"Xan!"

I don't need to hear her to know she's calling for me. I have no idea where I am or how I got here—here being the epitome of hell—within an arm's reach of my girlfriend, Lila Walker, but not able to touch her. Not able to hear her.

"Lila!" I pound on the thick barrier that separates us. I have to stop her from blaming herself. I need to stop her from wondering if she could have saved me had she done one thing differently.

She doesn't flinch, and my hands should be bruised. They're not. They don't even hurt. I strike harder than the time I shattered the glass when I locked my keys in the car. It's like I'm an exhibit at a museum, watching from behind a piece of soundproof Plexiglas as the world continues on, oblivious to my existence.

Lila has just finished covering my casket with lilacs and orchids. There have to be hundreds of them. With my coffin covered in flowers, she can pretend it's not me being lowered into the ground. She can—even if it's momentarily—push the fear of being forgotten by the person she loves more than life itself out of her head.

I could never forget her. Ever.

The cemetery is reminiscent of a mythical land I read about in eighth grade. I keep expecting Spartacus to jump out from behind one of the unfinished stone structures and threaten Lila with a sword. Snowstorms and sweltering heat have begun to crumble the massive pieces of rock while vines and spongy moss compete to be the one to get to cover the only proof that these people ever existed. “A magical oasis next to the Great Lakes in Milwaukee,” that’s what Lila calls it.

We went to the park next to the cemetery I’m being buried in on our first date two years ago. She danced under the trees, blending in with the swaying branches while I tapped out beats on an old tree stump. She wanted who gets married in this park. Now I don’t know if she’ll ever let the roars of Lake Michigan transport her to that world where she is invincible again.

Where I am now, it’s what I imagine solitary confinement to be like. No, I think even in prison they give you lights. Here I have a tiny window in the otherwise dark realm, a porthole to the present, reminding me what I’m missing. No lights. No sounds. No answers.

I’m not looking forward to nightfall.

“What the—?” I rub my eyes. It doesn’t help. The window is shrinking. Lila is fading. “No!” I try to knock on the glass. I can’t. It’s gone. There is no wall. No window. Just space, lots and lots of dark space.

It takes a few minutes for my eyes to adjust. When they do, I see a new, different light, similar to a big-screen TV. My brother Adam and I made a pact: When our demo got picked up by a record label, we’d get an awesome flat-screen. This is much, much bigger than the one we picked out.

I’m on this giant TV screen in front of me.

The image that flashes across the screen, I remember the day. All I wanted to do was visit Lila, but the stupid hospital receptionist wouldn’t let me through because I wasn’t family. I was pissed.

The picture changes and the receptionist is gone. I'm happy to be looking at Lila, but this isn't how I want to remember her. She looks like a corpse lying in her hospital bed. She was so skinny. My hand goes through her when I try to touch her. I never told her I felt this way, but I believe getting injured saved her life. If she had kept dancing, she'd be the one who is dead.

Before I'm ready to say good-bye, the image changes and Lila is gone. It's me back on the screen. Only this time I'm older than I am now—older than I *was*. Maybe twenty-one or so, definitely not seventeen, the age I was when I died, when I was buried today. The version of myself on the screen has the same body and structure that I had when I died, only my long hair is much longer and lighter and incredibly straggly. I can't be sure, but I think my eyes are green rather than brown. And I'm thinner—scrawny, even. I'm drunk. And dirty.

Another change. Lila's back, and she can't be more than fifteen. Except that her hair is jet black instead of blond, she looks identical to the Lila I met when she was fifteen, two years ago. Why is she covered in blood?

Who keeps channel surfing? "I'd like to see more than a second!" I yell, looking around. Somebody has to be doing this. Magical TV screens don't appear out of thin air and change channels by themselves. The latest scene shows both of us dressed in orange jumpsuits. We have to be over eighteen; those are not juvie jumpsuits. Once again, aside from a few minor feature changes, Lila and I both look the same as we did two weeks ago. A change of hair or eye color, a different haircut, and different styles of clothes—it's like someone has been playing paper dolls with our bodies. The next image catches my attention more than any of the others. There is a tiny baby surrounded by tubes and machines, fighting for her life in a clear plastic box. I know that baby. Why do I know that baby? How can I feel her tiny fingers wrapped around mine?

I try to touch her as she fades. She's gone. The confusing

images of Lila and me have disappeared, but they remain ingrained in my brain.

"Hello, Xan."

I jump three feet in the air when I hear an Australian say my name. I look left to right, up and down. Nobody. A heart that no longer beats thumps inside my empty chest. Adrenaline searches for a living vein to flow through. Together they form a perfect melody of death.

I'm not a fighter, but my fists are clenched guarding my face, ready to strike whatever it is that's coming my way. I have never understood the appeal of scary movies, and now I seem to be starring in one. "I'm not afraid of you," I lie, preparing to defend myself.

His energy surrounds me, holding me in place with its barbed-wire restraint. He is everywhere. "Put your hands down, Xander. Stop being ridiculous," he says. "I'm here to help."

I do as I am told. I lower my hands from covering my eyes just in time to see a featureless figure coming toward me. He looks like that statue of the naked guy thinking, only this guy/thing is not smooth like marble. As relieved as I am not to be alone, I have no idea what he is. Why doesn't he have a face? I touch my face and find I still have my nose, mouth, and eyes. Where did he come from?

"Where am I?" I don't give him much time to answer before asking again, this time less hesitant. "Where am I?"

"You must have done something right, mate. You've been given a final chance," he answers.

I think he just punched me on the shoulder, like Charlie and Adam used to do after I rocked out a song.

"A chance to what?" What the hell is he talking about, and why does his voice sound familiar? I don't know anybody from outside Wisconsin. I don't even know any foreign-exchange students.

"Make it right," he replies, stepping to the side so I can see through the window that has reappeared.

Lila's back.

I breathe a sigh of relief.

Then I remember I'm dead.

"Make what right?" I ask.

He doesn't answer.

He doesn't need to. For some unexplainable reason, I understand his silence, and the confusing pieces surrounding my death come together. "She will never believe it."

"Love will make you do crazy things," he says. "A good drink will make you do really stupid things."

I think he is trying to make me feel better about the situation. I've done stupid stuff before. Lila knows I would never choose to leave her, to put her through this. "She won't."

Again he doesn't acknowledge my need for reassurance. "The girl"—he points to Lila—"the way you look at her, it's as if you are looking at the most spectacular thing you've ever seen."

He isn't looking at me anymore; he's looking at her. He sounds intrigued, in awe.

"She is." Before I met Lila, I don't know, something was missing. I came to life the day she walked into class.

Jason has finished loading the rental chairs into the truck. The only chair left is the one Lila has been sitting on for the past twenty minutes. Everyone else has moved inside to celebrate my short life with cake and punch. Motionless, she watches her future be lowered into the ground, all contained in one big brown box.

My fear of the unknown no longer seems important. I shove past Shadow Man so I can get closer to her, to comfort her. I can't. I can't get past the invisible wall. It is no longer me protecting her from the world; it's him. Jason Montgomery. It's his chest she's clutching. I want it to be my flesh she is digging her nails into. I need to be the one taking away her pain, promising she'll be okay. "It's over, isn't it?"

"Not necessarily." His words of hope interrupt my thoughts

of hatred toward Jason. I've never understood why Lila is friends with him; he's a creep.

The electricity radiating from Shadow Man is less intense. Cautiously, I take another look at the dark, featureless figure that is inches from me. Invisible pins run up my spine as I feel his unidentifiable face studying mine. He is as incomprehensible as the place I am in. I force myself to look away.

"Is it time to make a deal with the devil or something?" I wouldn't think twice about trading my soul for one more day with her.

"Your soul is spoken for. But you do have a choice to make," he says.

I should have known. Mr. Australian Shadow Man is here for business. "Okay . . ."

"Option one: You stay like this." He motions to the nothingness that surrounds me. "You'll be able to see Lila for the rest of her life." He stops me before I can speak. "Until the day she dies, you will see her, not touch her, not hear her, and not smell her."

As he tells me what I feared, an eerie wall of storm clouds moves in from the east in the outside world. I may not be able to hear, but it is clear Jason is trying to get her inside, away from the trees before the storm hits. "Just Lila?" I question.

I've been dead for a while. Twelve days to be exact. All I've thought about is Lila. She is the one I worried about when they couldn't find my body. Every minute I see her, I thank God that I don't need sleep, because I couldn't close my eyes. What if she wasn't there when I opened them? Why haven't I missed my parents? My brother? Charlie, my best friend since kindergarten? Only Lila. I miss her so much. I miss the things that seemed so little, like holding her hand.

He nods. "The connection between two stars that fall at the same time is very powerful."

I'm about to ask where we fell from when images similar to

the ones I saw earlier start playing out in front of me. This time, though, they are not on a screen. They're in my head.

Oh my God. "How is that possible?" I ask, watching more and more recollections fly out of my mental file cabinet. They are memories.

"What do you notice?" he asks. He's a nosy shrink prying for information.

I remember all of it. Every single moment of every life we've lived together. All five. I remember all the mistakes. So many mistakes. "I don't know," I decide.

He crosses his massive arms across his even bigger chest and calls my bluff. "By the look on your face, I am guessing you remember quite a lot."

"What does it mean?" I ask. Why is this the first time I am recalling all of this?

Taking an unnecessary deep breath, he delivers my fate. "It means if you don't get it right this time, it's game over."

The only thing I can offer him is my hands up in the air. I don't know what I would say even if I could speak.

"You just saw five versions of yourself," he continues, sounding like a broken record. Like this is the millionth time he has given this speech.

I did.

"You've used five human lifetimes trying to find your way back." He shakes his stony head. "You always find each other, but then one of you makes a stupid mistake and you accrue more karmic debt. I don't know how you've gotten so many chances."

"Karmic debt?" Where are we trying to get back to? This is not happening. Maybe I'm in a coma. That's it: I'm dreaming.

I must not be doing a very good job disguising my skepticism. He continues to face me, I think. I imagine if he had a face, he would be staring at me with such disappointment and frustration—frustration that I am just not getting what he seems to think is obvious. I feel like he is struggling to find a way to explain the unexplainable. That's the energy I feel. I throw my hands up again, giving him the go-ahead to continue his attempts to make me a believer. What choice do I have but to hear him out? What can it hurt?

After taking a deep breath, he continues, "You lost sight of your true self, causing your divine glow to dim. As a punishment, you were sent to a world of imperfection and temptation to rediscover your purity. Lila was sent at the exact same moment, and as the two of you fell to earth, your souls merged."

This sounds like something I didn't pay attention to in philosophy class because my parents told me to ignore anything that questioned Christianity. "So we're, like, soul mates? Like, literally?" Did he just tell me that I was a star?

"You've yet to live out a full life with Lila. In order to return to your original state of celestial purity, you must be at peace when you die. It's impossible to be at peace when you're missing half of your soul."

"What happens when we die in peace?" I ask, not sure I really want to know the answer.

"You move on to the final realm." He points up, to where the stars would be if I could see the sky.

Is this guy serious? "Reincarnation?" I ask.

I think he is waiting for me to react. I want to tell him he's lost his mind, but if what he's saying is bogus, how am I, the dead guy, able to see Lila, the living girl? And why do I suddenly have a million memories of things that have never happened, or so I thought? "The memories?" It's my turn to ask the questions.

"Anything from previous lives is not easily accessed while you're alive," he starts to explain.

But I cut him off. "Lila's déjà vu." This is insane. It's insane because it makes sense.

"Yes, from past lives," he confirms.

"What's my second choice?" I wonder what could be better than seeing her when I am, well, dead.

"You can have it all. Hear her voice, smell her perfume, feel emotions, and even touch her."

"And?" Wait for it, wait for it . . .

"And you can have all that while you are here. But if you want a chance to live one more life with her, you must find a way to show her that you are still connected, that you haven't left her."

There it is. I think the last time I blinked was five minutes ago. I would never leave her. "What kind of idiot would choose option one?" He may not have any features, but I'd bet a million dollars he just rolled his eyes at me. What's his problem?

"The kind of idiot who likes to play it safe," he snaps. "If you go with choice number two, smart-ass, and fail, you will be judged and be forced to spend the rest of eternity paying for your ignorance. You may never see Lila again."

"Ever?"

Ignoring my question—again—he says what he wants. "Keep in mind that whichever choice you make, you will feel everything your soul mate does until the day she dies. Each time she cries, you will feel her pain; when she is happy, her joy; and when she falls in love again, you will feel that too."

I'd rather suffer for all of eternity knowing I did everything I could to be with her. What about her, what will happen to her if I fail? Is it better to wait sixty years for a guarantee, or do I try? This sucks. It would make my decision so much easier if I didn't have anything to lose.

I have everything to lose.

"You can make it right, Xan."

I can't help but be drawn to the outside world. The wind has picked up and the swells of Lake Michigan are violently engulfing the rocky shoreline. A sliver of sun hovers above the giant churning clouds as beams of light shine out to the exact place where I lie. *God lights*, that's what my mom called them.

My casket is nearly out of sight when I see Jason trip and

fall into the hole. If my coffin were to open, we'd be face-to-face. "Awesome!" I mutter under my breath.

"You made the right choice, Xan." He pats me on the back the way my old band teacher did when I nailed a song no one else could. "Did you see her react when she felt you make that breeze during the funeral?"

I don't know at what point he assumed I was going with option two, but he did. I don't think I would have risked it if I'd had to make the choice on my own. I know I wouldn't have. "I didn't do anything."

"You did. And the light on her hand, nice touch!" he says, voice trailing. "Thirty days isn't going to be a problem for you."

What? I know he's gone, but I yell at him anyway. "How am I supposed to figure this out?" I shout into the darkness, which has once again turned cold. He can't just leave me here. "Coward!" He couldn't tell me I have thirty days to my face? People can't learn a new language in thirty days!

"Xan." Lila's voice chokes out my name. With an impressive amount of strength, she pulls Jason out of the ground so she can crawl in herself.

Does it surprise me to see her curling up in the dirt next to her dead boyfriend? No. She would do anything to be close to me. "I love you," she whispers.

"I love you," I whisper back.

"I will always love you." Talking to my casket, she traces the exact perimeter of my face, as if she can see me lying under the closed lid. "We'll be together again." She gives me one last kiss before climbing out of the muddy hole. "Until then, you are the air I breathe. You have to be, because without you, I can't survive."

I watch her succumb to the tears that have become too much for her to hold off as Jason helps her up and guides her away from me. I don't panic.

I don't panic, because I heard her.

TWENTY-EIGHT DAYS LEFT

I wonder if it's possible to trick death into coming for me. If I look and smell enough like a rotting corpse, will he show up at my door? It's not the dying part of suicide that scares me; it's the possibility of surviving.

"Don't even think about it!" Jason shouts. The boat rocks as he slams the heavy glass door shut. Quickly I put my finger gun to my head and pull the trigger before he gets to my bedroom.

I should have known he'd be here soon, and that he'd know I'd be contemplating my own death. Since Xan died, he's been checking on me daily. He uses an extra-large cup of mint tea as his excuse. Sometimes it's twice a day.

"I'll be out in a sec!" I yell back at him. He can't come in here. I took my clothes off to shower and never made it in. I catch my reflection in the mirror. He can't see my translucent skin clinging to my bones. I look like I've been covered in saran wrap and put in the microwave, my skin suction-cupped to my body, keeping my organs from falling out of place.

I don't need to step on a scale to know that I've lost six pounds. My cheekbones look fabulous. So do my arms.

I pull on an oversized sweatshirt and my favorite pair of stretched-out yoga pants to cover up and stop myself from thinking about how good I would look if I lost a few more pounds. I can't go down that path again. Yesterday I had to add another hole in my belt so my pants would stop falling down.

I knew Jason wouldn't wait for me to come out. "I'd never do it," I say, grabbing the doorknob from inside the bathroom as soon as I hear him hit the familiar creak of the stairs. Habitually, I push the button in to lock the door so he can't reach for the handle and walk in before I'm ready. I hold on to the handle for what feels like minutes before unlocking the door. I wish he would just leave the cup of tea on the stairs and leave me be. Not forever. Just for a little bit.

That will never happen. I open the door to the boy I've known since I was ten. The boy I Jet-Skied with. The boy I played cards with for hours; Uno and bullshit were always our favorites. The boy I used to watch horror movies with every weekend. The boy I've taken countless walks through the marina with. The boy who finally gained the courage to tell me he wanted to do more with me than share licorice, but by then I had found the love of my life. The boy who then never looked at me the same, or told me his secrets again—instead he told them to drugs and alcohol, because drugs don't reject you. I wish I could say I didn't understand why he turned to chemicals, but I do. Things don't hurt you—people do.

I take a sip of the warm tea he's brought me and turn back to the mirror. I used to be pretty. I used to know where I was going, what I wanted. Now I'm broken and have no idea how to put the pieces back together. I don't know where they belong.

"It wouldn't do you any good. Suicide is an automatic ticket to hell." He takes a loud slurp of his coffee.

If he said that to get me to stop focusing on my body, it worked. Even for Jason, that was low. "I'm in hell no matter what I do." If Xan is in hell, I'll happily take a one-way ticket.

The thought of being with Xan again one day is the only thing I can think about. I welcome that time to come sooner than later. I'm sad. Sad. Sad. Sad. I wish I could think of another word, but right now, that's all I can come up with. Okay, maybe

I'm angry, too.

Jason wraps his arms around me. His chin feels nice on my shoulder; it's warm. Someday he'll learn that he can't take back his words. "I can guarantee Xander Hemlock isn't waiting for you in hell," he whispers, twisting my hair up so he can see my long neck and clavicles, the only two parts of my body I like. "Plus, you can't leave me."

I pull away from him and grab a T-shirt of Xan's. I've been sleeping with it since the day he disappeared; it still smells like him.

I keep hitting rewind, going over and over the last few months. What did I miss? Why couldn't I see him suffering? What did I do that pushed him over the edge? Life must have been awful for him. I've been so selfish. I thought I loved him before. That was nothing compared to what I feel for him now. That's what makes this so tragic. If I'd shown him how much I loved him, this could have been avoided. He would still be here with me.

Jason sits next to me on the bed. "It's going to be okay."

I want to cry or yell or throw up, anything to release the pressure inside of me. But I can't. "Why can't I cry?"

"You won't let yourself."

I want it all to come out, to go away. It's so close to the surface, but it just can't find its way out. I take another drink. At least, I *think* I want to cry. "It doesn't make sense."

"What?" Jason asks. He has gotten off the bed and is obnoxiously dousing me and the entire boat with grapefruit body spray.

I fan the thick mist away from my face so I can breathe. "Xan, killing himself."

Jason freezes mid-spritz. I don't think he was expecting me to talk about Xan's death. It's been fourteen days since he went missing. Ten days since they found him in Lake Michigan. Six days since they declared it a suicide. Two days since I watched my reason for living be lowered into the ground. Fourteen days with the awkward white elephant in the room.

"Maybe he had demons you didn't know about." Nervously he fumbles around with the spray bottle, pretending it's suddenly stopped working. He's an even bigger idiot than I thought if he thinks I'm buying it.

No. I knew Xan inside and out. "Does it really surprise you that I'm questioning the fact that he killed himself?"

"No. You stink," he says, pushing past me. Changing the subject, he tells me that the front of the boat is ready for a day of lying in the sun and that if we don't get out there soon, the water bottles are going to be boiling.

Since when does he lie in the sun? "I'm sorry." I stop him from leaving. I weasel my way into his arms and allow his body to warm mine.

I cringe when I catch a whiff of myself. I should be embarrassed. I'm not. Jason and I have been having sleepovers since we were ten. It used to be Jason who kept me company when my parents were too drunk to make it home. Being alone at night has always given me the creeps, especially when I can't see the stars.

I shudder, recalling the day we moved into the house on Lake Drive. Weird things happened in that house. I told myself there were logical, scientific explanations for it all. That's what got me through the night. When my parents split up this spring, I couldn't get out of that house fast enough.

A crash pulls my attention away from my creepy thoughts. "Why did you do that?" I ask, reaching past him to the ledge next to my bed.

"Do what?"

"This." I pick of my favorite picture of Xan and me, which has been knocked over. It was taken the morning after homecoming this year. We'd just woken up: I don't have any makeup on, and he is wearing his favorite Notre Dame hat, which is supposed to be white; it's not. It's a dingy gray because he refused to wash his "lucky hat." It's our eyes that I love so much. We were so happy.

I run my finger over his face and hope by some miracle he will walk through the door and tell me this is all a bad joke. The photo laughs at me. I wish Xan were here to laugh at me. "Why did you knock it down?" I ask Jason without taking my eyes off Xan.

"I didn't."

To his credit, he does look confused. I'm trying so hard not to overreact, but this picture is the one item I would grab if the boat were sinking.

"Honest, Lila, I never touched the photo. I swear."

A cool breeze chills me to the core. The air-conditioning must have kicked in. In the photo, our cheeks are touching. I was safe. I try to remember how it felt to touch him, to feel connected to another human. I can feel something on my cheek, like I am resting on a pillow of ice, which is oddly comforting. The cold air circles my face, and I imagine it's Xan somewhere, somehow, telling me he loves me.

Will I ever be happy again?

"You haven't eaten in days; you're hallucinating."

"You're probably right," I say to appease him. I am still clutching Xan's shirt in my hand. I dread the day his scent evaporates completely. It's only a matter of time before I forget what it felt like to be wrapped in his arms. The sound of his voice will eventually no longer echo in my head. At some point, I will no longer be able to see the eyes that led me straight to his soul.

Out of the corner of my eye, I can see Jason cautiously approaching. My mom and my so-called best friend Hannah left as soon as the funeral was over. They did their duty. Jason stayed. He isn't afraid to give me what I need, even when it's not what I want.

One finger at a time, he loosens my grip on the colorful wooden frame. Carefully, with one hand, he sets it in its proper place on the shelf, wedged between two rolled-up towels so it doesn't fall over when the boat rocks.

I disintegrate into his arms as we collapse onto the bed. His grip is fierce, and I contemplate pulling away. Instead I let him save me from myself.

I am so tired, but afraid to sleep. I am terrified that when I wake up the wounds will somehow not be as fresh, the pain not so potent. The air is like Novocain flowing through my lungs as I take deep breaths. The numbing sensation has been trying to take over since I watched Xan be covered in dirt. I'm not ready for the agony of living without him to disappear, not yet.

I've never been able to resist the sound of water lapping against the side of the boat. Today is no different. Between the rhythmic pattern and the security of Jason's arms, it's not a question of whether I fall asleep; it's a matter of when.

The next thing I know, I'm waking up to the feeling of Xan's body curled up behind mine. No, I can't be awake; I have to be dreaming. How else could I feel his beating heart pressed against my back? Wait, I can hear him breathing. I allow my heart to skip only one beat before rolling over.

"Jason!" My heart sinks in my chest like a bowling ball in the sea.

He has the same look on his face his sister had when I accidentally told her Santa Claus wasn't real. "You thought I was Xan."

He doesn't move, and for some reason, neither do I. Who does he think I thought was spooning me?

"Sorry," he insincerely apologizes.

We've been sleeping together in the same bed since we were ten. We've woken up close before, but today, just now, it was intimate. "It's okay." I scoot toward the edge of the bed and decide not to tell him how furious I am at how the warmth of his body deceived me. How much I thought it was Xan's body pressing up against me. "How long was I asleep?"

Taking the hint, he hops down off the elevated bed. "A couple of hours. You were out cold. Next time I'll sleep in there," he says pointing to the next room. We both look into the room, where there is a set of bunk beds. Tiny bunk beds.

"I don't think you'd fit." He hasn't been able to lie in those bunks fully extended since he was twelve. There is no way he is going to squeeze in now, at seventeen.

I wish I could believe he didn't mean anything by it. I just have this overwhelming feeling that he's happy we woke up in such a compromising position. Our sleepovers have always *started* with me clinging to him, so why does it feel so wrong now?

The clinging usually, okay, always happens after we watch a scary movie. I hate scary movies, yet I watch them anyway, especially with Jason. Afterward, I am too afraid to sleep alone, so he stays with me. He is the one who brings the movies over, even after I started dating Xan two years ago. Now that I think about it, he has always been more than willing to slip into bed next to me. Still, it felt different today. Waking up and finding his leg intertwined with mine, I felt violated.

"You were talking a lot today." Jason adjusts his skin-tight gray T-shirt over his ridiculous eight-pack. He thinks that just because he stopped getting high six months ago that it means he isn't an addict anymore. He is still an addict. He's just replaced weed with weights.

"Nice way to change the subject." I slide down the side of the bed and search the closet for my swimsuit.

"No, really, Lila. It was pretty intense. I had a conversation with you."

"What do you mean you had a conversation with me?"

Jason has been trying to decode my sleep talk since the night I started speaking in French a few years ago. I don't speak French.

He hands me a pair of knit shorts and a tank top. I take them and stop looking for the swimsuit I don't want to wear anyway. It's sweet, and it reminds me that he knows me almost as well as Xan does. I always wear shorts and a tank top instead of a swimsuit.

He pretends to be fixing his hair while I slip off my yoga pants and put on the shorts. He's not fixing his hair. "I thought you were awake," he continues. "We were talking about how crazy it was that you suggested taking the long way around the lake instead of the bridge to Hannah's end-of-the-year party."

I throw my pants at his face in hopes of distracting him long enough to change my shirt. "What did I say?"

Rolling his eyes as he pulls my pants away from his face, he playfully pushes me to the side. "I knew." He says it so quietly I barely hear him.

"You knew what?" Does he know something about that night he isn't telling me?

"Not me, you. You said you knew. Then you started snoring." Picking up the yoga pants I just tossed onto the floor, he tells me, "You should never ever wear these again," and walks out of the bedroom with my pants in hand.

Where is he taking those? Wait. "I knew?" What is he talking about? And why is he paying more attention to my yoga pants than he is to me? The pants can wait.

"Yup, that's what you said!" he shouts from the kitchen.

The sound of cans being moved around in the pantry hypnotizes me. "I knew," I repeat, just loud enough for him to hear me. This feeling, that I am not real, has become more frequent since I met Xan. I try to revel in the out-of-body sensation that has taken over, but the overwhelming feeling of having been here before is distracting me from fully enjoying the numbness.

"Yup." He has come back downstairs holding two different sodas and no pants. I will have to remember to pull those out from the trash when he leaves.

"I knew everything that was going to happen that night," I say after watching a replay of the bridge crumbling in front of me. It's a replay because I've seen it before—not on the news, but in my mind.

"You're not talking about that déjà vu crap again are you?" Jason hates it when I talk about having déjà vu.

But I do. A lot. I knew the bridge was going to collapse the night of that party. I knew something wasn't right. Gasping, I cover my mouth. I feel sick. How did I forget that this happened? "Jason, did I pass out at Xan's funeral?"

"Yup, you dropped in two seconds flat."

Oh, God, it wasn't a dream.

It's not possible.

There is no way I've buried Xan before. The spine-tingling goose bumps are telling me otherwise. The ray of sun that left his coffin and found its way to the promise ring Xan gave me two months ago—what if it wasn't simply a shift of the clouds?

My heart stops. I quit breathing. Unconsciously, I rub my thumb and forefinger together, feeling for the splinter his casket gave me.

There is no splinter.

There is no splinter because it was an unfinished pine casket that gave it to me. His casket two days ago was mahogany.

"Hello, Earth to Lila." Jason waves a Diet Coke in my face.

I can't react. My body is frozen in time. My fingers burn with icy nervousness, and chills reach for the nape of my neck. Logic once again tries to tell me it's because the air-conditioning just kicked back in; the vision of Xan's body peacefully sinking to the bottom of Lake Michigan tells me otherwise.

Xan

TWENTY-EIGHT DAYS LEFT

I can make wind. Let me rephrase that: I made wind, the kind that blows papers off the table and leaves around the yard.

I feel like Harry Potter minus the magic wand. Oh, and I don't have a teacher.

I'd rather have sulfuric acid poured in my eyes than be forced to watch Jason come to Lila's rescue. With me out of the picture there is no reason for her not to fall for him. He knows it. I know it. I know she will eventually fall in love with someone other than me. It just can't be him.

I don't know why I hate the guy. It's not like he tells Lila crap that isn't true about me or throws me under the bus every chance he gets. Oh, wait, he does. I've lost count how many times he's tried to get her to hate me.

I'd like to shove him into a shark-infested tank. It took all I had to not dive off the stage during our concerts and pummel him. I'd watch through the nearly blinding stage lights as he did everything he could to lure her to the side of the room with him. I even caught him trying to grind up on her—repeatedly. Now I can't do anything about it even if I wanted to. I should've knocked him out when I had the chance.

Look at him, staring at her from afar like a crocodile stalking its prey. That or a character from a crime show—the shows that claim they are not based on real situations—the ones that dissect the inner workings of a psychopath. I don't need to be a mind reader to know he's plotting his next move, how he is going to trick her into sleeping with him. How can she be so oblivious?

"Did you see that?" Shadow Man asks, once again reappearing out of nowhere.

"Stop doing that!" In two days, he is the only thing that has approached me, but it still scares the crap out of me when he comes out of thin air.

"Jumpy," he so obviously points out.

You think? I'm locked in a cell that is 90 percent black. I think I have the right to be a little freaked out. "Can you give me some sort of indication you're coming next time?"

He wraps his arm of stone around my shoulders and, as usual, ignores my question to ask his own. "Did you see it?"

"What?" The ass trying to make a move on my girl? Yeah, I saw it.

He points to Lila lying on the beach. Somehow Jason has convinced her to leave the boat and go to the beach. I'm not surprised that they are at the beach, Lila loves the beach. I'm surprised that he was able to get her to leave the boat. "The magazine."

I know. I would be embarrassed getting caught reading that crap too, but seeing which celebrities have cellulite makes Lila happy. "And?" I ask.

I should be looking at the magazine to see which celebrity without makeup he is talking about, but I can't take my eyes off her. Her unusually pale skin has a slight glow. She is sparkling. Her giant black sunglasses cover half of her face. They cover the part that shows she is suffering. She looks fantastic.

"It's open." Shadow Man has impeccable timing for interrupting me when I am craving her the most. He isn't going to leave it alone until I look.

So I do. It's open and facedown. "So?"

"You flipped it over," he says.

If he didn't have that proud-father sound in his voice, I'd tell him he is full of it.

I take a deep breath; the smell of Lila's coconut sunscreen takes the edge off. I got all of my senses back when I accepted the challenge of contacting her. It has been great, but very distracting. I need to kiss her so she knows it's going to be okay. I have to tell her I'm going to fix this. I will fix this.

"I can't believe there aren't more people here," Lila says to Jason. She doesn't move, not even a tilt of her head in his direction.

"It's Tuesday," he reminds her.

Idiot. She wants to talk. He says he knows her better than I do. If that's the case, why can't he read a simple nonverbal like that? Lila doesn't ask for help.

"When you knocked over the photograph, what were you thinking about?" Shadow Man asks, peering over my shoulder.

I don't know. I still have questions of my own. Like, where the hell am I? Why is this our last chance? How did this happen, us being reincarnated and all? Why us?

He plants himself in front of me when I don't answer his question.

"Is everyone reincarnated, or just us?"

He moves an inch to the left, completely covering the porthole. "If you were not going to try, you made a very bad choice, Xan."

"How am I not trying?"

He sounds like Lila's dad reminding me that he knows more than me, therefore I shouldn't ask questions. How can I figure out what I need to be doing when he won't answer any of them? "I don't even know what I am supposed to be trying to do."

Backing away from the window, he lets me see her. "I thought you were a fighter, Xan, at least when it came to Lila. But hey, if you want to let that jerk have her, be my guest." He walks away.

I'm starting to figure out how to tell the difference between Shadow Man's front and back. His face is smooth; it has no texture. The rest of him is rough, like one of those things you make guacamole in.

"Wait!" I shout. He's right. I never sat back and let Jason have her before. Why should now be any different, even if I am dead? She's deserves to be fought for.

He comes back. This time he doesn't stand in front of me; he stands next to me. Silently, we watch Lila. I love it when she unconsciously digs her hands and feet in the sand. I hope she's drinking enough water. She needs more sunscreen; her nose and shoulders are getting red. She needs to start taking care of herself. Jason isn't going to.

It's been two days since I first made things blow around. Doing things the wind can do isn't going to convince her of anything. "I haven't done anything Mother Nature couldn't have done herself," I say.

"If you keep thinking about what you haven't done, how are you going to make what you want happen?" he points to Lila.

Who is this guy? "How is any of this possible?" I ask.

"Do you think it's a coincidence that when you met Lila you had an out-of-this-world, unexplainable connection?"

I never thought about it. But I guess it was kinda weird. I knew within a few seconds of meeting Lila that I wanted to spend the rest of my life with her. I just knew.

"The two of you may keep making mistakes that get you sent back to human form, but you do the thing that matters. That is what is giving you another chance."

"What's that?" I ask.

"You find each other."

"What did I do wrong this time?"

"Nothing. She's anorexic, Xan. She was trying to kill the human form she was given. That's not okay. That body is not hers to kill," he explains.

Then why am I the one who is dead? Not that I wish she was, but if she is the one who made the mistake, why am I here trying to save us?

As if he read my mind, he answers my question. "Once you have repaid the karmic debt you've accrued by living a complete life with your soul mate, you can return to a celestial state of purity. However, your soul must be at peace when you die."

I wasn't at peace when I died. Lila is my peace.

I hate to admit he's right, but he is. I can't change the past, and if I keep dwelling on it, today is going to turn out exactly the same as yesterday, not any closer to showing here I am here.

"Why can't she see he'll never love her?" I ask, jealous that Jason is there with her.

"He's helping her get through losing you . . ." His voice tapers off.

He doesn't need to finish. I know what he is thinking. "He's alive."

"You knocked down the photograph." He holds up his finger, asking me to hear him out, when he sees me start to speak. "What was going on in the outside world?"

He's trying. I'm starting to think there is a reason he hasn't handed me an instruction manual: some kind of self-discovery lesson to be learned.

"He touched her," I answer.

Sounding more upbeat, he clasps his hands together. "How did that make you feel?"

What is this, therapy? How do you think it made me feel? I was mad! I don't want to talk about my feelings! I want to get Lila back! I wanted to punch Jason in the face. While she was falling apart, he was copping feels. He held her much tighter than necessary. I cringe at the thought of him touching her. "Angry." No, he didn't kiss her, but his lips were much too close to her chin for my liking. I don't want to think about his mouth anywhere near her body.

More questions. "Were you angry when the magazine flipped over?"

Yes. I was watching him stalk her from the water. "Is that it? I have to get pissed off?" That shouldn't be difficult, since Jason never leaves her side.

He shrugs. "Jason really makes your skin crawl, doesn't he?"

I get that Jason is pissed Lila chose me over him. I do. I would have been furious if she had chosen him. But she didn't; she chose me. At least, she did then. I lied. I wouldn't have been furious, I would have been crushed.

"How did he react when he found out you gave her a promise ring?"

Jason knew before we told him. I don't know if it was because Lila was talking more than normal or the fact that we couldn't take our eyes off each other when I was onstage. Maybe the ring caught a stage light and he saw the blinding glare. Whatever it was, he saw it, and she winced when he grabbed her hand.

She was too busy looking at me, trying to convince me not to jump off the stage and kill him to see the look of death Jason gave me before running out of the old barn where my band was playing. I could be wrong, but it looked like he wanted to destroy me. Since then, he has tried every day to find a new reason Lila shouldn't be with me. "He tried convincing her that I was a jerk."

"Xan, he can give her what you can't."

The truth burns like rock salt on a fresh wound. Habitually, my jaw clenches, and the invisible adrenaline begins to flow. "You think I like watching her come out of her depression and crawl into his psychotic, manipulative, conniving arms?"

I shouldn't, but I can't help myself from getting closer to the giant piece of rock that is pissing me off. "I want to jump in front of her and tell her I'm here. At the very least, I want to tell her to stay away from him. But I can't! I can't do anything but sit back and watch, because I'm dead!"

I see it happen while coming down from my rant. An unopened bottle of water rolls across the sand and hits her arm. Jason is still in the water. There hasn't been a trace of wind all day. "Don't you see? She's looking for you," Shadow Man says, assuring me that I consciously made it happen this time.

I'll buy that she is wondering how the heck it rolled into her; however, I'm not convinced that she thinks it was me. Not yet. She does seem to be looking for something. No. I can't allow myself to believe it's me she's looking for.

The pleased tone in his voice is similar to the one I used to secretly pray for at night. It's not that my dad wasn't proud of me. He just paid more attention to my brother, Adam, the golden child who could do no wrong—even though Adam barely finished high school and currently works at an oil-change place.

"You did it!" Shadow Man screams, jumping up and down and pumping his fist before clutching me.

I'm not going to pull away from him, even if he is crushing me. He is too excited. I'm trying not to smile. I don't want to get my hopes up. All I did was move a bottle of water. It was pretty frickin' cool, though!

"Doing things that will remind her of you will help her figure it out quicker," he suggests.

The bottle of water; I was always reminding her to drink. She never drinks enough. The picture next to her bed; it's her favorite. The magazines I used to tease her about and the sunlight on her promise ring at the funeral. I wasn't thinking about it, but I've already been doing it. "Do I have to get mad each time?"

He shrugs.

"Did you throw this at me?" Lila asks Jason. She holds up the water bottle, which she has already drained. I knew she was thirsty. Why is she so stubborn?

"Yeah, I carry a spare with me when I swim." He doesn't let her sudden interest in him pass this time and makes his way to the sandbar. He catches the beach towel she throws at him as he gets out of the water. Instead of drying off like a normal person, he shakes off like a dog and drapes the towel around his neck, flexing his abs. I liked him better when he was a scrawny pothead.

He isn't looking at her like he cares what she has to say or that she is finally talking. No, I've seen that look before. I've seen it in myself. I had that look on my face when we got studio time after I was told we'd never get a record deal. She's been an out-of-reach goal of his that just got a whole lot closer.

Lila slaps her ankle and kicks her leg up at the same time Jason starts to sit down. He falls flat on his face. "What the hell, Lila?" he asks as he spits out a mouth full of sand.

"I'm sorry," she says, trying not to laugh. It's nice to see that smirk on her face. He doesn't think it is funny. "I'm sorry, Jason. I felt a spider crawling up my leg, I swear." She looks around the ground for the creepy-crawly that just tickled her leg. When she can't find it, she explodes into laughter.

Her deep belly laugh gives me the fuel I need to keep going. I needed to hear that laugh.

Reluctantly he gives in. "At least I got you to laugh."

Arrogant prick.

She stops laughing. She doesn't want to be okay. She doesn't want to move on. Neither do I.

TWENTY-FIVE DAYS LEFT

Xan and I came here for frozen yogurt the day I was released from the hospital. I freaked out when I thought mine wasn't fat-free. I immediately lost my appetite and wanted to throw my cup of chocolate-vanilla swirl into the trash. But I didn't, because I'd made a stupid promise to Xan that I would stop punishing myself, that I would get better. I am better.

So much has changed since I made that promise. My parents aren't who I thought they were. Finding out my dad was having an affair with my best friend's mom was bad; my mom telling me she was okay with it, incomprehensible. Tracy Kensington, Hannah's mom, has taken over the house I used to call home. My white, fluffy down bed now belongs to Hannah.

Accepting that my ballet career is over hasn't exactly been easy. I will never dance on a stage in New York City. Instead, I am going to have to go to college like everyone else.

Never. That seems to be the only consistent thing in my life: a bunch of nevers.

When Hannah and her mom showed up at my house with a moving van, my mom moved to Chicago to be a flight attendant again. For me it was a no-brainer: I moved to the boat. I was worried my parents wouldn't let me live alone; after all, I am only seventeen and have a habit of finding myself locked up in the psych ward. Then one morning I found a set of boat keys on my nightstand when I woke up. When I went outside, a shiny new Mercedes sat in the driveway. It was their peace offering. I had no choice but to be on my own. The only way I can understand it is that they believe as long as I have a stocked fridge, a place to live, and a bank account fully loaded, I'm good to go. Parents of the year.

My parents never cared before. Why should now be any different?

I'm still trying to get used to the fact that Hannah's the one not coming back to school in the fall. I was the one who was supposed to spend my senior year at the performing arts boarding school. But when you get injured, they give your spot away. They even give it to a person who wants to use her perfectly proportioned dancer's body for Broadway instead of *Swan Lake*.

She got out of Wisconsin. I didn't.

Hannah might be self-centered, but within minutes of finding out Xan died, she booked a flight home. She missed a week's worth of rehearsals. At a ballet summer intensive, that is equivalent to years. Somewhere underneath all that beauty is a heart. Somewhere. Deep, deep inside.

Xan is gone. My ballet career is gone. Hannah is gone. My family is gone.

Gone. Never. Alone.

Jason is the only thing that hasn't disappeared. He's always been here for me. I think we met at the beach; I know we were ten. His dad had a question about repainting the hull of his boat, and my dad obviously had the answer. If it weren't for Jason, I wouldn't have gotten out of bed for Xan's funeral. I'd still be curled up in the fetal position.I should be nicer to him.

Why couldn't my dad have been the one they found floating in Lake Michigan? Nobody would miss him. Not me. Not Mom. Maybe Tracy. I've danced the lead in twenty-five ballets over six years. The last time my dad saw me dance was when I was twelve; I was a snowflake in the Nutcracker. My mom isn't much better. She only came when I had leading roles. I was the prize she put on display to prove her worth. The ladies who lunch are like that.

Neither of them saw the performance that got me accepted into the New York School of Performing Arts last November. I was good—no, I was amazing.

I wasn't the star in my last production, so obviously they were not there. I'm surprised they came to Xan's funeral.

The last few months have been a mess. I was too busy pushing Xan away to think about the possibility of never seeing him again. Why would I? Why would a seventeen-year-old think her boyfriend was going to die? I did stupid things. Xan did stupid things. I did really stupid things.

"Huh," I say to Jason as he holds the door open for me.

"What?" Jason asks, mid-bite of his melting rocky road cone.

"This summer, while the rest of us were acting like complete morons, you actually became a better person." I playfully bop into him as we walk toward the boat.

Jason and I used to be close. Things changed when I met Xan. We both became junkies. My drugs of choice: Xan and ballet. Jason's: marijuana, cocaine, and tequila. I became obsessed with perfecting my body, perfecting every move I made in the ballet studio. Every free moment was spent with Xan. Jason discovered that altering the chemical balances within his mind and body allowed him to feel nothing. Similarly, so did my obsession with ballet. The paralyzing fear of being rejected was too much.

Jason playfully hugs me.

I pull away.

I elbow him in the ribs as hard as I can as he yanks me back into him; then I wrap my arm around his waist and rest my head on his shoulder. I pull myself close. He may be a jerk sometimes, but he knows when I'm heading down a dark path. He knows when I need to be held, even when I don't want to be. "Thanks for being here, Jason."

He hugs me back and kisses the top of my head. "You don't have to thank me."

I back up so I can see his face in the streetlight. "No, I do. I'd still be in bed if it weren't for you." How is it possible that my entire life has come crashing down in the last six months?

Everything is gone.

Lifting my chin, he forces me to look at him. Xan used to do that. Xan never let me run from myself.

"You're not going to lose me," he says, reading my mind.

I wish I could believe him.

We stand awkwardly in silence waiting for the light to turn green. I am about to comment on how chilly it has gotten when I first see it. I couldn't turn away if I wanted to. An electrical force pulls me away from Jason toward the fluorescent light across the street that reads *Psychic*. I don't bother looking for cars as I cross the street to the eerie building nestled between two flickering streetlights.

"Lila, no!" His voice wakes me from my hypnotized state. "You are not going to see a psychic!"

I pretend not to hear him. Maybe she will be able to explain why this all feels wrong. Déjà vu is one thing. Feeling like I've buried my boyfriend before is another.

"Stop!" His heart is racing; I can hear it beating in his voice.

"You don't have to come," I say before walking toward the dazzling sign I swear is calling my name.

"You'll believe what she says." He sounds desperate to keep me from walking into that house.

His strong body touches me from behind when I pause briefly. "Why is that a bad thing?"

He breathes down my neck like a hungry lion.

I'd like to think he isn't saying anything because he's trying to find the right words, but Jason never thinks before he speaks. He blurts out whatever comes to his mind. No, he's not thinking; he's avoiding saying something, and it's starting to piss me off.

"Spit it out!" I spin around so I can see his face when he says whatever it is he doesn't want to say. A thin layer of air is all that fits between our noses. "You've never hesitated saying what you want before—why start now? Say it!" I yell, pushing him away from me.

He doesn't get very far before yanking me back in. "What if she says something about Xan's death?"

"Jason, you're brilliant!" What if she *can* tell me something about his death?

His breath reeks of chocolate. "What if she makes up something about how you could have saved him? What if she says that if you knew how to use your déjà vu dreamy thing you could have saved him? How are you going to feel then? Or what if she implies something about your future that you don't want to hear? I just don't think it's a very good idea, Lila."

Why would he say that? In all the years I've known him, he has never brought up my déjà vu. Why would he even suggest that it was my fault? Yes, I've thought it, but that's for me to think, not for him to say.

I back up the steps. I don't want his hands on me. "Do you remember that time on the beach when we played light as a feather, stiff as a board and the Ouija board?" I take his blank stare as a no. "We were fifteen." It was two weeks before I met Xan.

"Oh, yeah, I forgot about that."

"You forgot about it?" Some seriously freaky stuff happened that night, and he claims he doesn't remember? It was the first time he looked at me like I was a freak. I haven't been able to go near a Ouija board since.

"Lila, it's a piece of cardboard and a plastic cursor." I try to ignore the mockery he is so diligently trying to hide. "Our hands were shaking. That's what moved the cursor," he insists.

Why am I the only one who believes something happened that night? I'm not getting anywhere. I'll try the other game.

"Jason, you were holding my head; your sister, who was eleven, sat on one side of me; and Brian, who weighed less than I did, sat on the other side. You seriously believe the three of you lifted me above your heads with two fingers?"

"You weighed like eighty pounds."

My weight had nothing to do with it. He can't ever admit he is wrong. The dumbass liar just said he didn't remember that night. I don't know why I am compelled to make him believe in any of it. But I am. It's a compulsion and I can't stop. "Jason, it was only the two of us playing the Ouija board! We were barely touching the cursor when it shot across the board back and forth. It answered our questions."

Let's say he could explain that; how would he explain the fact that it levitated? I'll save that refresher for another day. Even in the dark of night, he looks pale. I am going to take that as a confirmation that he has just remembered how things really went down. "How often do you think about that?" he asks.

More than you want to know. I think about taking his arm and letting him lead me back to the boat, forgetting about the psychic, and watching a movie. Not because I don't want to go in, but because this is the first time Jason has asked me a sincere question since that night two years ago. I've missed him.

"Jason, something isn't right about me." I mean, why am I the only one who felt the cool breeze at the funeral and in the boat the other day? "Why did my favorite picture get knocked down, and how did the water bottle know to roll to me the very moment I thought, *I'm thirsty*? If my déjà vu is from dreams I've had, why do I get the feeling something isn't right about Xan's death?"

The unseen magnetic force of the neon light begins pulling at me again. I allow it to bring me toward it, and I open the screen door. A wind chime makes our presence known.

The panic in Jason's face is out of place. You would think I'd threatened to tell his mother he started smoking pot again.

He looks petrified and is holding on to my hand too tightly. "Couldn't you call the psychic hotline or something?" he asks.

I pull my hand out of his and apprehensively push the main door open. No doubt about it, this place is creepy. I choke on my own spit when I see her standing in the hallway. Panic and regret surge through my body like a pinball on the loose attempting to score as many points as possible before falling into the gutter. I am going to get myself killed.

That wouldn't be so bad.

Her smile is somewhat unnerving, like she has been expecting me. More necklaces than I can count adorn her neck. Each strand of beads has a specific meaning, I suppose. I once wore six different-color beaded bracelets, hoping they would bring me the strengths I wished to acquire. The headscarf she wears isn't a bold enough pattern to distract from her disgusting mouth full of rotting teeth.

"Welcome, my children. I am Madame Tula. Come." Her rich voice puts her into the stereotype movies have imbedded in my head about psychics and witch doctors. I'd recognize her thick, almost-impossible-to-understand accent anywhere. It's Russian. It's the same voice I've been decoding since I was twelve, when Marina first came to the ballet school to teach. I suddenly feel less nervous.

I look behind me as she guides me through a narrow hallway lined with ancient artifacts. Jason is following. Thank God. The house smells good. Incense. Xan's room smelled nearly identical: lavender and vanilla.

She leads us into a small, cold, and empty room. One large round rug sits in the middle of the cement floor. A well-used red candle burns in the center of the room. "Sit," she instructs. She sits on a smaller rug close to the candle. We sit on the opposite side, on the freezing cement floor, very, very close to each other.

She isn't saying anything. She hasn't taken her eyes off me

since we sat down. It is really dark in here. "I'm Lila and this is Jason," I say, unable to take the uncomfortable silence any longer.

Squinting, she speaks. "I know, dear. I knew that you would be back." She lights more candles.

The familiar, comfortable feeling her voice was giving me is gone. I'm not sure what scares me most: the fact that she thinks she knows me, her swollen gummy smile, or her eyes that now penetrate me without the slightest waver.

I take a deep breath and match her stare. I wait for her confidence to falter. Without words, I tell her I've never been here. That maybe she has seen me at the ice cream shop across the street. I've been going there since I was eight. Has she been watching me?

She continues to invade my personal space with her eyes. Instead of growing more uncomfortable, I'm beginning to relax again. She is trying to find a way to tell me something. It's no longer Madame Tula herself that makes me nervous; it's what she might say.

I should have listened to Jason. He was right. I was wrong. I don't want to know what happened to Xan that night.

Madame Tula has started a tarot card reading for Jason. He's fully engrossed. "What's up?" he finally asks when he notices I am no longer sitting next to him, but standing behind him. He doesn't look away from the cards she has flipped over.

I hate walking out of a store not buying something, especially when I am the only customer. This is the epitome of that. I'm trying to be subtle about wanting to leave and he is not getting it. He is sitting there staring at me like I'm speaking Japanese. "You were right. Let's go."

He doesn't move.

Are you kidding me???!?! Get your ass up! "Fine. I'll wait for you outside." I give him a nasty glare. I can't believe he is going to let me walk out of here alone. What if she has a trusty sidekick on the other side of the door waiting to chop me into pieces?

"When the two of you calm down, come back and we will talk about why you really are here." Her tone of voice startles me. I should have known better than to think I might get away without her trying to get me to buy something. She no longer sounds like the lovely ballet teacher I pretended she was. The pleasant charm is gone, and the harshness that has replaced it sends shivers up my spine.

A lump of terror closes off my airway. I don't turn around. I can't.

"I'm fine," Jason says.

She chuckles deeply. I'm not sure if she is amused because Jason is an idiot or because she knows I know what she is talking about. Whichever it is, I'm missing the humorous part. "Not you, dear." She seductively touches Jason's leg, never taking her eyes off of mine. "Your pain is breaking my heart, Lila."

I turn to find her long, crooked finger pointing first at me, then I watch as she moves it to my right, where there is nothing but open space. "And the beautiful boy standing next to you, he is filled with so much anger."

I gasp. I didn't mean to; it just happened.

"Do not be afraid, my dear." Her eyes grow wider by the minute. She pauses, and I wait.

I wait to hear her tell me how much Xan loves me. How much he misses me. My heart feels bruised from trying to escape from my chest.

"He has an unnatural amount of love for you. Deeper love than I have seen in all my years," she says instead.

Goose bumps attack my body over and over again.

"What is she talking about?" Jason looks up at me and then to her.

"It cannot be," she continues. Her hands cover her mouth as her doubt turns to glee. "There is a force between you not of this Earth."

I know I should be freaked out, terrified, even. But I'm not. I'm the exact opposite. Everything suddenly feels right. I sit back down next to Jason—who, by the way, is filled with shock, confusion, and, dare I say it, fear.

Madame Tula blows out the candles and folds up the mat, which contains all of her supplies: tarot cards, stones, magical things. I wonder if she saw my heart drop. She crouches down close to me, so only I can hear. I don't flinch when her icy hands touch mine. "For you, my dear, I do not need magic. You are the one who brings the magic to the table tonight."

I don't know what I expected to find when I came in here, but it wasn't this.

Xan

TWENTY-FIVE DAYS LEFT

Ten minutes ago I would have agreed with Jason: nothing good could come of Lila seeing a psychic. But somehow, instead of being a total disaster, this creepy old Russian woman might be what I need.

Lila can see her.

She can see me.

I can see both of them. I wouldn't have wasted the past six days trying to find a way to contact her if I'd known psychics actually worked!

"Tell me, dear, when did it start?"What's really weird is Lila hasn't said much, yet Madame Tula knows what to ask. "Tell me, dear. When did it start?" she repeats.

"When did what start?" Lila is picking at a zit on the back of her neck. She picks when she's nervous. Lila knows exactly what Madame Tula is talking about.

"When time stops," Madame Tula clarifies before pausing just long enough to get a reaction out of Lila. She wants her to look at her. No! It seems she *needs* Lila to look at her. "When you're sure you've been somewhere before, yet it's impossible."

Lila doesn't hesitate. She begins to divulge information she usually keeps to herself. "I was twelve." She looks at Jason. "It was winter. We were skiing." Lila points to herself, then to Jason, in case there is any confusion as to whom she is talking about. "The snowflakes hovered around us as the chairlift stopped. Silently, it swung back and forth. I could have sworn I'd been there before, on that chair, watching people effortlessly glide down the hill in slow motion. I could hear the fresh snow squeaking under their skis."

Jason scoots closer to her and wraps his arms around her waist. She doesn't push him away. "You never told me that."

"You'd have thought I was crazy," Lila says to him. "It was our first time skiing together and I had a crush on you."

Did she just blush? I crouch behind Lila and try to hug her. My arms go right through her torso. Wait. I'm not behind the glass wall! I'm not trapped in a box. When did this happen? I'm in their world. They can't see me, but I'm here, sitting next to her. I hold my hand above her thigh. The heat radiating from her body warms my cool hand. My fingers sink under her kneecap as I try to rest my hand on her leg.

She straightens out her leg. Did I do that? I do it again. Nothing. Shadow Man was right; it's like I am with her. Only she can't see me or feel me or hear me, and, oh yeah, I'm dead.

I stretch my arm out to push Jason out of the way. I can't get close enough. He has some sort of protective armor surrounding him. Damn, I can't rip his heart out. And my hand hurts from trying.

Lila is much braver than I thought—brave or desperate. Madame Tula is scary and dirty. Lila hates dirty people. Madame Tula smells like stale patchouli oil, and I don't even want to think about what has accumulated under the scarf she is wearing on her head, which looks like it's never seen soap.

What if I'm wrong and she can't see me? Just because she can read Lila like a book and knows I'm angry doesn't mean she can see me. I wave. Is she looking at me? She is. She can see me. Can she hear me? "Hi," I say.

If her bug eyes bulge any more, they are going to pop out of her head. She's freaking out, hyperventilating. The woman lives in a house that has to be at least a hundred years old. Her choice of décor includes jars of eyeballs, organs, and who knows what other kinds of gooey crap. I find it hard to believe that she is afraid of dead things. I'm willing to bet one of my days that she didn't buy those teeth hanging around her neck.

The bewildered psychic looks between Lila and me. One, two, one, two, left and right, left and right, it's rhythmic.

"You can hear me, can't you?" I ask, standing and taking a step in her direction.

I take her breath away. She grins, and without taking her eyes off me, she questions Lila. "Why did you come here?"

She wants to know if Lila knows I'm here or not. Why? "Why haven't you told Lila I'm here?"

All she has to say is, "Hey, your dead boyfriend is standing right behind you!"

Madame Tula looks at me with a sneer that would scare the devil. "Shhhhh," she hisses.

Lila and Jason look at each other, confused because neither of them said anything shush-worthy.

"Come closer," she orders them as she offers each a hand.

They do as she requests. Together, the three of them hold hands. Why does she need to summon the dead? I'm already here! Madame Tula closes her eyes and chants something. When she finishes, she drops their hands and tells them to leave. "Thank you for coming, my children."

Wait! "No! No! You can't be done!" I scream, jumping in front of Lila, trying to stop her. She walks right through me. Why isn't Lila saying anything? She knows it's more than a coincidence that Madame Tula knew about me and her déjà vu episodes. Doesn't she?

All I need is one tiny slip from Madame Tula. Just one. And Lila will know I'm here. "You hear me and I know you see me."

She doesn't flinch.

Maybe if I block her she will acknowledge me while Lila is still here. "Tell her I'm here!" I step in front of Madame Tula.

Like Jason, she walks around me.

"Please! Please! Tell her I am here," I beg.

She continues to ignore me. Lila hesitates before walking out the door. She knows something weird is going on; she just doesn't know it's me. If she did know, nothing could make her walk out the front door.

Madame Tula practically pushes them out and doesn't waste a second locking the door once Lila's feet hit the pavement. Jason looks relieved to have made it out alive and is trying to get Lila away as quickly as possible.

I don't blame him. First smart move he's made with her.

Wait, she didn't make them pay. What kind of psychic doesn't make someone pay?

Unnaturally, Madame Tula cranks her long neck around so she can see me. She didn't make her pay because she found something much more valuable than money.

Me.

She baited Lila. She gave her the tiniest taste, just enough to make her want to come back for more.

"You," she says, jutting her crooked finger at me. "When I tell you to shut up, you do it. Your incessant begging just won't stop."

The endearing accent is gone. Now she sounds like she is from the Bronx. She circles me three times before walking through a beaded doorway. "What took you so long?"

Like Lila, I've seen the neon sign. I've never been here either. I make sure we stay on the opposite side of the street. People like us don't go into places like this unless we have a death wish. I follow her. "Why didn't you tell her?"

"Why don't you?" she throws back at me. My words effortlessly rebound off her as she slams a stepladder against the wall. Rows and rows of shelves line the room.

"She was right there; you could have told her." I try not to sound like I don't know what I am doing.

Madame Tula speaks quietly to herself. "Ah, that's right. You're down to twenty-five days, aren't you?" She peers over her shoulder in between rummaging through the shelves.

"How do you know that?"

She climbs down the ladder with half a dozen bottles in hand. One by one she dumps them into a pot and mixes together the pink goo, red powder, brown slime, what appears to be sand, black sticks, and bleach. "I told you, I've been waiting for you."

The concoction seems to boil instantly, and she takes the pot and then pours it over ice. The steam rising isn't white; it's black like a shadow—it's the color of death. "Lila already knows."

No. She *wonders*. I need her to *know*. "Please." I don't know what else to do but beg. I know shortcuts are never the right way to do things, but this is different. I'm not asking her to do all the work for me; I just want her to help Lila see I'm not gone.

She turns to me, holding two glasses full of sludge in her hand. I take one as she raises her glass, giving me a toast. She doesn't appear to be concerned about my luck. Her mouth opens; she pours the liquid onto her tongue and allows the mixture to crawl down her throat. One gulp and it's gone. "You help me. I help you," she proposes before wiping her mouth.

"Me?" It's the only word I can get out before she grabs my cheeks, squeezing them together, forcing my mouth to open. The mixture is hideous and, as soon as I swallow, my organs begin to spasm. Every twist of my stomach brings me closer to my knees. As poison begins spewing out of my mouth uncontrollably, I can barely move and can't help but think this is the end. I know I'm supposed to be dead, but this reaction is very human.

Cackling uncontrollably, she hovers over me. "Do you know what this does to you?" Circling me like a hyena on its prey, she points to the pool of black tar that sits in front of me.

I am too weak to get up but I find the strength to utter a few words. I'm not sure she will be able to hear me. "What do you want?"

She pours another potion over the top of my puke. I watch it bubble and turn into vapor. "You want me to tell your sweet Lila that you are here so you can live happily ever after, right?"

I nod.

"Then you will give me what you have."

"I'm dead." What could I possibly have that she wants?

If she can bring me to my knees with a simple drink, what is she going to do to me when I can't give her what she wants? Twenty-five days is not enough time to save Lila. Now I have to add this psycho to the mix?

"Leave, Xan," Shadow Man warns from somewhere in the distance.

I don't see him. I feel his energy. "She can help me." Though she may scare the crap out of me. "She can tell Lila I'm not gone."

"Xan, leave now." His energy is stronger and more hostile than I've ever felt. He is filled with rage. A kind of rage that is ready to destroy. I don't move, partially because I'm not sure I don't want her help. Plus, I can barely lift my head I'm so weak.

Shadow Man doesn't waste any more time before yanking me from the familiarity of Wisconsin and throwing me back into my box of darkness, where once again I am left with nothing but a tiny window. "You are the only one she can see," he tells me once we are alone.

He offers to help me up. He's calming down, but I keep my distance.

"The psychic?" No way am I the only nonhuman thing she can see.

Taking a deep, airless breath, he explains more clearly the things he should have the day I first met him. "When a soul loses sight of why it exists, its purity is tainted, causing it to fall. The soul is forced to rediscover what makes it shine if it wants to return to its original state of purity."

He continues, "A single life isn't enough time to fix the karmic debt the two of you have accrued. Think of it like this:

Your parents told you what goes around comes around when you and your brother would fight, right? That if you hit your brother, he would come back and hit you twice as hard. Same concept here, but on a much, much grander scale. Every wrong the two of you have ever done, to yourself or another person, in every life you have lived, has built a mountain of wrongs that must be righted. Every time you told a lie or committed a crime, you betrayed Lila or she betrayed you. Everything counts—think the seven deadly sins. It's a snowball effect, and the two of you have built the world's largest snowman." His gaze narrows, "remember, this is your last chance, Xan."

"Why now? Why is our run over? Not that I'm complaining about having so many chances to spend all of eternity in peace and happiness with Lila."

After a brief pause, his demeanor changes. I still can't see his face, but I feel like he is looking at me with a puzzled yet enlightened look. "There is no way for another chance," he says through a deep exhale.

"Then why us, why have we gotten so many chances?"

"If two souls merge that were created for each other, it creates an unbreakable bond. I've seen dozens of souls that fall at the same time and merge." He stops to, what I can only assume is think. "Not one of them has gotten more than two, maybe three chances at life to clear their karmic debt and be returned to the sky with their soul mate before their lights go out completely."

Lila and I passed lifetime number three decades ago. "Assuming I succeed, we will be living life number six."

He is pacing now, aggressively grabbing the hair on top of his head that is not there. I wonder if it feels hard when he touches himself or if it feels normal—whatever normal is. "If you are true soul mates, you sure as hell better not mess up this time or you'll never see each other again. You are being given one last chance to get it right, to not do something stupid. Just love each other, love life, don't worry about the rest of it. Most importantly, don't screw up."

"Why six? Why not one or three or twelve?"

"When a single star falls from the sky, it simply fizzles out. When two stars merge on the fall down, their light doesn't go out completely. They have a slight glow that keeps them alive. Each life and death causes the light to dim, until it eventually goes out. I've never seen a pair that have merged last more than three lives before their lights go out," he says, sounding like he's not quite sure he believes what he is saying.

"Until us?"

He nods and continues. "When souls merge that were created for each other, there is nothing more powerful in the universe when they are together. Separated, each soul is incredibly vulnerable. There are five points on a star. Each point represents a chance, a lifetime to find the other half of the soul and live that life to completion. Each of you dying a natural death. Simply being together, not sinning, being honest and true to who you are, is what will slowly clear that debt. It can only be cleared when the two of you are together."

It's a team effort. Lila and I are an amazing team; this makes me smile. I can't believe this is starting to make sense. "The psychic, she can see our glow, can't she."

"Yeah, I've never seen anything like it. The fact that you are dead and Lila is alive appears to have no effect on the glow. It lit up like a firework on the Fourth of July the second the two of you were in the same room."

His disbelief now looks like happy confusion. Like he can't keep up with the slew of information that appears to be flooding his brain. Does he have a brain? Do I still have a brain? I make a mental note to ask him about that later. I'm not sure now is the time to start asking questions unrelated to Lila and me and souls and eternal lights. "But then why are we getting a sixth chance if we completed the star?"

"Let me finish," he says, not with authority but rather with a need to hear out loud whatever is running through his head; he needs to hear it himself to believe all of this. "I never said it was completed. Each one of the five lives you have lived already"—he chuckles, then finishes his thought—"you started those off with a blank canvas. It should have been easy to find each other and not screw up."

I take the hand he has extended in front of me. I am regaining my strength quickly, but I am a long way from being able to stand up on my own. "You said all the stupid-ass things we've done over the years are going to come at us twofold. Wouldn't the first or second life have been the only easy ones?"

"The karmic debt, it's like a cancer. It doesn't go away on its own. When it's not treated properly, it grows. It spreads. Eventually killing you. So yes, each time you begin a new life, it becomes more difficult. Each time your human bodies die, all the karmic debt, the mistakes you made in that single lifetime, are taken from your individual souls and are added to the already massive pile of mistakes you have made in previous lives." This dims your individual lights and increases the light when you are together, the completed soul."

"But you also said our lights dim with each life and death."

"Karmic debt is poison to pure souls. The light is taken from your individual soul and because its toxic, with it lingering in your system, moving on to the next life would be impossible. So, the karmic debt is taken from you as individuals and is placed, along with Lila's karmic debt, in space, next to your completed soul. It's being redistributed to a place where it will remain until the two of you come to defeat it, to overcome and destroy the debt together. When the two of you are physically together, and can defeat the accrued debt, the soul will then be returned to its purest form. The soul will be complete. The two of you together is what the soul was created for, and it begins to rejuvenate you, giving each of you some of your individual light back, giving you strength."

He looks like he has more to say. "But?"

He shakes his head no. "When your soul is merged with Lila's, it will give the two of you indestructible strength."

There is more than a hint of fear in his voice he is trying to mask. Isn't that a good thing?

I follow Shadow Man's lead when he sits down and leans against the tiny window to the outside world. We sit together, side by side in silence. Although if we could crack open our heads and hear what was going on inside, it would be louder than any show I've done. It might be louder than all the shows I've done combined. "If I succeed and Lila and I get this final chance to be together, we will not only have to find each other, but we'll have to do it carrying all the negativity and karmic mistakes we've made in our previous lives?"

His body slumps a little lower.

"Impossible." It's impossible. We've tried five times already and we couldn't do it. Five times we've tried entering with a clean record. How are we going to succeed when we have every bad thing we've ever done trying to prevent us from being together?

Shadow Man is still eerily quiet. Either he doesn't have anything to say or he doesn't want to say what he thinks. It's probably only been thirty seconds, but it feels like ten minutes have passed. I keep waiting for him to say something, to lean his heavy stone body into mine and reassure me that we don't have anything to worry about. That our love is so strong it can conquer anything that is thrown at us.

He doesn't reassure me. He doesn't even attempt to encourage me. "Are there others, like Lila and me?"

He subtly shakes his head, which is now tightly cradled by his giant hands. "There can only be one complete soul on Earth at once."

"If I somehow convince Lila that her dead boyfriend is the one making all the weird things happen around her and we get one final chance as humans to come together and purify our souls so we can be together forever, what happens when we die the last time?" I'm not sure I want to know the answer.

"You don't die. One of two things will happen. You will both be enlightened and spend the rest of eternity together, or you will be cast into eternal suffering, separately."

Is this some kind of sick game God likes to play with us mortals? Maybe it isn't God; maybe it's the devil who did this. Am I even mortal? "What happens if I can't do it?" I don't plan on failing, but let's be real.

"If you fail to convince her that you are still here with her—which you won't—you will be put on Earth again immediately. You will not hang out here until Lila dies so you can be put back into human form for your final life together. Lila will not know who you are. You won't know her. You and she will live your lives out, most likely separately. The cycle of reincarnation will be broken, and your chance at spending all of eternity together will be gone. Your destinies will be redecided before your souls are placed into bodies for the final time."

"How will my soul not recognize its other half?"

"If you fail, the two souls that created that perfect union will become individuals, no longer two parts of a whole. You and Lila will be given back whatever karmic debt and memories belong to you. When the lights are given back to the owners as individuals, it weakens the complete soul, causing it to fade, completely. The perfect, complete soul will naturally destroy itself—out of sadness and devastation. Any memory the two of you will have about each other will be too weak to recognize what was once the thing that kept it alive."

Cutting him off, I ask, "What if we do find each other in the next life, after our perfect complete soul has been destroyed?"

"Even if you do find each other, and by some miracle it

works out, the best-case scenario will be that you get to live the rest of that life together. When the two of you die, that will be the last time you see each other. Two more stars will be dropped to Earth and given a chance at eternal happiness with their soul mate."

Seventeen days since I died. Seventeen days without Lila has been torture. I can't stomach the thought of spending an eternity without her. "And if I do get her to see me in time, what then?"

"*When* you do," he corrects me, "the two of you will be placed in holding until it is time to return to Earth for your final chance."

"Where we won't know each other," I add. This is all so messed up. "Will we know each other in holding?"

He nods. "In holding, not only will you be together, but you will remember everything you've ever lived through. There, you have a chance to figure out what you've been doing wrong. You can make a plan."

"A plan?"

"You have to have a plan, Xan. Once you get back into human form, you won't remember anything! The only difference from all the other times is that your memories will be more easily accessed. It will be easier for you to find each other and, hopefully, not make mistakes."

Lila and I knew the second she walked into Public Speaking 101 that someone or something brought us together. We never thought to question it. "You want us to win."

"Almost everyone wants you to win." He has a bit of the anger like when he found me in Madame Tula's house.

"What if we mess up again? We've done it five times—what's stopping us from doing it again?"

"Don't."

Easier said than done.

"Don't you want to live your lives out the way they were

intended, together? Then when you are old and your physical bodies can't take it anymore, you will die. Your souls will be transported to another realm, where your eternal glow will be returned. That is where the two of you will remain for the rest of time."

I have to get us back there. Is that why we liked to look at the stars so much, wondering where the moonlight would take us, because we are stars? "Are there others in the realm we will be going to?"

"Everyone who has succeeded before you."

"Do you have a name?" It would be nice to call him something other than Shadow Man, which implies evil. After today, I see he is anything but.

"Wesley. Call me Wes." He extends his hand.

I shake it, and to my surprise, his hand of stone feels human. "Okay, Wes, how do you know so much about all of this?"

"I failed."

TWENTY-FOUR DAYS LEFT

How people believe in something they have no proof of is beyond me. Trusting that an invisible force has a master plan for all of us sounds like the definition of insanity. It's not that I don't believe in God; I do. I just think hard work and sacrifice gets you what you want, not sitting around praying for it.

I thought churches were supposed to be safe zones—you know, evil can't cross over the threshold and all. That's how it is in the movies. This isn't the movies. Something is definitely lurking in this hallway. Something other than these disturbing statues is definitely watching me voluntarily walk into its lair, where it will no doubt come to life and attack. A ripple of ice runs up my spine. I turn. Nobody. My paranoia about being watched has become a constant since Xan died.

A piano is playing Pachelbel's Canon in D in the sanctuary. The stained-glass windows are the only source of light. If it's a cloudy day tomorrow, the guests of this wedding are going to need night-vision goggles to see the bride. It's a shame; she's pretty.

I peer around a large marble pillar and watch as the happy couple rehearses their vows, practicing words that are ultimately just that: words.

"Lila?"

Crap, Pastor Gary has spotted me and is coming in my direction.

"Are you here to see me?" He looks at his watch and tries not to look annoyed; it's almost six. I nod. I probably should have called first. "We'll be finished in a few minutes. You can wait in my office if you'd like," he offers as he is guiding me out of the chapel.

He wants me to think he's being polite. He's not. He wants me as far away from this wedding as possible. He doesn't trust me. I don't blame him.

I don't like the fact that he knows my name. I like it even less that I know where his office is.

I'd never been to this church before I met Xan, other than when I was baptized. "It might help to talk to someone other than a therapist," Xan used to say. He wanted so much for me to see that my life wasn't over. That just because I couldn't dance anymore didn't mean there wasn't a future of possibilities ahead of me. I think he hoped that Pastor Gary could bring back the passion and faith I used to have in life. It was sweet of him to try.

I never told him that talking to Pastor Gary did help. I'm still not sold on the whole "There is good in all the bad that happens to us" spiel. But he is more inspiring than my shrink. It's all pretty much the same, though. Dr. Jacobs tries to fix me with psychobabble from his medical books, while Pastor Gary tries to heal me with words of inspiration from the Bible.

The church raised Xan. Not literally—it was just always a huge part of his life. His mom is a youth pastor and his dad runs the business office. There are pictures of Xan in the church nursery from when he was like two weeks old. Xan got the whole God thing. His parents taught him that if he had faith and gave people a chance, he would find that everyone is essentially good.

My parents taught me that when you think things can't get any worse, you're wrong.

I stopped going to my shrink when he asked me what I wanted to be doing ten years from now. I wanted to strangle him. My world had just been pulled out from under my feet. I didn't know what I was supposed to be doing the next day—how the hell was I supposed to know what I wanted to be doing in a decade?

After I stopped seeing my shrink, Xan somehow convinced me that it might be helpful if I talked to Pastor Gary. Xan meant well, he was worried about me, so I agreed. On my first visit Pastor Gary told me there was a reason dance didn't work out for me, that losing the only thing I'd ever known was part of the master plan. He assured me that one day I would see this reason and be grateful for the lessons it taught me. That day was the first and last time I visited him. I've come today to tell him what I think about master plans. I want to hear what ridiculous explanation he has for why Xan was taken from me. What good could possibly come from this?

The Church on the Lake is huge, as is Pastor Gary's office. I thought the purpose of collecting an offering Sunday mornings was to help people in need. By the looks of it, I think Pastor Gary has been using that money to build himself an empire. I run my hand along his glossy, smooth desk. Cherry.

"Lila, what a surprise."

I jump and step away from his personal things. I follow his gaze down to his desk and see a sweaty handprint slowly fading away. So embarrassing.

He no longer looks annoyed that I have barged in this late without calling, or that I've left a disgusting mark on his beautiful desk. He looks happy. He is always happy. Always.

He was happy at Xan's funeral. Who's happy at a funeral?

Ugh, he wants a hug. I don't want a hug, especially from a lingerer who holds on much, much longer than necessary. But how can I pretend I don't see him standing in front of me with his arms wide open?

Quickly, I give him what he wants before plopping into one of the giant plush armchairs—which seem to be made of quicksand—sitting in front of his desk. I let the chair take me. Like a sticky marshmallow, I imagine it pulling me in, transporting me to a place where there is nothing but white space filled with fluffy white stuff. The gentle click of the door closing pulls me out of my fantasy.

"How are you?" His hand inappropriately brushes my shoulder as he passes by me on his way to his desk.

Taking his chair, Pastor Gary looks more like an arrogant king sitting on his throne than a worker bee of God. Reclining in his fancy suede chair and resting his elbows in the grooves of the well-worn armrests, he waits for my answer.

Why do people ask that when they already know the answer? He should take a picture of me; it would last longer. Why do people keep staring at me?

"Is that Bruce Willis?" I blurt. I can't believe I never noticed that photograph before. Since when do pastors hang out with celebrities?

He clears his throat and turns the oversized photo so I can't see it. "That was at the hurricane-relief drive," he attempts to explain.

I might believe him if he wasn't wearing a tuxedo and standing on a red carpet in front of a backdrop that says *Gala Event*. Plus, they are nearly blinded by the sun. Sun doesn't shine like that here in Wisconsin, especially in not March. He obviously doesn't remember that Xan and I volunteered at the hurricane-relief drive the church hosted two weeks before the date on the photo.

"Look, Lila," he says, changing the subject. "I know we don't know each other all that well. But I knew Xan. I know he wouldn't want you to be hurting so much."

Oh, I'm sorry, is your wife dead?

Sitting up a little straighter, he gives a different kind of smile. A real smile. "I remember when Xan and his brother, Adam, came to me and asked if their band could play on Sunday mornings. At first, I was reluctant. I wasn't sure how the rest of the congregation would respond to drums and guitars instead of organs and the gospel choir."

If this is some sort of go-for-your-dreams speech, now is not the time.

He continues: "The point, Lila, is that you have to be open if you want change to happen. You can't move on until you are open to the idea of things being different."

Oh no, he's shifting in his chair. Is he going to get up and come over here? *No, don't get out of your chair. Stay. Stay. No!*

Here we go. I know, I know, change doesn't mean bad. I've heard it a million times. I don't need you closer for me to hear you.

Thankfully, he sits back down. "Like you, I was comfortable with the way things were. It worked. Being comfortable isn't what life is about. Life is about feeling alive."

Don't you think I want to pray for something other than for God to take me?

"I took the risk of putting drums and an electric guitar in a Sunday morning service." His happy smile is gloating. "If I hadn't been open to change, Xan's memorial service wouldn't have been outside by the lakefront."

Why do these therapy types always know what to say to get a reaction? It's where Xan wanted it. "I wouldn't have come if it was in here," I lie. I would have stood by Xan that day even if he were being buried in a swamp.

His unsuccessful sigh is a good sound. "Why did you come today?"

Finally a question I can answer.

But I don't answer. I stop lounging in the chair and sit up straight. Someone or something has taken over: an angry person, not a good thing right now. I'm more than angry. I feel enraged, and the butterflies that surprised me the first time Xan said my name have migrated back to my stomach. I need to stand up. Thoughts and memories of Xan flood my mind and make my blood boil, bringing me to my feet. Suddenly, I have so much to say that I don't know where to begin.

Leaning across his desk, I do everything in my power to make him uncomfortable. "There are psychopaths in this world who meticulously calculate how they are going to kill their next victim. They stalk them. They torture them. They rape them. And finally, when they become bored, they show some mercy and slaughter them. These murderers deserve to die. Xan didn't deserve to die."

He doesn't back away or tell me to get out. Instead he leans in to me, meeting me halfway across the desk. "I don't care if you believe in God, Lila. I don't care if you are Catholic or Lutheran or Jewish or Buddhist. Believe in something. Have hope."

"What kind of god takes a person like Xan?" I ask. The demon inside me who wanted to tear him a new one is gone. I no longer have the urge to fight. I honestly want to know what kind of god does something so horrible.

Taking my hands in his, he kneels in front of me. "It wasn't God who got to Xan." The heartbreak in his voice tells me he believes it's true.

I can't. I won't. Don't cry, don't cry . . . God, I miss him so much. So, so, so very much. The tears climb out of my heart, up my throat, and hit the back of my eyes without warning. "He didn't kill himself," I whisper. I don't care if there is no evidence of foul play. He used to get so upset with me when I got close to the edge of the rocks; they are always so slippery, and the water is rough. He would never willingly jump, not there.

"Evil is smart. It knows our weaknesses before we do." Now he is defending the religion he's devoted his life to.

I yank my hands out of his before he can get too far into his next motivational speech. "No, he didn't. He wouldn't. He wouldn't do it to himself and he wouldn't do it to me. He believed you went to hell if you commit suicide. He wouldn't." He wouldn't. He couldn't.

Pastor Gary waits for me to calm down before touching

the top of my hand again. "You didn't come here to yell at me."

I take a deep breath—a really, really deep breath. I can't let any more tears escape. Xan deserves more than that. "Do you believe in ghosts?"

"Ghosts?"

Did he just laugh? "Yes," I answer, straight-faced.

Rubbing the back of his neck, he takes his time before answering. "I believe that your soul goes to heaven, so I guess I believe in angels. But you're talking about the white things that float around, right?"

I swallow the lump in my throat.

"No," he says.

That's it? No? This is why I hate such religious people. They are so closed-minded about anything that is outside of what their holy little book says. News flash: Someone wrote that book, and I don't think it was God himself.

Pastor Gary is aggressively rummaging through his desk. What is he looking for? I'm not letting him get off that easy. "What about unexplained phenomena?" *Don't look at me like that; you know what I'm talking about.* He is going to make me say it? "The Virgin Mary statue that cried bloody tears? The guy who found a Jesus-shaped rice cake? Jesus in the Cheetos?" I could go on and on if he wants; I've googled. I know he reads the trashy magazines as much as the rest of us. He has a picture with Bruce Willis, for Christ's sake.

Clasping something in his hand, he closes the drawer. "Those are miracles."

"If those miracles can happen, why can't there be ghosts?" I push.

"Are there ghosts in the Bible?" he rebuts.

I have no idea and I don't care. The Bible says that two guys can't be together and, well, have you looked outside? Everyone knows someone who is gay. I'm going to keep my mouth shut on that one. I don't think he has the chops to argue that with me.

I tried. I did. I gave Pastor Gary an opportunity to give me hope that there was some biblical explanation as to why I feel like Xan is still here with me. "I didn't mean to keep you from the rehearsal dinner." I stand up and push my chair under the desk. "Tell the bride and groom congratulations."

Once again, I am reminded why I avoid organized religion.

"Lila, take this." He holds a small satin pouch out to me.

I am one foot out the door. It's a rosary. "I thought only Catholics used those." I don't take it from him.

He pulls a burgundy strand of beads out of the pouch. It looks as meaningless as a necklace I once bought at a craft fair. "If you really believe there is something following you, this will keep evil away."

Now I feel bad. Like everyone else, he's trying to help; he just doesn't know how. I shouldn't have been so rude. Who knows, maybe this can do something; it's pretty. I hold it up to my neck before turning to walk away.

I make it halfway down the hall this time.

"Lila!"

I want to keep walking, but even I'm not that coldhearted.

"Hang the rosary on your headboard or on your bedroom doorknob. *Do not* wear it around your neck," he instructs.

It's a necklace.

"Trust me, it's bad, sacrilegious," he says before disappearing back into his office.

There's no doubt in my mind I would have put this around my neck before bed tonight. I may have my doubts about God, but with my luck, I'm not taking any chances. I slip the beads into their satin pouch and tuck it safely into my back pocket.

I stop at the end of the hall and watch the fire of the large white candles dance. At night, they light the dungeon. It's actually a smaller sanctuary for people with babies or the ill, but it looks like a jail cell from an old castle. The tall one in the middle flickers the most. Its flame is large, and four smaller ones try to keep up. The smallest one tries the hardest; it stretches tall three times before burning out. I look behind me and hope that Pastor Gary didn't see that.

A thin line of smoke trails from the freshly extinguished flame as the red embers of the wick try to reignite before giving up and turning black. I hurry to the table and search for a match or something to relight the candle. Nothing. Crap. I don't need him thinking I am the one who put these candles out. Who am I kidding? I am the only other person here, and he sure as hell didn't blow out a holy candle.

Another flame begins to flicker and jump. I quickly cup my hands around it before it goes out too. When the flame is steady, I pick it up and pour the pooled wax into an offering envelope. I touch the lit flame to the wick of the dead candle, and when the two flames are strong enough to be separated, I put the candles back where they belong.

The chapel catches my attention on my way out. Now that I look at it, it wouldn't have been such a horrible place to get married. It was something Xan and I used to argue about, where we would get married one day. I didn't want to get married in a church, and he really couldn't imagine getting married anywhere else. I never told Xan this, but I would have married him in a church—this church, even. We could have gotten married in a landfill. It wouldn't have mattered, because I would have been with Xan. I stare, fantasizing about what will never be, and the feeling that has become all too familiar starts. Time stands still and the world begins to spin around me. I know for a fact this has never happened before. I would not be caught dead in a dark church alone at night; thank goodness it's summer and it will stay light for another few hours. Even so, it's eerily dark in this hall. Staying here in the dark right now, this is an exception.

Something is different. Next to the thing that looks like a birdbath, where they do baptisms, a young couple appears.

They have a baby. A baby girl. They hand her over to the pastor, who pours water over her head. The baby begins to scream, and the mother and father rush to comfort her.

I struggle for breath. I know those people. It's Xan and me.

"Lila! Wait!" Pastor Gary is running toward me, and I can't move. I can't stop staring at the spot where I just saw something that clearly isn't there. "You're not ready now, but someday you will be." He hands me a business card. Like the twelve he's handed me before, this one too will end up in the trash.

I make it to the colossal water-absorbing rug in the main entryway when I hear his rubber soles come to a screeching halt on the stone floor.

He reappears out of the darkness, much slower, less on a mission. "Lila, the candles."

Oh crap.

"They are lit the night before a wedding as a form of good luck. Why did you blow them out?" He sounds almost as disheartened as he did when he was trying to convince me Xan killed himself.

I knew he would blame me. Wait, what? Still feeling the effects of whatever I just saw, I snap myself out of it and walk back to the dungeon. I look at the table. There is no light. I can't help but smirk. "I didn't." I give him back his string of religious beads. He probably thinks I blew out all the candles trying to destroy someone else's happiness. I'll let him think that.

"You should go," he tells me with a hint of fear in his voice.

I happily oblige and head to my car.

"Jesus, Jason, you scared the crap out of me!" I scream when I see him standing next to the drivers side door.

"You shouldn't use the Lord's name in vain, especially at his house."

While trying to make sense of what just happened inside the church, it occurs to me that I never told Jason I was coming here. I told him I was going to the mall.

Xan

TWENTY-THREE DAYS LEFT

Lila is standing in the kitchen of the boat eyeing up the junk food in the pantry. I can see she wants to give in; she won't. She needs to. She's lost a lot of weight. She closes the door and reaches for a banana. In her mind, I can only assume that life seems to be proving her theories true: the only thing she has control over is what she puts in her mouth.

This is where I am supposed to step in. Why hasn't Jason noticed how skinny she's gotten?

She stumbles backward when the boat rocks. My mom just climbed aboard. The fiberglass pops, the distinct sound of footsteps. Lila takes one small bite of the perfectly ripe banana and buries the rest in the bottom of the trash. Old habits die hard.

My mom sizes up the massive boat Lila now calls home. She has a disgusted look on her face, the one that she wears when looking at something she believes to be unnecessary. In her opinion, any extra money should be given to those in need. Not spent on a yacht the size of New Hampshire.

This is the first time she's come to see Lila since I died. Why didn't she come sooner? She knows Lila is alone.

"Mrs. Hemlock." Lila slides open the heavy glass door. She is trying so hard to hide the relief she is feeling that my mom is here to see her. "Come in."

To my mom, walking through that door is as dangerous as stepping through the looking glass.

Lila has never rolled her eyes at my parents' absurd beliefs, and she doesn't try to make them like her. She steps outside, knowing it is where my mother is more comfortable, and begins to roll up the unzipped screens that are flapping in the warm breeze. "How are you?" she asks my mom.

"Lila!" I shout.

Lila winces as her face turns beet red. She knows how my mother is and is mortified for asking. If I know Lila like I think I do, she thinks she is now just as stupid as all the idiots who ask her how she is.

"Say something!" I urge my mom. My parents have tolerated Lila's family. Well, "tolerated" is being generous. I've never seen two families who were so different produce offspring so in love. My parents have very old-school, traditional beliefs, like being married before having sex, dating someone with the same religious beliefs, and not giving alcohol to teenagers. Lila's parents, on the other hand, are a bit more free-spirited. We used to drink with them all the time—they gave us drinks the first day I met them, and Lila and I slept together in her bedroom. The expectations they put on Lila to succeed are ridiculous. But at the same time, they allow her to make and learn from mistakes. As messed up as they are, they have allowed her to discover who she is. Are we like Romeo and Juliet?

Denial keeps my parents happy. All the nights I spent at Lila's, they thought I was at Charlie's. I can't believe the charade went on as long as it did. I think Charlie's parents were in on it. They had to have been. If I hadn't stupidly left my phone lying on the kitchen table one morning, and if my dad hadn't happened to pick it up just as Lila sent me a text that made it kind of obvious we'd had sex, they would have thought I died a virgin. But they knew. That single text prompted them to read months of texts between Lila and me, which shattered their delusional perception.

I wonder how Charlie is. Charlie and I have been friends since kindergarten. Why hasn't he come to check on Lila? He didn't like the fact that I spent so much time with her, but he knew how much I loved her.

Why is this the first time I've thought about anyone other than Lila?

My mom looks good standing on the back of the yacht. She is tall and thin. If she took the time to do her hair and makeup, she would turn heads. Maybe that's another reason she never meshed with Lila. What my mom doesn't understand is that Lila's not vain; she's insecure. If my mom could see past Lila's quest for perfection, she'd see they are more alike than she is willing to admit.

"I want Xan's things back."

I wait for a smile, a laugh, a smirk, anything to indicate she's kidding. It doesn't happen. The only movement is the growing size of Lila's eyes, which stare through my mom to the calm water. Lila tends to zone out when she is replaying something in her head.

"What?" The devastation on her face is unbearable to look at. She heard my mother the first time.

Aggressively backing Lila into the corner, my mother repeats herself. "The things you have of Xan's. I want anything you have of Xan's back before you move on. I don't want them stuffed into a box or thrown away."

Who is this person jabbing her finger into my girlfriend's chest?

Lila's back hits the wall, and she allows my mother to slide her across the rounded fiberglass until her spine presses into the metal door handle.

My mother is inches away from her face. She looks like she wants to eat her. "I am his mother. His things belong with me."

Why is Lila taking this bullshit from her? Lila has never taken crap from anyone. She isn't even giving her a dirty look.

Lila reaches behind her back, searching for the door handle. The door weighs as much as she does, but she usually opens it with ease. This is the first time I've seen her struggle with it.

I don't follow her inside. It kills me not to be able to help her. I stay with my mother, the liar. She isn't selfless. She isn't kind. She doesn't appear to even have a heart. I get that she is sad; she lost her child. But how does she think Lila feels? I am the one Lila was supposed to spend forever with.

Lila lost everything.

I step close to her. Like with the psychic and Jason, I am stopped by an invisible barrier. I can't touch her like I can Lila. It's a good thing. I might strangle my own mother. Has she always been a hypocrite, or did my death do this to her?

She never thought Lila was good enough for me. Even so, she was always kind to her, at least to her face. She picks up a picture of Lila and me that is sitting next to the sink on the back of the boat.

A couple of weeks ago, I would have assumed her reaction to it was due to the fact that, in the photo, we have glasses of champagne in our hands. That's not why she's upset.

She blames Lila. She thinks Lila killed me.

I sense Lila pause on the other side of the door before coming out. She should have climbed out one of the front windows and hid until my mom left. I would have, but Lila's not weak.

Lila hands my mother what she came for. I peek into the bag along with my mom to see what she is willing to part with: my lucky hat, two photos (one of us on vacation in Hawaii with her family and the other of my band at one of our concerts), my nylon black running pants, and a shirt I haven't worn in years.

Lila didn't give her anything of value, and my mom knows it. She kept everything that has ever meant anything to me: my favorite concert tee, a pair of drumsticks I used during a show when I dedicated a song to her, a million more pictures, my fishhook bracelet, my leather necklace, and every letter and note we have written to each other (there are thousands). A few months before I died, Lila suggested that I not keep any of our notes or letters at my house. After the texting incident, we didn't need my parents reading any more about how we felt about each other.

I smile, not because I'm proud of her for not giving in to my mother—though I am. This is what Lila needed: proof that she can control things. It's small, but I see the twinkle in her eye she is trying to hide.

Lila's promise ring has been in my father's family for years. My mom is staring at it like a hungry vulture. Grandma gave it to me last year when Lila and I visited her in Pasadena over spring break. Like me, she knew Lila was the one for me. My mom has never said it, but I know she has always been hurt that Grandma didn't part with the ring when my dad proposed to her. It would kill her to know that she gave it to me the first day she met Lila.

"Do not give it to her!" I shout, pushing my face halfway into hers. A beach towel hanging over the railing flies toward her. She catches it without moving anything other than her arm. Our faces are still one disturbing blend of the impossible. A surge of excitement rushes through me. Did she hear me?

I separate myself from her. "Lila! I'm right here!" I take a few steps back and wave my hands frantically in front of her. Desperate, I place my hand on hers and pray with all my might that she can feel me, sense me, whatever. She cannot give my mother that ring. She can't take it off her hand.

A single tear runs down her cheek. "I know you've never liked me. And you're right, I'm not good enough for him," Lila whispers.

What the hell is she saying?

I take a step closer, and my hand becomes one with Lila's. "He could have had any girl he wanted. But for some reason he chose me. He chose me to spend forever with." I feel her sadness flowing between our hands. "He wanted to spend the rest of his life with me." She's not talking to my mom, but reminding herself that I did, that I was to spend forever with her.

It's my mom's turn to be speechless.

Lila's body moves forward; her hand stays back. She doesn't separate it from mine. "I can't imagine what it would be like to lose a child."

Part of my nonexistent life goes with her when she takes her hand away. It doesn't bring me to my knees, but I'm drained, like when the psychic drank that potion.

"Xan was my future," Lila continues, looking at the photo my mom still clutches in her hand. "Every time I see a pregnant woman, I see the kids we'll never have. When I sit here"—she points to the chair where we used to sit, wish on stars, and talk about how lucky we were—"sometimes, if I focus enough, I can remember exactly what it felt like to have his arms around me, promising to protect me from everything—even myself. How when we looked into each other's eyes, words were never needed—we knew what each other was thinking. We would have conversations with our eyes, and when we held hands, my soul vibrated. Each and every time he took my hand, my soul was happy to be home. Xan is my home, and my home has been taken away."

Lila is getting to her. I just saw my mom clench her jaw.

Lila continues. "I panic when the sun sets, because during the day I can pretend everything is okay. But at night, when it's dark, I can't hide from the fact that he's gone." Lila extends her hand. She wants the picture back. "The truth keeps me awake. Each night I go to sleep knowing he isn't going to be there when I open my eyes in the morning."

I have always loved watching her sleep. She is so happy and

peaceful when she isn't overanalyzing things. I think it freaked her out the first time she woke up to me staring at her, but I'm pretty sure she also loved it. I was the luckiest guy in the Universe to be able to wake up next to her. I should have told her when I had the chance.

I used to pray every night for my mother to see the Lila I fell in love with. She never did in my lifetime, so seeing it happen when I am out of the picture, when she has no incentive to like her, it's more than I can take.

The coldhearted woman who took over my mother's body has vanished. Tenderly she sets the photo on the counter and wraps Lila in her arms. Lila allows the mother she always wanted to love her, and my mother holds the daughter she never had.

"What happened?" Wes asks. His potent energy is getting less noticeable.

I hold my hand up to stop him from talking. Lila and my mother are not competing for my attention. They are not trying to prove who loves me the most. In this moment, they seem to have put everything aside other than the fact they have both lost me. I don't know if this will ever happen again.

I assume the bizarre tender moment will be over when the hug stops. I'm wrong. They're not looking at each other through enemy eyes. Instead they seem to have a mutual understanding.

Picking up the things she was so ungrateful to have a few minutes ago, my mother thanks Lila and tells her not to be a stranger. That if she needs anything, anything at all, she should call. Lila says she won't be a stranger and she will call. All three of us know she won't do either.

Lila watches my mother walk down the dock and drive out of the marina. When she's sure she's gone, Lila picks up the picture my mom was holding. Sliding our chair out of the shade, she spins it to face the setting sun.

"Why did I get weak when I felt her separate from me?" I ask Wes.

"You *felt* her clasp your hand?"

"Yeah."

Lila is looking less tense. The sun must be warming her up. It's the beginning of August, but she still needs to wear sweaters to keep from freezing. I wonder if she is thinking about me or my mom.

"Why?"

Wes pushes himself between us like my mom used to step in front of the TV when she wanted my attention. "Xan, you've got to be careful! Humans—even *your* human—are stronger than us. She can tolerate you floating through her all day long. But when she touches you back, and you feel it, you can only handle so much of that, man."

With the amount of worry in his voice, you would have thought I'd jumped into a shark tank with a bleeding leg. If it was such a big deal, why didn't he tell me about it? I didn't know it was bad for me. "It just happened."

He backs off. "You can't let it just happen. You have to control it, or it will kill you."

"Kill me?" He's kidding, right? How do you kill someone who's already dead? "I don't understand why I can touch her but she can't touch me. Isn't that the goal here, for me to get her to see or feel or hear me? Isn't it the same thing, me reaching for her and her reaching for me?"

"No."

"No. That's your answer, no." Are you kidding me?

"No, it's not the same thing. Lila doesn't have access to everything you do. She doesn't remember all the lives you've lived. She isn't currently holding on to any karmic debt other than what she's accrued in her current lifetime. She can withstand things you can't. You are not human, Xan. You are a raw soul—when she touches you, in the glow that illuminates when the two of you touch, you feel everything you've ever felt in those five lifetimes. It's too much. She feels connected and complete."

I want to say something. Anything. All I can come up with is . . . nothing. The thought of Lila hurting me when she touches me, I can't comprehend it. She used to touch my cheek to bring me back to her when I would get distracted or lost in my thoughts. The greatest feeling in the world was her hands on me. Now her touch can kill me.

"You tossed the towel to her when you were angry," I barely hear Wes say, trying to change the subject.

I can change the subject too. "Why don't I miss anyone other than Lila? I mean, I know she is my soul mate and all, but I hadn't even thought about anyone else until today, when I saw my mom."

"You've known Lila for almost one hundred years. You've only known the rest of them for seventeen."

Oh my God. A hundred years.

"Something happened today. What made her not pull away from you?" he asks.

He's right. My touch has always given her chills. Today she didn't flinch. *Think, Xan, think.* I didn't want her to give the ring to my mom. I wanted to stop her from losing any more of me. "I was feeling protective?" I ask, unsure if it even makes any sense.

He starts to say something about five times but stops before the words leave his mouth. "If you were alive, you would have jumped in front of her and stood up to your mom, right?"

I would have taken Lila by the hand and left my mom on the boat, but not before telling her to go to hell. I would have fixed the damage my mother caused by reassuring Lila that my grandmother wanted her to have the ring for a reason. A buzzing sensation takes over my body. The invisible blood pumps through my collapsed veins, and I get it. I know how to get to her.

TWENTY-TWO DAYS LEFT

It's three o'clock, the sun is shining, and there isn't a cloud in the sky. Yet, to me, walking through this graveyard is as haunting as it is on Halloween night.

I wonder who I'm stepping on. Are their dehydrated hearts beginning to race with excitement when the ground above them crunches? Are their palms sweating as they bang on the walls of the small boxes they are stuck in? Are they screaming, begging for me to hear them and set them free?

I can't help them, because I can't hear them. What if there really is someone buried alive under me and I just walk away?

It's quiet here today. An elderly woman talks at a headstone. I assume it belongs to her husband. She is recounting every detail of the home run their grandson hit yesterday and how their granddaughter, who is now fifteen, has a new boyfriend.

That's how it should be: a ninety-year-old woman contentedly telling her husband the events of the day he missed.

Xan's grave is on the far side of the cemetery. On my way to it, I watch the gardener take care of those who've been forgotten. The back of his muddy golf cart is filled with carnations bound together by reeds of grass. They are pretty, natural. Xan got me some like them once from the farmers' market. That, or he picked them from his own backyard.

I watch from behind a life-size tombstone as he looks around to see if anyone is watching. When he thinks he is in the clear, he places one of the bouquets on a neglected grave. He says something, I'm not sure what, as he brushes the freshly cut grass away so the words on the headstone can be read. How often does he do this? Today he makes four people smile.

Xan isn't one of the ignored. This is my tenth time here, if you count the day he was buried, when I visited twice. The heat has already wilted the flowers I brought yesterday. It's pretty morbid. His parents have recently hung a wreath that reads *Beloved Son*, and someone else put up one of those stand-alone plants. I rearrange the flowers and clear away the loose grass from the lawn mower. I sit where I think he might be lying under me.

XANDER MICHAEL HEMLOCK
11.20.1998–7.14.2015
Until we meet again.

The short, thick grass is soft under my hands. I slip off my flip-flops so I can feel the grass between my toes. Xan loved it when I took my shoes off, especially in the car. I hope there is grass where he is.

I pretend it's his warm body I'm leaning against, not a slab of marble. I can no longer tell the difference between sadness and pain. I've turned into a robot, mechanically going through the motions of life. I keep waiting for the weight of the world to crush the already-dented shell that protects my vital organs.

"Why did you leave me?" I ask, more than half expecting a response. "You could have told me something was wrong."

Why didn't I see it? I know things were messy right before he died, but I thought we fixed all the really bad stuff. I was getting better. He gave me his grandmother's ring. He promised to love me for the rest of his life. I guess he held up his end of the bargain.

"Ouch!" I dig through the grass to find what just poked me.

I hope it was a poke, not a bite. I have to dig into the dirt to get it out. It's stuck. I rub the matted dirt off. It's a comb, the toothy kind people used to wear in their hair. My grandmother wore one.

The silver is tarnished and most of the blue rhinestones have fallen off. It's been here a while. I wonder if it fell out of someone's hair or if it was buried where the one she loved lies, so he would always have a piece of her with him.

I dig a deeper hole and place the comb in it. It belongs with someone, not me.

Across the cemetery a random yellow balloon bobs among the trees. I don't remember seeing any kids here today, although the cemetery is surrounded by playgrounds. I'll jump up and grab the balloon if it comes close enough, and find its rightful owner.

I watch as the string gets tangled in a cluster of branches and fights to get free. I guess even pieces of rubber don't like being trapped. Once free, the balloon finds an open spot in the center of the cemetery. It hovers, catching its breath from the near-death experience. I can't believe it didn't pop. As if it knows I am watching, it drifts in my direction.

The balloon is close now, close enough that I can see what is beneath it. When I do, I squeeze my eyes tightly and promise to eat more. I read about this. Like the nuns who fasted for days, I must be hallucinating. I don't think they really saw Jesus or God; they were starving. They'd go days without food or water in order to get as close to God as possible. Yeah, they were getting close to God all right. They were dying!

My mind has played tricks on me before, especially when I weighed less than eighty pounds. My eating disorder told me things that weren't true, and like a fool, I believed it.

I open my eyes. Xan is still walking toward me.

I stop being a chicken and stare into the face that I've missed so much. His transparent hand offers me the balloon. I watch in disbelief as he bounces the string up and down, trying to get me to take it. When I do, I feel his hand pass through mine. We both gasp.

I back up.

I let go of the balloon as the cool slime of his hand coats my bones. Xan reaches up, catches it, and hands it back to me. I bunch the string into a ball and clutch it tightly in my fist.

The iciness of his hand touches my brow, and my face immediately relaxes. Xan hated it when I'd bunch up my face; it drove him crazy. He was always touching it to remind me to relax. If that didn't work, he'd tell me I was getting premature wrinkles.

I reach for him and lose my breath when my hand disappears into his chest. He looks as solid as the last time I held him, but he feels like a cold bowl of jelly. I pull my hand out. He drops to the ground. My hand looks exactly the same as it did before I shoved it into my dead boyfriend's chest. I kneel down beside him, and for the first time ever he puts his hand up to stop me from coming any closer.

He doesn't want me near him.

Heartbroken, I scoot back so I can lean against his gravestone. "I'm losing it," I say out loud, burying my face into my knees. My desire for him is a constant ache rather than something of pleasure. I know this is all happening in my head. I know that, but I can't ignore the fact that seeing his face has eased the pain. And I can't pretend it doesn't hurt that he just backed away from me, even if it was a delusion. "Do you want me to let you go?"

I feel the balloon trying to tug itself out of my hand. I might have believed it was a force of nature if it was a windy day. But it's not. It never seems to be windy anymore. I lift my face from my lap and see Xan crouched in front of me shaking his head no. The air is suddenly so heavy I'm starting to hyperventilate.

"Lila?" Jason is approaching behind Xan.

"Jason, what are you doing here?" I panic. Can he see Xan too?

Jason gets closer and Xan steps to the side so Jason can get to me. "You weren't at the boat. Lucky guess that you'd be here."

I hear Jason talking, but I don't take my eyes off Xan. He is saying something, and he looks concerned. He is pointing at Jason. I can't hear him. I jump to my feet and cry as he begins to fade. Frantically, I search. He's gone. What if I never see him again? He can't disappear. "Xan!" I scream before collapsing onto my knees.

Jason runs to my side and scoops me up. "Why are you here?" I sob. "He was here and you made him go away! You made him go away!" I pound his chest, trying to escape the prison his arms have trapped me in.

"He's gone, Lila." Jason tosses me to the side as steps away from me. "He's not coming back. He's gone!"

I stand motionless as Jason screams at me while violently pulling at his own hair.

"You think this is healthy, coming to his grave every day?" He is speaking to me, but he won't look at me. "Did you just hear yourself? You said he was here! The scary thing is that I think you mean it. I think you believe you saw him just now. I think you thought you were talking to him."

He's wrong. It wasn't an illusion. I look at the balloon I'm holding on to for dear life and deflate.

Jason's face isn't as red, and he's stopped ripping his hair out. "Lila, you've gotta let him go."

The fire he was just filled with has been transferred to me. "Let him *go*? Jason, he just died!"

"I know, I know he did." He takes a calming deep breath and steps closer to me. "There's a few weeks left of freedom before school starts. Let's do something, go somewhere," he suggests eagerly, and takes my hands.

I back away. Do they make a medication for people who don't think before they speak? "God, Jason!" For someone who is so supportive at times, he can be a real jerk. "I don't *want* to move on! I don't want to wake up and not feel the pain of living without him! You don't get it! I don't want to think about living without him!"

His face is starting to glow again. Why is he so mad about this? "Lila, you've gone to a psychic and a pastor, and now you are talking to dead people. That's not normal."

"I'm not normal!"

Forcefully, he steps close again. "You don't want to be."

"I've always been different, Jason." I slap his finger out of my face before walking away. I get three headstones closer to my car before I turn around. "You think I wanted to freeze in the middle of my boyfriend's funeral because I felt like I'd been there before? You're right." I throw my hands up in defeat, still clutching the balloon Xan handed to me. "I love it. I also like being in a constant state of anticipation, wondering when it's going to happen again. Oh, and I really love being terrified to open my eyes at night."

"What?" He grabs my arm. I try to take it back, but he is holding on really tight. He has gotten really strong. His nails scrape along my skin as I wriggle out of his grip.

"What is your problem?" I ask, rubbing the red welts on my triceps. His eyes are devilishly on fire. That's not what catches my attention. It's that he isn't sorry for hurting me. If anything, I think he's disappointed in how little damage he's done.

He thinks he can scare me. I stopped being afraid of humanity the day I had nothing left to lose. It's not what I can see that terrifies me; it's the unknown, the unanswered.

I forget about bringing the balloon back to the kid who lost it. I'm keeping it.

Xan

TWENTY-ONE DAYS LEFT

Can someone please explain to me why she is listening to the jackass who branded her? She usually wears long-sleeved shirts in the middle of August because she is cold. Today she has to wear one in order to hide the large handprint Jason temporarily tattooed on her arm.

He's getting to her. He's trying to convince her that it's her desperation to see me that's causing her to sense my presence.

She saw me. I know she did.

I walk away from the window that keeps me from her when I violate some rule I'm unaware exists. It's not that different from Earth here. I still have to learn from my mistakes. I can't stop myself from turning around and looking back when I can no longer hear her voice. From where I stand now, her world is nothing more than a faint flicker, the first and only star in my endless night.

I don't know where I am going or what I'll find. Anything is better than watching her with Jason.

I've been in the dark too long; I'm seeing things. Like a well-kindled fire, a speck of light seems to be growing ahead of me. I follow the flickering. It's not another porthole like I thought. It's a door. I push it open and shield my eyes. Wes is here. He seems unaffected by the buzzing intensity of the fluorescent lights. I've never seen him in the light before. His face is still the color of granite, but I can see that his mouth moves as he speaks. His nostrils flare when he sees me. Can he see me? Or does he sense me? He almost looks human here—almost.

It doesn't take long for my eyes to adjust. I check to see if I have turned to stone like him. Negative. I'm as pale as the day I died.

Wes is rummaging through an oversized file cabinet. Dozens of them hover over the opaque floor. "About time," he says, slamming the drawer shut. As he does, they glide away, as if on tracks. But there are no tracks. The room is empty. And white. Literally hundreds of file cabinets just vanish into thin air.

He offers me a glowing folder. "Your file."

It's thick and heavy. I search for something in the photos to tell me what I'm looking at. Like a history book, they progress in time, scratchy black-and-white to modern-day glossy. I remember some of them. Most of them I want to remember. Some I hope are in the wrong folder.

I stop when I see one I recognize. It's impossible.

"It's the first time you and Lila found each other, in 1914."

The next is from the present. I close the folder and give it back. "I don't want to see any more." I feel sick.

Wes takes it and rummages through. He is looking for something. "You need to." He hands me a thin stack of photos.

I remember the night in the first photo. It was the night we decided we would get married. We were planning to do it the summer before we started college, right after we turned eighteen so we wouldn't need permission from our parents. We laughed at how furious my mom and dad would be and contemplated eloping. I was the one who vetoed eloping. But all I really wanted was for her to become my wife.

We loved going to the park next to the lake. She wanted to get married there, next to the weeping willow tree, not bury me in the neighboring cemetery. Lila talked about turning the park into a princess-like world of white, pink, and silver. Instead it was covered in black. Now she will forever remember it as the place where we were separated, not joined.

The moon was full the night this picture was taken. I could see every freckle on her nose in the light reflecting off the water. She tries to cover them up with makeup. I miss those freckles. She was content that night, at peace. It had been a long time since I'd seen her that happy.

I take a closer look at the picture. "Is that Jason?" I bring the picture closer to my face, squinting to make out the image. Jason is lurking behind a tree several feet behind us. "I had no idea he was there." That's how he knew we planned on getting married.

"Look at the second one." Wes pulls a new photo out of the stack.

Jason and I are arguing in the parking lot of the marina. I hated that he was there. He was always there. His family has a boat too, so he was unavoidable, and that night he was mad.

He said I was pushing Lila into something she wasn't ready for, that giving her a promise ring and talking about our future together was only setting her up for another devastating life change.

I didn't push her into anything. Lila wanted to be with me. "He went crazy." I'd never seen him like that before. It was like a switch flipped in him, and he finally realized Lila chose me, not him.

Wes takes that photo and gives me another.

This picture can't possibly be from my folder. There is a body with a black garbage bag covering the head; Jason is tying the hands behind its back with a zip tie. I do a double take: Lila gave me that same watch two Christmases ago. Those are my overly worn black soccer shoes bound together with another zip tie. And I would recognize anywhere the rope being wrapped around the body to secure his arms to his side, so there is no chance of escape.

I've used that rope a million times tying Lila's dad's boat to the dock. He special-orders it: extra-thick nylon, black and white.

It looks like I'm fighting.

I don't remember this.

I've barely had time to process this information when Wes switches the photos in my hands.

I see Jason overconfidently stuffing the ropes, zip ties, and trash bags into another black trash bag. Three gallons of bleach wash the rocks and his hands clean. He restrained me so he wouldn't have to hold me down himself. Another photo follows. He sits on the rocky shore watching, making sure my lifeless body sinks to the bottom of Lake Michigan.

"Time is running out," Wes says, patting my back.

No shit, Sherlock.

It's like a bad car accident. I keep telling myself to look away from the photo, but I can't. I also can't stop picturing myself sinking to the bottom. Lake Michigan is deep and cold. But even it can't hold bodies down. I feel bad for the dudes dredging who found me floating four days later. I imagine myself floating effortlessly to the surface like a bubble of air.

He thought about it. It was calculated. He was smart.

Wes tries to shake me out of my state of shock. "You can't let her kill herself, Xan."

"Why?" I ask. "Other than the obvious reasons."

"Don't let it happen," he warns.

Wes is right. If she thinks I'm in hell, it's only a matter of time before she decides that's where she wants to be too. Keeping Jason away from her would be a lot easier if I could do something about it.

"You saw what she can do to you," Wes cautions, as if he heard the thoughts of going back to Madame Tula entering my mind.

Do I like the idea of asking someone who tried to kill me for help? No, but as far as I can see, she is the only one who can see both Lila and me. She could be the person I need to actually succeed at making Lila see that I am still here. I bounced back quicker after Lila stuck her hand through my chest. Maybe I just needed to build up a tolerance. "She might be able to help."

"I had to help you to your feet, Xan."

"I know. I know that, but I'm running out of time. Every minute not spent trying to get Lila to see me is wasted time. I don't have any extra time to waste."Wes doesn't argue with me. He knows I'm right. I'm hoping his silence means he's starting to see it from my point of view.

"The psychic has nothing positive to offer you. She makes concoctions designed to destroy you, to take your inner glow—that's what she is trying to do, destroy you so she can have it. Lila makes you whole. Remember, when the two of your souls are together, you are indestructible. When you separate, that's what is making you collapse. The single perfect soul your two souls make together is completely drained when they are torn apart. The power doesn't know where to go. It kind of floats around looking for its home. It has to find its way back to you."

"What good is our power if we have to be touching for it to work?"

"You don't have to literally be touching, smart-ass." He opens the door that leads nowhere. "I know you want nothing more than to be with her, but don't be stupid." He pushes me out the door, leaving me once again in the dark.

I head back to Lila. The tiny speck of light quickly turns into a clear vision of her sitting in our chair on the back of the boat, drinking a cup of tea. There has to be an easier way, I say to myself.

"I can help," a purring voice offers.

Great, now I'm hearing voices. "How?" I ask, ready for a conversation with myself. It doesn't take long, though, to realize that I am not alone.

Whatever the voice is coming from doesn't come close enough for me to see, but like with Wes, I can feel its presence. I'm not hearing things. I'm not alone. All of the sudden, I'm pulled away from Lila and into Jason's basement. He is pacing like a madman. He *should* be nervous. What does he think she's going to do when she figures out what really happened to me? Run to him?

"What would you do to him if you could?" the voice tempts.

I play along. "Anything?"

"Anything."

Easy. "I'd plant drugs." His parents would find them and he'd be shipped off to rehab the next day.

Her laughter is getting closer. "You can do anything you want without being held accountable and *that* is what you choose?"

"I want him to suffer." Death would be too kind.

"Okay," the voice pathetically agrees.

How did I get into Jason's car? The black leather of his BMW is warm. It reeks of cigarettes. You know you have a smoking problem when three pine tree air fresheners can't cover it up.

A knock at the window startles me.

"You can see me?" I ask the woman running her finger along the side of Jason's sleek car. Judging by her tight leather bodysuit, I don't think she's someone who hangs around Jason's house. She does, though, appear to be someone who likes the finer things in life. I get a very strong feeling that she isn't afraid to do whatever it takes to get them.

"Life would be easier if she were with him," she says, stroking his expensive car parked in the three-car garage that has heated floors.

Thank you for pointing out what has always lurked in the back of my mind. Life would be easier with him. Jason's family could provide her the life she's used to. She wouldn't have to give up the things she believes are essential, like designer purses and traveling multiple times a year. She wouldn't have to think about how she was going to afford something if she was with Jason. "Who are you?" I snap.

Handing me a sandwich bag filled with marijuana through the opened window, she answers, "Irene."

I've never seen so much pot in my life.

"You're not going to let him win, are you?" She asks shaking the bag in my face.

I take it without asking where she got it. Her smirk makes me nervous. Bad girls get turned on when good boys do dangerous things. She looks very excited. Wes would have told me about her if she were good, wouldn't he? He does seem to be omitting a lot of crucial information, though. What if *he's* not who I think he is?

"Plant it."

"What?" I don't move fast enough for her. She aggressively opens the car door and reaches across my lap to open the armrest. With her body touching mine, she snatches the baggie out of my hand and drops it in.

Still not sure what is happening, I get out of the car and follow her. We walk out of the garage, not back into obscurity, but down the street. The cement is hard beneath my feet. I haven't felt ground for almost three weeks. I never knew how hard cement was or how nice humid air felt.

She catches me staring. I'm not staring because she's beautiful, which she is, in an Angelina Jolie movie star kind of way. I can't stop gawking because she doesn't look like a rock. Her green eyes match the grass, and her hair is the color of the outside of a York Peppermint Pattie. "Who are you?"

"I told you. I'm Irene," she says without so much as a glance in my direction. She knows where she is headed. I wish I knew.

"What are you?"

"There are other ways to get what you want." She is avoiding the question.

Why doesn't anyone here answer anything? She turns and steps uncomfortably close to me.

"How many days do you have left?" Her breath is hot and

smells like strawberries. Her firm breasts are pressed against my chest. Those can't be real.

"Twenty-one," I answer.

She weaves her fingers into mine, causing my stone cold heart to pump. "Have you touched her yet?"

I can't speak, so I nod.

I don't move, not even when her lips touch my neck. "So she knows it's you?" She is kissing me in ways I've only seen in movies.

Again, I nod. "I think so."

The air that comes between us when she pulls away is cool, even though it's got to be a hundred degrees out. "You *think* so. Have you told her it's you?"

I'm still not moving. Now it's not because she's making me nervous; it's because she's right.

"Has she heard your voice or not?"

No.

With a dangerous gleam in her eye, she continues: "I can help her hear your voice. I can also help you get rid of your problem." She points to Jason's house.

It sounds good, too good. "What do you want?"

She clenches her jaw the same way my dad used to when I'd disappointed him. "To get to Jason, it will cost you one day."

"That's it? One day?" If I do it right, get Jason away from her, all it should take is one time. Wait, did I just do something to Jason or did she? "Did I just give up a day?"

Tracing the outline of my body as she circles me, she breathes into my ear the words I hoped she wouldn't. "You did," she continues, giggling, touching me like I am her boy toy. If a woman like her had come on to me when I was alive, before I met Lila, it would not have been hard to resist her.

But at the moment sex is the furthest thing from my mind. When the sun rose today, I had twenty-one days left. Now, instantly, I'm down to twenty. Shit. "I didn't put the drugs there; you did."

"Technically, you are right. But I am not the one who is racing the clock here. This is about you. You are the one making wagers with a strange woman," she says, looking at me like she is thrilled she was able to pull that over me.

Shit. "What about talking to Lila?" I ask.

Wrapping her arms around my waist, she pulls me in. Her lips are so close to mine I can taste her cracking lipstick. "That'll cost you three days, Romeo." She bites my lip. "Choices, choices, what will you do?" she sings jovially as she walks away.

I can't lose three days. What if it doesn't work and I'm down to seventeen? Then again, what if it does? I don't seem to be making great progress on my own. "This sucks!" I grunt, punching a lamppost.

She stops but doesn't come back. "With every choice comes a sacrifice, Xan. The question is: Which you can live with? Never seeing her again, or watching her live happily ever after with him?" She points toward the mansion where Jason is most likely sitting on his ass watching reality TV.

Neither is a good choice. I can't live without her, and watching her with him would be torture, but at least I'd be able to see her. Three days isn't an option right now, but one more could be worth it: If I can get rid of Jason, she will start to believe in what she is seeing again. "I want to make Jason go away," I agree.

In a flash so fast I don't see her move, she returns to my side. "All right, then, let's have some fun." She snaps us into Jason's basement. Irene is wearing a pathetic, pouty face, the one so many girls give their boyfriends or daddies when they don't get their way.

I'm not letting her trick me into losing three days. Not yet.

"Can I touch him?" I'm standing a foot away from the only person I'd ever consider strangling with my bare hands.

"No."

Are you kidding? "I just gave up another day and I can't even touch him?"

Checking her blood-red nails for flaws, she answers, "You should have asked more questions before you bought."

"That's bullshit," I argue, getting in her face. "Completely false advertising, I didn't give up two days for nothing."

She barely looks up from her nails. "Just because you can't literally push him out of the picture doesn't mean you can't scare him away."

The damage is done. I'm one day closer to losing Lila. I look around the room. I need to do something. There is a TV, a pool table, a vintage pinball game, bar lights, and some beer.

I inspect the collection of imported beers that is displayed over the plasma TV. Lila told me once that Jason's dad thinks these bottles are priceless, that he won't drink them, because they cost like three hundred dollars a bottle.

Ever so gently, I tap each label as I walk by. I can't keep the smile off my face as the amber liquid seeps out of the bottles and drains onto the TV.

A stream of beer running down the screen catches Jason's attention. He gets up from the couch and walks up to the screen. He wipes it off. Another drop follows. Frantically he tries to stop the bottles from leaking. His dad is going to kill him! If the pot doesn't get him shipped to rehab, this will.

Jason picks up one of the bottles and slams it onto the bookshelf. He turns to face me and growls, "Xan, I know it's you, you bastard."

"Can he see me?"

"No, but clearly you are on someone's mind." She is disturbingly excited about all of this.

Thoughts of me should be eating away at him. He killed me. He steps toward me but has to go around me when he gets close. I follow and watch him yell into thin air. "You don't get it! I won!" He isn't scared. He is gloating.

"Are you going to take this from him?"

No.

Sweeping my arm through the cables that hold up the vintage bar light hanging above his head, I sever them. Shards of glass shower him and nestle themselves into the carpet. I hope he steps on them with bare feet.

Rolling with laughter, he raises his arms to the ceiling and turns in circles. "You're dead!" he screams. "Who do you think she is going to choose, Xan? She may love you more, but guess what? I'm *alive*!"

His taunting laugh has turned into something much more malicious. He wants me to know he has a plan. And now I only have nineteen days to stop him.

NINETEEN DAYS LEFT

I'm not crazy. I saw Xan. I think she did too. So this time, I don't hesitate when I get to her door.

"I want to see him!" My voice echoes in the vacant foyer. Bits of white paint fall from the door as I slam it shut. "I know you can hear me!" I say, choking on dust particles. Millions of them fight for a turn to dance in the warm, final minutes of the sunlight shining through the window.

The smells of stale tobacco, burnt coffee, and mothballs waft toward me. The scent seems to be pulling the psychic along on a leash. No hello. No questions as to who I am or why I'm here. No warmth in her face. There is, however, an invitation to follow her through the doorway of tacky beads.

I suck in my stomach as I try to squeeze by without touching her. Changing clothes in an airplane bathroom and not touching the walls would be easier than not brushing up against her or her creepy plastic beads, which seem to reach for my face as I try to get through. Gross.

I haven't seen this many artificial lights since I had my tonsils out. Hundreds—no thousands—of clear glass jars line the shelves. They appear to be in some kind of order. Behind me are the liquids, every color imaginable. To my left are herbs, maybe. Bugs, eyeballs, and things that look like she robbed the hospital's trash are on the right.

My God, it's cold in here!

"I knew you'd come back," Madame Tula says, sizing me up, looking for something. She is scary as hell.

I can't let her know I'm afraid.

Her slew of necklaces smacks me in the face as she reaches over me to a shelf above my head. Was she this tall before? God, she stinks.

"I know you saw him." I quickly duck my head so her beads don't hit me again.

As she gathers ingredients, she nonchalantly replies, "Could have." She doesn't even look at me. Instead she scans the section of eyes, looking for the perfect pair.

What was I thinking, coming to a psychic who spends her days mixing twigs, slugs, and eyeballs? She can't bring Xan back. "I shouldn't have come." I need to go. I can't keep prolonging the unbearable devastation of accepting the truth. He isn't coming back.

This time I'm certain the beads hanging from the door frame grab at me like serpents as I walk through them. I have to shake them off. I should run as far away from here as I can. But I don't. I sit on the front step and let the hot cement warm me up. That room was freezing. I didn't think houses that old had air conditioning.

Where did she get all those eyeballs? Are they human?

Across the street, a young couple fights over whether their baby should wear a sun hat or not. "Who cares?" I mumble. It's not like she's in the sun anyway; the sun is gone and the moon will be on its way up soon. The stroller canopy covers every inch of the baby but her toes. I wave at the adorable baby blowing raspberries.

I want to fight over stupid things like whether or not our baby needs more sunscreen or if she is too young to be eating frozen yogurt. I never even got to fight with Xan about how many kids we'd have.

I didn't get to say good-bye. I would pay anything if it meant being with Xan. Why didn't Madame Tula try to stop me from leaving? She didn't even try to rip me off by filling me full of bull. All she cared about was her chemistry experiment, which smelled worse than a landfill on a hot day like today.

The baby across the street squeals with joy. She can't see her parents making out behind the stroller, but she seems to know everything is going to be okay. And it will be.

For them.

When did I become such a pathetic loser? I came here for answers. I don't take no for an answer. I am not a quitter. I take one deep, controlled breath and while I slowly exhale, I turn off my emotions.

I've been avoiding shutting down, emotionally. I've been too afraid of not feeling the pain of missing Xan. Before him, I was a human rock. I didn't let anyone in. Then we met, and well, it was just perfect. There was something unspoken that wouldn't let me walk away from him even if I wanted to. All it took was one touch for me to know he was the one I wanted to spend forever with.

It didn't occur to me to worry that it wouldn't work out.

I should have known better.

I get off my butt, which is now toasty warm, and go back inside. She looks like a mad scientist, that is if mad scientists wore muumuus. She is hovering over the gas stove, watching the orange and purple flames cradle a beaker of furiously boiling liquid. "What kind of psychic can't tell me anything?" I approach her without an invitation.

She doesn't flinch. Looking over her shoulder, she answers me with as few words as possible. "I can. I won't."

"Why not?" I plead helplessly. I haven't felt in control since Xan died.

Madame Tula reaches into the pot, scoops up the steaming, lumpy concoction, and plops it into a paper cup. "You are not ready."

Ready for what? For someone to tell me my boyfriend is

dead? That it's time I start getting on with my life and stop talking to ghosts who aren't there? There isn't anything I'm not ready for.

"Was it real, what I saw in the graveyard?" Please tell me I'm not crazy. Please.

I am crazy. I sound ridiculous. I just asked a psychic to confirm that I saw my dead boyfriend. I lean in to the wall and slump to the floor. Jason is right. I want to see Xan so badly I'm willing to believe anything, even my own insanity.

Her back may still be to me, but I swear I just saw her ears perk up. "You saw him?" Suddenly she seems very interested. She turns around and offers me a drink of the sludge that is no longer bubbling. "Drink."

I take the cup. It smells like muddy paint; it looks like it too. "Do I drink or chew this?" I ask as if I'm actually going to put it in my mouth.

With a twisted twinkle in her eye, she tells me what I've been praying for. She guides the cup to my mouth. "Drink and you can see your sweet Xan."

She knows his name. I didn't tell her, did I?

I open up.

I watch her shake the clumps free so they can tumble out of the cup and into my mouth. I pretend it's Greek yogurt zinging my taste buds instead of what looks like blended-up black whale blubber. My tongue holds the chunks against the roof of my mouth, not by choice, but because I can't figure out how to get them down without throwing up.

"Swallow."

I do as I'm told.

"Good girl." She makes sure I consumed everything in the cup.

Something doesn't feel right. I probably should have made that observation before I drank something made by a voodoo psycho. Xan would be so mad at me. But he's not here. And really, worst-case scenario, I die. Not a bad outcome.

A small jar tucked behind the dehydrated frogs and salamanders catches my attention. Moss-covered sticks bounce around like a box of magic jumping beans I had when I was little.

Madame Tula becomes irate and starts breathing heavily when she sees what I'm looking at. Violently, she tells them to stop. They listen. The sticks stop moving and look like sticks should.

What is this place? Who is she and why does she all of a sudden sound like she is from New Jersey instead of Russia?

As soon as the sticks are under control, she turns her attention back to me. Why is she looking at me like she can't wait to see which trick I will perform next?

Never mind. A darkness, an evil is forming in my stomach. It's churning.

The unexplainable déjà vu feeling I've had so many times arrives as the darkness climbs out of my stomach and into my bloodstream. As always, I feel like I should be on display at a house of wax. Something is different. This time I can think clearly.

"How long has this been going on?" asks Madame Tula, who is crouched down by me, examining my every move. Watching. Waiting. I just wish I knew what for.

I don't pretend to not know what she is talking about or ask how she knows about it. "Since I was twelve." Random images begin passing in front of my still-open eyes. They don't make any sense. I feel like I know them. Like I've been there. Each one contains Xan and me, but from different time periods. We look like us—our weight or hair color might be different, but it's clearly me in each one of these pictures. Xan, too. The slide show stops, and I remember something. "The day I met Xan, it happened three times."

I cannot believe I forgot that. No, I didn't forget. I didn't know.

The tingling numbness of my body increases as my memories and déjà vu moments begin fitting together like a jigsaw puzzle. I didn't live those lives. I couldn't have. Terrified or enlightened, I'm not sure which, I confess, "I saw my grandfather the night he died."

"Okay," Madame Tula says.

I try to rationalize. Try to make logical sense of what cannot be real and why I haven't remembered this until right now. My heart is beating so heavily it is making my whole body pulsate. "I saw him standing at the foot of my bed. I thought it was a dream. When I told my mother about it the next morning, she turned white. Then she told me my grandfather had died the night before. I was six." My mother has never looked at me the same since.

I didn't notice Madame Tula take my hands into hers; they are as corpse-like as mine. "Lila, think." She rubs the tops of my hands tenderly. "This is not something new. You have always been able to sense things; it started long before you were twelve. Now you have a reason to *want* to see them." Another one of her personalities emerges as she shakes my arms around like wet noodles.

She's right. I have always been afraid of what I can't see. I've always felt like someone—or something—is with me, lurking. I've gone as far as using the Lord's name, shouting it out when I'm really scared.

"You, my child, are not from this world."

Excuse me? "I'm an alien?" Aliens terrify me.

Her bony hands act as handcuffs. She feels around the underside of my wrists until she finds a pulse. "Not an alien," she reassures me. "But not from this time. You've lived many lives, Lila." She seems to be pleased to be the one enlightening me with this bit of information.

Yeah, okay, I've thought it, but that's the most absurd thing I've ever heard. "I don't believe in reincarnation." I wriggle my arms free and stand up.

This time she tries to stop me from leaving. "Maybe not.

But tell me, did you feel like you already knew Xan the moment you saw him?"

His name is all I needed to hear. I'm listening. I've always told myself we felt like that because that's what happens when you find *the one*.

I pause in the doorway. Her knees crack as she stands up. I twirl a dangling strand of blue beads around my finger.

"The déjà vu only happens when it involves him, doesn't it?"

My heart skips a beat. "Where is he?" I turn back. I have to see the expression on her face. I need to know if she is telling the truth or not.

She looks like she just won the lottery. "There is only one bond that could be strong enough to keep him where he is. A single life wouldn't be enough love to fight for." She unwinds the beads from my now-purple finger.

"He's still here?" I ask, searching like crazy for a sign of him.

Her fingers creep around my body like my mom's used to do when she'd sing "Itsy-Bitsy Spider."

"You are the gifted ones," she seductively whispers into my ear, her hand on my head.

"Ouch! Gifted ones?" I rub my scalp.

She doesn't answer. She is too busy stuffing the long blond hairs she just ripped from my head in with the jumping twigs. With extreme care, she places the jar next to an empty one. This jar is like nothing I've ever seen. Two separate glass tubes twist and turn until they become one.

Is she for real? There is something seriously wrong with me that I am listening to this and actually hoping it's true. "And I'm one of them?" I mock.

I have been given more than enough disapproving looks in my life to know when I am silently being disparaged. She doesn't need words to make me feel like an idiot for questioning her. "Every now and then, two souls merge on their way to mortality."

"So, Xan and I merged on our way to Earth?" From the sky,

where we were once perfect star souls?

"I don't think so." She has started mumbling. I don't think she is talking to me. I can't make it all out, but something about running out of time and to stop playing around.

"What?"

Her laugh makes every hair on my body stand up, and she turns back to me.

I recognize that laugh. I let out the very same cackle when I got into the New York School of Performing Arts. When it finally happened, I couldn't believe it. I had finally gotten what I wanted. What has she been waiting for?

She is examining me, looking for my cracks, my flaws, my weak spots. I haven't felt this violated since the last time I was in ballet class. "In the beginning, every soul starts whole. Then, just before they are thrust into the sky, a selected few are divided: two parts, one perfect whole."

"Xan is my other half?" Unlike everything else she's said, this feels strangely right. It makes sense.

"Literally." She caps off a small test tube of what appears to be dirty water. "This is incredible! That is why you've been given so many chances to get it right!" She begins aggressively shaking the liquid.

I don't get a chance to ask what we are trying to make right or how many chances we've been given. I am too transfixed by the swirling tornado she is holding in her hand.

"Drink this when you are ready to feel Xan in your arms again," she says as she offers me the magical bottle.

"What do *you* want?" I might be desperate, but I'm not stupid.

"Your ring." She is forcing me to hold on tight to the tiny jar, which is singeing my hand.

This ring is the only thing I've got left that ties me to Xan. As long as this ring is on my finger, I am his. A cool, invisible force pries my hand open and warms my heart. "No." I give the vial back.

I don't look back, even when her friendly accent miraculously returns.

"Tell me, Lila, before he died, did he speak to you as if he knew he would be leaving soon?"

I stand torn between the voice inside me telling me to leave and the curiosity luring me back in. If she isn't legit, how does she know things I've never spoken of to anyone?

Xan

NINETEEN DAYS LEFT

I feel like a five-year-old child who doesn't know what they did to get into trouble. Only my punishment isn't being put into the corner for a time-out; it's having the invisible wall that separates me from Lila put back up. I've tried breaking through the barrier twelve times already.

"What were you thinking?" Wes sounds like my mother berating me after she's caught me drinking or sleeping on the couch with Lila.

Me? How is this my fault? "She said she could help me!"

"Irene is not one of us," he warns. He's been pacing for so long I'm starting to see the path he's worn into the ground.

"I think you're pissed because I found someone else who is willing to help me." My legs dangle off the ground as his rock-solid fist clenches my neck.

"I know how badly you want to be with her. But you just gave up two days in an already impossible time frame."

My vocal cords collapse in his grip, and the look on his marble face is terrifying. I don't know why he decided against ripping my head off. But he did. "You're going to get yourself killed, Xan." He drops me to the ground.

I pick myself up and chuckle at the bad joke he's just made. He doesn't laugh. He's serious. "Why are Madame Tula and Irene so interested in me?"

"They want the eternal glow." He says it as naturally as ordering a cheeseburger.

I can't stop laughing. It's not funny, it's really not—I only have so much time left to get to Lila—and I'm trying to stop, really, I am, but c'mon! Eternal glow? If I have some kind of glow, why can't I see in the dark? Iron Man has light in his chest where his power lies. Being a self-sufficient night light would come in handy here.

I check myself for any sort of light I may be emitting.

"You can't see it, idiot."

I was kind of—okay, *really*—hoping to see myself completely illuminated.

"I don't know why *I* didn't see it before." I watch as Wes places his hands on the barrier, and his energy changes.

I'm such an ass. I keep forgetting he's been in my shoes and things didn't turn out well for him. I drive my fist into his bicep of steel. "C'mon, you're telling me you didn't look for a glow at first?" I am trying to lighten the mood. It's not working.

"That's why you've been given so many chances to get it right with Lila. Xan, you and Lila are much more than two souls looking for each other. You're different. You started as a single, perfect soul and were separated for reasons we don't know—long before you were sent to earth. You are the same soul searching for its other half, trying to become whole again. What we do know, is that you belong together."

"That must be why we fit together so well!" I say, still trying to get a laugh out of him.

He's quiet and calm. I've never seen him like this. "Xan, be serious. You gave away two days to do what? Rile Jason? He doesn't seem like the kind of guy who backs off when threatened."

Jason doesn't know what it means to back off.

Wes looks weak. I don't like it. His head seems too heavy for him to hold up. The massive, indestructible creature that just moments ago was ready to crush me into pieces is now using the wall to keep himself from falling down. "They make you weak." The way Wes is holding his hand to the glass, it's as if he wants to get to her as desperately as I do. Jason has "accidentally" found Lila slowly walking along the beach. "If Lila drinks that potion Madame Tula made for her, you will be able to make physical contact."

He doesn't sound happy, but I can't help but perk up. That's all I've wanted. "I've made contact with Lila, and the psychic has used her potions on me. It brings me down, but I always rebound."

He wasn't finished. "Done separately, it's fine. Done together, it brings you one step closer to becoming mortal. Done together in the presence of Madame Tula . . ." He doesn't finish. He doesn't need to; the shake of his head says it all.

Does it never end? Ten minutes ago I woke up to Wes standing over my limp body looking at me as if I had just given chemicals to a terrorist. It isn't the frustration plastered across his face that bothers me. It's the fear. It's making his already rigid body ready to crumble.

He doesn't think I can do this.

"If you become mortal before Lila acknowledges you, before you have a real two-person conversation, you're just that: mortal."

His words play ping-pong in my head as the pieces fall into place. Mortality equals death. Game over.

"If Lila drinks that, you'll be too weak to survive Madame Tula's power. You haven't been in a human body for weeks. Yes, you will be strong because you and Lila are together, but it takes time to regain the use of that power. You can't run after you've been in a horrible accident and lost the use of your legs—same idea. You have to relearn how to use your strength."

"I thought she needed my light to gain power."

"She does. Madame Tula has been around as long as you have. Maybe longer. When a star or a soul fails to reach its original state of perfection, it is judged by God. The severity of the accrued karmic debt decides its fate, and it is sentenced to Earth to suffer. She must have done something really bad."

"Why do you say that?"

"Because she's been on Earth waiting, perfecting the potion she needs to destroy the gifted ones. It's the only way she can get back home—she has to have the light of a pure soul." Wes has come out of his pity party. He sounds less defeated and more like the motivator I need.

If she's been alive this whole time . . . "She has to be over a hundred years old."

He nods. "She is lucky a hundred years is all she had to wait. It's been centuries since the last two parts of a whole fell at the same time and merged. It just doesn't happen."

What the hell kind of magic is she doing? I'm not the best at guessing ages, but no way does she look over forty.

"See the large jar on the shelf next to the one with Lila's hair and the jumping twigs? The one that has two tubes that twist together becoming one? It's ready and waiting for the eternal glow."

I suddenly wonder if they are working together, Irene and Madame Tula.

"I may look like stone, but inside, jealousy, envy, and regret are what keeps me alive." Wes says.

He's not angry. He's heartbroken. He's trying to save me from making the same mistakes he did.

There is a perfect half-moon tonight. In a couple of hours it will illuminate the sky and make a beautiful reflection on the water. Like Lila and me: one half bright, full of life, and the other half completely dark. Tonight, though, it's not me on the beach with Lila; it's Jason. And because of my stupidity, I can't warn her. I can't tell her how creepy he is, walking three steps behind, checking out her ass.

God, her ass looks good. Jason wouldn't be human if he didn't look.

"What would you say . . . ," Lila starts.

He splashes her, urging her to continue.

"If I said I knew a way that I could be with Xan again?" She bunches her face up.

Is she drunk? Why would she ask him that?

His eyes glare into her back like a dagger shoving into my heart. "I'd say you're crazy and you'd better not be thinking about killing yourself again." He takes another look at her butt before catching up and taking her hand into his.

She holds his hand, believing he is really worried about her mental health. She stops so her bare feet wiggle as the sand and water flows between her toes. When she was dancing, she would aggressively dig her feet into the sand until all her calluses were scraped off. "I don't think I am."

He pretends to trip and fall into her. If she thinks that was an accident, she is more oblivious than I thought. He tucks a stray curl behind her ear and steps even closer to her. "Do crazy people ever think they're crazy?"

She ignores his question and allows her eyes to follow the moonlight on the water. I wonder where she's imagining the lighted path leads tonight. To marvel about things that have no logical explanation is one of Lila's favorite things to do.

"I'll take back my words if you answer one thing."

That gets her attention. The hope in her eyes breaks my heart. She wants so much for him to believe her. "Anything."

"Have you ever actually *seen* anything?" He is making ghostlike gestures with his hands.

This is her chance. Tell him. Let him show you who he really is. She bites her lip and digs her feet deeper into the sand. She wants to but knows she shouldn't.

He doesn't give her the time she needed. "Lila, he's dead!" He doesn't waste any time cutting to the chase. "Do you not see me standing here?" He beats his chest like the ape he is before raising his arms as if to praise God, who has to be waiting for the right moment to strike him down. "I'm alive, Lila. I've been bending over backward to help you. And how do you repay me? By telling me that you've come up with a plan to have a relationship with your dead boyfriend?"

"He was more than a boyfriend."

He backs down. It might be a first for him. "Whatever, Lila, you have him on such a pedestal. You don't even know the truth about him." He kicks through the water and sand as he walks away, loud enough so she is sure to hear him.

I push past Wes and bang on the window. I pray he can hear me. "Shut up, Jason!"

Turning to Wes, I beg, "I could really use one of those passes to do something to him right now."

"He's just trying to get her to doubt you," Wes tries to reassure me.

She has reason to.

The Lila I know comes out of her shell. "You've always been jealous of him! You should be, Jason, because even dead, Xan is more of a man than you will ever be!" She screams so loud half of Wisconsin has to have heard her.

Jason picks up the pace. He is still walking away from her. What is he waiting for? I know he's going to do it.

Lila doesn't like to be ignored. Screaming at the top of her lungs, she throws her shoes at him. They are the very same pink satin wedges she wore to the winter dance this year. I know this because her face lit up when she showed them to me—she said they felt like ballet slippers. "If you're going to throw out accusations, you'd better be able to follow up."

He stops. That did it.

Oh God.

The momentum he gained from running away is now directed at her. She is the red flag as he charges like a bull. He backs her into the water. "You want to know what the rest of the world knows about your perfect Xan?" he hisses, driving his finger into her chest.

The water is up to her shins. She looks scared. I know that look, and I wish I could say it's because she's afraid Jason is going to drown her. It's not that kind of terror that fills her eyes. "What, Jason? What does everyone know?" She pushes back at him. Her voice is trembling.

He shoves her with both hands and she stumbles, barely catching herself from falling. The moonlight exposes the devil he is. "He slept with that nurse."

I collapse.

She doesn't yell. She doesn't try to tell him he doesn't know what he is talking about. She's known it in her heart all along. She drops to her knees and lets the waves crash up over her back, covering her like a blanket.

Shocked, Wes points out the obvious. "This isn't good, Xan."

"You think?"

Lila and I lie equally devastated in two separate worlds until she smells the sweet stench. Then, like a zombie, she drags herself out of the water and goes to him. Jason and I don't move when she snatches the joint out of his mouth and puts it into hers. The embers crackle as she inhales deeply, finishing it with one breath.

"Don't say it."

The three of us watch her grind the ashes into the sand with her bare foot. When she is sure the fire is out, she extends her hand to Jason.

Jason reaches into his back pocket and gives her what she wants: a pack of cigarette papers, a lighter, and a very full plastic bag of sticky, sweet-smelling clumps of drugs.

"I'm going to pretend this didn't happen." She snatches the items from him. We watch her disappear into the night, carrying the bag of drugs that I planted in Jason's car.

In the midst of his jealous rage, he hurt the one he loves. Right now, Jason and I are very much alike.

Lila

SEVENTEEN DAYS LEFT

She isn't in the room with me. She isn't even across town sleeping in the bed that used to be mine. Hannah is halfway across the country preparing for the New York School of Performing Arts summer showcase.

She didn't get the roles I would have.

She has probably already forgotten that my boyfriend died. She took my spot at the summer intensive this year. She took her mom's side instead of mine when we found out our parents were sleeping together. I should think about those awful things she's done to me. But I don't. I think about the time I slipped in ballet class and she caught me. We were eleven. We've been best friends ever since.

That's why I called her.

"Wait, what?" It's good to know that some things never change. All it takes for her to pay attention to me is to say something that makes my life less perfect than hers.

"Did you know Xan slept with Julia?" I repeat. It is so quiet I can hear the clock ticking in her apartment. Her silence tells me she knew. "Why didn't you tell me?"

"What was I supposed to say?"

I don't know. She should have said something, though.

"Was I supposed to bring it up after you got out of the hospital, or maybe after he gave you that rock? Which looks more like an engagement ring than a promise ring, if you ask me. You really wanted me to be like, hey, Lila, guess what? The love of your life screwed the nurse who knows all your deepest, darkest secrets." Hannah does this when she knows she is wrong. She gets defensive.

What did I do to deserve all of this? Seriously, what did I do? If Xan were here, he'd tell me to pray, to go talk to Pastor Gary. I wish I could. It might help. God has a plan, right? That's what people keep telling me. You know what? I'm sick of his plan. I'm sick of pathetically begging for help from the thing or entity or being who is single-handedly responsible for ruining my life.

I hate you. You hear me, God? *I hate you!* I hate you for taking my ballet career away. I hate you for giving me a best friend who cries when she finds out her nail color doesn't match her outfit but doesn't shed a tear when everything I've lived for disappears. I hate you for allowing me to walk into my house at the very same moment my father was nailing my best friend's mom. Most of all, I hate you for taking Xan without me.

The last is unforgivable.

All of this could have been avoided. One trip to the doctor's office when my mom found out she was pregnant with me could have prevented a lot of heartache. My dad wouldn't hate us for trapping him, and my mom wouldn't hate me for ruining her life.

"My life sucks," I pout. I sit on the bed and hope the boat sinks. Maybe I should untie it and let the current take me away.

"Stop feeling sorry for yourself, Lila."

I'm sure she is standing in front of her full-length mirror, watching herself, making sure she looks pretty. I shouldn't judge. She needs to look pretty to be a successful dancer. Her dancing certainly isn't going to get her noticed.

"Yeah, things have been a little rough for you," she continues. "Deal. I am so sick of hearing about poor Lila. It's like you choose when to be sad. I don't know why you are getting so upset about Xan. You're the one who should be ashamed of yourself."

What is she talking about? "Me?"

"Xan *just* died, Lila. I don't know how you can sleep at night."

"Hannah, what are you talking about?"

"Seriously, you are going to make me say it? You spend your days pathetically throwing yourself at Jason."

I know Hannah's a bitch. I've known that since the day we met. She tries so hard to make everyone think she is a badass. She is even more afraid of appearing weak than I am, but she's been different since we found out about our parents. It's like she is full of hate and on a vindictive mission to destroy anything and everything in her path.

"You're right, Hannah. It was my plan all along, to get Xan out of the picture so I could have a selfish prick like Jason. He'd be perfect for you, though, Hannah. You should call him. Oh, wait, you tried and he rejected you." I know it's not right to rub his refusal to date her in her face. But it's the only thing I've got right now.

I know that Jason and I have a strange relationship. One day we are two peas in a pod; then weeks, even months, can go by without so much as a hello to each other. But no matter how much time passes, it always feels like no time has passed at all.

He had so many opportunities to tell me about Xan. Why now?

Is anyone who they seem to be?

Until Xan, my life felt forced. Everything changed the day I met him. I knew he was the reason I was born. Is it possible that I imagined everything? That I wanted a happily ever after so badly that I convinced myself it was actually happening to me?

"I'm sorry. I didn't mean that," Hannah painfully spits out. She would rather have a root canal than apologize.

"Yes, you did."

"I didn't tell you, because you were doing so well," she says quietly.

Is it possible she actually feels bad? Is she actually thinking about what to say before she says it?

"You and Xan had just gotten back together when I found out. You weren't hesitating to put food in your mouth. You were happy. It didn't matter."

She is trying to justify herself. Everything was perfect. That's why it doesn't make sense that he'd kill himself. "Maybe that's why he did it," I half ask, half say. "He knew it would kill me if I found out he'd slept with her." He took the easy way out. Coward.

Right now, in this moment, Hannah starts to sound like a best friend should. She is trying to protect me. "Do you remember when I said you guys were more perfect for each other than I thought?"

I'll go along with her random subject change. It's nice to talk to someone other than my dead boyfriend, who refuses to talk back. "Yeah."

"He said that he wanted to discover the world and all of its meaning with you! And you are so full of motivational philosophy crap!"

Like magic, the mood changes, and we forget any tension that might have been between us. "I wish you were here." I'm tired of doing this alone.

I am alone.

I'm the one who lost the love of my life. I wasn't supposed to have my soul mate taken from me, at least not at seventeen. I need help. Hannah is the only person still alive who knows I won't ask for it.

I've missed this.

"You found your prom dress that day."

"I can't believe I was the only person the dress fit. That had to be a sign, right?"

"Luck, Lila. It's what happens when you are in the right place at the right time."

"Yeah, maybe." I don't want to argue. That dress fit like a glove; it was weird.

"Hey, don't let Jason change how you remember Xan."

For a brief moment, I was able to forget the living hell I get to call my life. I shouldn't be shocked that Hannah wouldn't let me forget for long. But like a fool, I am. "You can't forget what you already know, Hannah. You can't un-hear things."

"Lila!" Hannah's voice calls to me until I press the end button.

I toss the phone on the bed and bury it under the pillow, then grab my iPod and scroll through the playlist, looking for something to drown out the noise in my head. I'll take anything but a love song. I collapse on the bed and let the vibrations from the bass zing around me.

It's me. I'm the problem. It's me the world doesn't want.

The sun blinds me as I leave my cave-like bedroom in search of trash bags and vodka. A sure sign I'm doing the right thing: I find both in the first place I look (under the sink). I raise the nearly empty bottle to the sky and toast God. "To the destruction of Lila." The vodka burns my throat and dribbles down my chin as I chug. When I've drained it, I toss the empty bottle in the sink and grab the box of industrial-size garbage bags.

Under the mattress of my nearly king-size bed are secret compartments where I keep the things I can't bear to look at but can't get rid of. Wedging my shoulder under the heavy mattress, I prop it up and begin pulling everything out. Leotards, pointe shoes, leg warmers, sweaters—I don't stop until every last piece covers the floor.

I don't look. I just stuff. If I look, I won't be able to go through with it. Every piece of clothing here has a story, a memory. I slow down when I come to my first pair of pointe shoes. The black three-quarter-sleeve leotard I wore to my audition for the New York School of Performing Arts slows me even more.

The song changes. Classical music begins before I can hit

stop. It doesn't matter: I've heard the first note of the "Waltz of the Flowers."

One time I broke down while picking out a tie for my dad at the mall. It was Christmas and I couldn't dance because my Achilles tendonitis was so bad. I dropped the tie and ran out of the store the second I heard it playing over the loudspeaker. While shoppers agonized over finding the perfect gift, I contemplated throwing myself over the second-floor railing.

Desperate to change the song, I don't look to see what is next. If I had thought for a second, I would have known. I know my iPod like the back of my hand. Above all, I know where Xan's songs are.

Xan's voice echoes throughout my fiberglass home. I stop stuffing the bag and grip my favorite pair of plum-colored leg warmers. I can't breathe. This is the closest I can get to him. He will never again introduce me as his. He will never again tell the screaming crowd of girls that he wrote this for me:

I remember the day I saw you standing there
That beautiful smile, pink ribbon in your hair
My heart would never be the same; I fell in love with you
We brought each other happiness; it was all so new

The years, they passed; you and I began to grow apart
But even through the worst of it you've stayed inside my heart
Now things are different; we still talk every day
But every time that we hang up, there's so much more to say.

I miss you in the morning; I dream of you at night
And when we're together, everything feels right
I miss you in the morning; I dream of you at night
And when we're together, everything feels right
Oh, even though you're far away still
Oh, even though you're far away still

No matter what the future holds, whatever we may do
You can always trust in me: I'm here for you
My heart would never be the same; I fell in love with you
We brought each other happiness; it was all so new

I miss you in the morning; I dream of you at night
And when we're together, everything feels right
I miss you in the morning; I dream of you at night
And when we're together, everything feels right
Oh, even though you're far away still
Oh, even though you're far away still

It was the song he wrote to tell me he would never stop loving me no matter what. We were in the middle of a fight and I had just gotten out of the hospital. I was still broken. In hindsight, I was just a little cracked. That night, I knew nothing could ever tear us apart.

The adrenaline pumping through my veins is insane. I can't stop shaking. He's gone. He's really gone. He isn't coming back, and I can't do anything about it. I don't even have a ballet studio to hide in. Everything I've ever loved is gone. "You're not coming back," I say out loud, acknowledging the thoughts running through my head.

I talk to the very person I'm trying to convince myself is no longer here. "I don't have a choice but to live without you." I hit the repeat button so his voice never leaves me. "I don't have a choice but to let you go." The words escape my lips, which are fighting to keep them in.

Ten minutes ago I wanted to reach through the phone and tear Hannah's vocal cords out. I hated her for saying that Xan is gone. Now I hear her. He's dead. I don't know how I'm going to do it, but I have to accept the fact that we can never be together again.

It scares me to death. I don't want to let him go, but a life free of constant aching sounds kind of nice.

My phone rings; it's Jason. I've been avoiding him. I shouldn't be mad at him. He isn't the one who slept with my rehab nurse. I do have one question I can't find a good answer to: Why didn't he let the secret be lowered into the ground with Xan?

I'm never going to find out if I keep avoiding him. "Hey."

Xan

SEVENTEEN DAYS LEFT

"Wes!" Calling out to a talking rock because I need his help is something I thought it was safe to say I'd never do. After watching Lila be buried under a pile of goo, I am in need of serious help.

"Wes!" Why is he never here when I need him? "Seriously, Wes, where is she?" This is worse than the first day. I didn't know what I was missing. I knew she was okay. I knew she was alive.

Is she dead or alive? Did a mixer really smother her with tar, or is the porthole just black so I can't see her?

"No, don't. I'm fine," Lila forcefully tells someone. The sound of her voice allows my panic to fade a bit. The fear in her voice scares me.

I wait for someone to answer, to hear who she is afraid of. The only thing I hear is the clacking of flip-flops. She's on the phone. "I know he's gone. It's been over three weeks since he went missing. I need to accept the fact that he isn't coming back. Just give me some time—next week it will have been a month. I need to try to understand it, to process it, to accept it."

She's talking to Jason. What is she saying? "Lila! Lila!" I scream in every direction, hoping for something, anything.

Nothing.

"She can't hear you." Oh good, Wes has decided to make an appearance after all. "She can't even feel your presence right now."

I look to the right, where his voice is coming from. I can't see him either. "What happened?"

"What did you do?"

"I didn't do anything!" I rethink the last few moments I saw Lila. For once, I didn't do anything. I didn't go to Irene, and Lila was nowhere near the psychic. I wasn't even touching Lila.

"You're one step closer to death." Wes sounds like he is halfway across a football field. If I could see him, he'd be wearing the cancer face. You know, the one doctors get just before they tell you the bad news. "What is the last thing you saw?"

"Lila was listening to a song I wrote for her. The next thing I knew she was being smothered in black tar." I recheck my memory one more time. "I really don't think I did anything."

Barely audible, he says, "She did."

"She did?"

"She acknowledged your death, Xan. Out loud."

I may not be able to see him, but I can hear his teeth grinding. He *should* be upset. He hasn't been a very good coach. "Thanks for telling me I wasn't the only one who could mess this up."

"You can't control what she says. It was only a matter of time before she began accepting what the world believes to be the end."

"I could have tried to stop her from saying it." From thinking it. How can she acknowledge something as it is when it isn't?

Wes's protective energy reaches out to me. "Think about how much pain she must be in trying to convince herself that you're not really dead, that you're somehow still with her."

It must be bad. Lila doesn't let anyone change her mind when she believes in something. "Now what?" I ask, not for my benefit, but for hers.

Dr. Wes delivers the ill-fated news. "Your powers have been reduced."

"Reduced?"

"Think of being totally wasted. You still have the ability to function; it's in your nature. But it is going to take more effort and focus to make things happen." He explains it in a way that makes complete sense for once. I could use a drink.

"So, how do I sober up?"

"Get her to react again."

"Isn't that what I've been trying to do for the last eleven days?"

"Yes . . ." He trails off.

Throwing my hands in the air, I say what we both are thinking. "That's impossible." I could barely communicate with her when I had all my "power." How am I going to do it when I can't see or touch her? Getting her to see me is going to be like cutting a watermelon with a plastic knife. Impossible.

"Not impossible—difficult. First, you need to stop pretending that you're not dead. It isn't helping anyone. Second, acknowledge what is: it's the only thing that can break you free from this cell."

"It would have been easier to die."

"Xan, you've been given a chance the rest of the world would kill for. When has anything worth having been easy?"

Where is he and why hasn't he made himself visible? He feels close, but all I find is thin air when I reach toward the sound of his voice. "Every time I get close, something new gets in my way. Bam! Now Lila can ruin us too. What's next?"

"Xan, you are the only one who can make the choice," he pleads to me.

"What choice?"

"If she's worth it or not."

What kind of stupid remark is that? "Of course she's worth it." That has never been a question.

"Then start fighting for her."

Fight for her? What does he think I've been doing, baking cookies? I run in the direction his voice is coming from. I need to get close enough so I can punch him in the face. I want to see how he does when everything is against him: Jason, Madame Tula, Irene, time, and now Lila.

"You do know, no matter how many advances Jason makes, she will never choose him. You've always known she is yours. Why do you hate him so much?"

A million topics he could choose and he chose Jason. "I just do," I snap.

"Why?" he repeats, unaffected by my anger.

"He knows things about her I don't." The hatred for him festers deeper than I will ever admit. "He's known her since they were kids. They have inside jokes."

"You had a past before you met Lila," Wes reminds me.

I know. I still don't like him. "A few months before I was killed, she pushed me away. I should have been the one helping her through the whole affair thing with her dad. Instead, she ran to him."

"Why do you think she pushed you away?"

"She was afraid I'd turn out to be like her dad." She told me it would be less painful to end our relationship before she fell even more in love with me. Stupidest thing I've ever heard.

"You did have sex with the nurse she confided in while being treated for anorexia."

Thanks. Does he think I might actually forget that? "Did you know she slept with my best friend?" I say. I feel the need to justify what I did. Even the playing field.

"I did. When did she do that?"

He isn't asking me; he is reminding me.

After she found out I'd slept with Hannah. But I hadn't even met Lila when that happened. "That doesn't count."

"Everything counts, Xan. From what I've seen, Lila has never been a priority at home. Her mom was too busy trying to climb the town social ladder to see that her own daughter was killing herself. Don't get me started on her dad."

Jason was there for her when no one else was.

"Why do you think she chose ballet? Because she loved it?" He pauses, but not long enough for me to answer. "Sure, after you tell yourself something enough times, it becomes your reality. As a dancer, she had control over her destiny. Her plan to run as far away as possible wasn't a bad one, if you ask me."

Things would have worked out for her if I'd never come into the picture. Jason was doing a good job of being there for her. "I messed up her plan."

He corrects me. "No. You made her feel things she'd worked very hard to suppress."

I did this to her. If I had been a better boyfriend, if I hadn't allowed her to push me away, I wouldn't be racing the clock to save our love. What have I done? "I shouldn't have let her push me away."

"Probably not, but you did. No sense in dwelling on it. You're jealous."

"I am not jealous of that piece of crap."

"Oh yeah, what kind of car does he drive? Who is paying for his college? I am willing to bet one of your days that you've thought Lila might choose him. Not because she loves him, but because life would be easier with him."

I am jealous. "How can I be jealous when I know he isn't part of the plan?"

"Who says he's not part of the plan?"

I've got to get her back. "I can't lose her."

"You know her better than you think, Xan. You've known her in five lives, and in each one, she is the same person at her core."

Jason may know what she liked to do when she was ten. I know her in ways he doesn't know exist.

"Listen to her heart beating; you can feel her mood," Wes suggests.

I listen. She's hung up the phone. The music is off. She is as calm as she can be.

"What is she going to do? How is she going to react to what

she has allowed herself to say out loud?" He guides me to her.

Not well. This is the calm before the storm.

I took a yoga class once. Lila made me. We were told visualization helps us attain our goals. I close my eyes and fill my empty lungs with imaginary air. After a few breaths, I hear a crinkling sound. Plastic. She is shoving the garbage bags filled with ballet stuff back under her bed. I knew she couldn't go through with it. I bet she is still holding on to the purple leg warmers.

The mattress flops down. She is pulling back the covers. She's crawled into bed. She is rubbing her feet back and forth on the sheets. It's not helping her fall asleep. She is restless.

I can hear everything.

I can see it all in my mind.

Curling up in the fetal position, she pulls her hood over her face and tucks her knees under my Notre Dame sweatshirt. The oversized sweatshirt hides her tiny body. She's holding the leg warmers close to her face. They are muffling her tears. It's not a sad cry like when she's watching a movie. This one is painfully silent. A cry so deep there is no sound to make.

I lose focus and imagine Jason barging through the door to comfort her. Just because she didn't want him to come over today doesn't mean he won't. He's right; he is the one who's alive. It's his flesh she can dig her nails into. It's his lips she will eventually kiss.

"Focus, Xan."

I wonder if Wes can see I've opened my eyes or if he feels my energy changes the way I feel his. "I can't."

"You've got to. You were close."

"How do you know? You don't know what I was thinking."

"I saw a glimpse of Lila. C'mon. Try again."

I close my eyes and try again. She is still curled up in a ball. Tears and eye boogers have nearly glued her eyes shut. She looks worse than the night she found her dad with Hannah's mom. She's lost weight. A lot. Her big knuckle is the only thing preventing her promise ring from falling off her finger.

She rolls into the arms that reach out to her. For a minute I think they are mine. They're not. I don't own a Rolex. She looks relieved in his arms. She looks safe.

"I can't."

"What are you talking about?" Wes is getting frustrated.

Every day I try to pull her back to me is a day she could be working on finding happiness. She's not going to let herself be happy as long as I'm around. "She deserves to be happy." I turn away from Wes and walk into the unknown.

FIFTEEN DAYS LEFT

Why did I think it would be safe to turn my cell phone back on? I've enjoyed pretending they disappeared: Hannah, Jason, my mom, all of them. Their false words of encouragement make my blood boil. I thought about throwing my phone into the lake, and then I remembered Xan's messages. Hearing Xan tell me he loves me is the only thing that gets me up in the morning.

If I don't resave the messages, the phone company will delete them. Somewhere between checking the million voice messages everyone has left, resaving Xan's, and deleting texts, I accidently answer the phone.

"Lila? Lila, are you there?"

"Mom?" The words scrape my throat like sandpaper. Logically, I know my throat is raw because I've spent the last two days screaming. That isn't why it hurts to talk to her.

"Oh my God, Lila, you sound awful. So much worse than she implied."

Thanks, Mom, it's good to hear your voice too. I can't think of a time my mother pointed out the positive in something. Ever. I mean *ever*. There is always something wrong with everything.

"I'm fine," I lie, clearing my throat. Why did it have to be her? Wait, what did she say? "Who implied what about me?"

"Hannah. She said you hung up on her and have been avoiding her for two days."

The condescending tone of her voice makes me want to

throw myself off a bridge. She is trying to make me feel guilty for being rude to Hannah.

How do I explain, to my narcissistic mother, that it feels as if someone has opened up my chest cavity and pressed a million pushpins into my still-beating heart? How do I make someone who is incapable of human emotion understand that the pain is beyond unbearable? "I'm fine," I repeat, and welcome the familiar pit back into my stomach.

"You don't sound fine. Are you eating enough?" I look at the bottle of water I just grabbed from the kitchen.

Telling her what she wants to hear is easier. It used to make Xan so mad that I let her get to me. I don't need to break Xan's heart any more than necessary now. "Really, Mom? My boyfriend just died and you are asking if I'm eating?" No, I haven't been, but I'm not about to tell her that. She didn't think I had a problem when I clearly did; why is she concerned now?

Huh. I haven't checked the mirror in a few days. I haven't thought about it. That's weird. "Ouch." A wave knocks me into the corner of the door. That's going to leave a bruise. The wind has picked up. The boat is rocking a lot. Nothing about this boat is safe. The sleek rounded appearance of the outside can be deceiving. Past the bulletproof glass door, there isn't a curve in sight.

"I'm sorry I care about you," she purrs in true shame-inducing fashion. Now she wants me to feel guilty for being mean to her.

I stumble back into my parents' bedroom and flip the lights on. "That's not going to work this time, Mom." I open the closet so I can see myself in the full-length mirror that hides behind the door.

"I bet you're sleeping well. You've always slept really well on the boat."

Are you kidding me? You're right! I've been sleeping like a baby. I get to have a bedtime story each night. It's the one where the girl wakes up in the same predicament every morning, alone. What could be more comforting than that?

The king-size bed behind me rubs in my face the fact that I sleep here alone every night. She would be mortified if she knew the truth of what I've done in her bed. Xan loved the mirrored ceiling. What's weird is that the boat came that way. "I can't sleep."

I check my stomach first. My ribs are visible. Abdomen is bloated. I find the nearest countertop—the bathroom sink—and roll the elastic waistband of my pants down. I imagine Xan staring at me from wherever he is, shaking his head in disappointment as I ram my hip bones into the hard marble.

"Do you need me to get you something to help?" my mom offers.

I shove my puffy gut in.

I cover myself up and vow to eat less. I haven't obsessed about it. I haven't even thought about it. I did have the banana-or-cookie debate the other day, but that was it. It doesn't make any sense. I've been hospitalized more times than I'd like to admit for starving myself. Why now, when my life is out of control, do I look amazing? I'm a little bloated, but other than that, I look better than ever.

Maybe Mom was right. I never had an eating disorder.

I think about asking her for some of the antidepressants she takes to pretend life isn't real. Instead I do what I always do. I open my mouth and know I am going to hate myself as soon as I hang up the phone. "I keep waiting not to be tired." The desire to sleep is endless, yet I'm lucky to get a few hours a night. Getting up to go to the bathroom takes effort. I don't want to die, but what am I living for?

"Do you want me to come? I could rearrange my schedule."

To the untrained ear, she sounds sincere. But sincerity is the furthest thing from her mind.

And have you hold over my head that you can barely make rent because I made you come and see me? I'll pass, thank you.

It didn't take long for Mom to go back to being a flight attendant after she and my dad decided to get a divorce. I think she knew that Dad was cheating on her; she was ready when he finally had the balls to tell her he was in love with someone else. I'm not talking about being emotionally ready: she had her ducks in a row. She had a job secured with a major airline within a couple of weeks. The fact that she got a job right away isn't what surprises me—she did fly before I was born, and she is still stunningly beautiful. What makes me question things is the level of flights she got assigned after being out of the business for seventeen years: international, first class. After that much time away, wouldn't you have to start on commuter flights on a low-budget airline to prove yourself before being trusted with the snobby, entitled elitists of the world?

Running away from my dad wasn't enough. She had to make sure she was unavailable to me as well. She quit flying when I was born to stay at home with me, and I think she's always resented me for it. Because of me, her life was ruined. I'm surprised she only moved to Chicago and not Milan or Paris. I give it a year before she meets a disgusting, arrogant millionaire no one can stand being around—and she will tolerate him, and he will ask her to marry her. Once that happens, she will be off to bigger and better things, most likely telling people she never had a child.

I hear Xan's voice, reminding me that my mom didn't think to call me until Hannah asked her to check in on me. She hasn't called once since Xan's funeral. I didn't think it was possible, but she is worse than Hannah.

"Hellooooooo?" she calls into the phone. She is irritated that I'm not paying attention to her.

"I'm here," I answer. "No, don't come. I'm fine." I put my hands over my stomach; it's starting to cramp. I must be getting my period.

"Are you sure?"

"Yes."

The conversation is over. She can continue living the delusion that she is a good mother. She offered and I declined like the unappreciative, spiteful child I am.

"I am so glad you've got Jason to help you through all this. The two of you have always shared a special bond."

She is using that tone, the one she gets when she's trying to make more of something than it actually is. She did it when I landed my first solo part in *The Nutcracker*, the part that lasted three counts of eight. She is so dramatic.

It's not always about making me look better than I am. She likes to make me look worse, too. For instance, when I broke into the ballet studio a few months ago, she made a huge deal of it.

Well, I didn't break in; I still had a key.

"We're just friends, Mom." I try to tame the fire before it spirals out of control.

"He's cute," she pushes. She is worse than a nosy teenage girl. *He's rich* is what she's really thinking. Wisely, she is keeping those thoughts to herself. I should remind her how well marrying into money turned out for her and suggest that she take extra caution the next time around. That's not entirely true. My dad was poor when they got married. When the money started rolling in, so did the problems.

She's right. There is no denying that Jason is gorgeous. Ever since he stopped using drugs and started working out, he's definitely hot. Yes, he has a trust fund the size of a small country. He used to make me laugh. We used to laugh so much. I could probably tolerate him. But I don't want to tolerate someone. I want it to be intolerable to be away from them.

"The two of you are so cute together." She still sounds like a giddy schoolgirl. I don't know why I'm surprised she has put Xan's death behind her. She's not one to hold on to any kind of emotional attachment. Amazing what a couple of months will do. In June she was in awe of Xan and me.

I let her continue to babble, playing matchmaker. I stare blankly at the TV. Breaking news cuts into the *Roswell* rerun I was watching before I accidently answered the phone.

A young couple, bound in chains, being transferred from prison, are being led to a bus. The news has never interested me before. I can't take my eyes off the neon-orange jumpsuits. The world freezes, and my heart begins thumping heavily. Each beat makes it harder and harder to breathe.

The girl stops, and the cop closely following her slams into her back. Goose bumps cover my arms when she looks into the camera. Time stands still as we stare into each other's eyes. The TV shuts off before I find out what crime they've committed or where they are being taken.

"Lila, are you listening to me?" The sound of my mom yelling for me is barely audible. "Are you daydreaming again?"

Frantically, I look for the remote. I have to find out what is happening to these people. Why they are being punished. That girl looked so innocent. *Where is the damn remote? Am I sitting on it?* That would explain why it suddenly shut off. I get on my knees and search every inch of the bed. The remote isn't here. I look closer at the TV. Sometimes the cable randomly reboots.

The electric-green 64 is still lit up. It wasn't the cable.

"Hello, Liiiiiiila!" She sounds more bored than when she used to listen to my dad talk about work. At least then she pretended to act interested. She had to; he was her lifeline. Well, his bank account was.

Daydreaming. That's what my mom calls my déjà vu moments. I used to think it was because she didn't understand. But now I don't think that's it. I think it's her form of denial.

Being crazy isn't an option for a Walker.

I couldn't wait to change my name to Lila Hemlock. Now I'll be Lila Walker forever.

My mom is a master at denial—and manipulation. They are

her strongest traits. Pretending she was in a happy marriage was one thing. Refusing to accept that her daughter had anorexia was another. The mentally ill person isn't supposed to be the one who says they have a problem and want help. The scale reading seventy-eight pounds should have been a big-enough clue.

"I went to see a psychic." Is it wrong saying something to deliberately piss her off? Is it awful that it makes me smile?

"You did what?" I think she just choked on her diet soda. "What did she say?"

You want it, Mom: here it is. "That Xan and I have been together for a long time, like a hundred years or something."

She starts laughing. "That's absurd." I let her get it out of her system. "Every time we'd walk by that creepy shop on the way to get yogurt, you would ask to go. I always said no because I knew you'd believe it. See, I told you—maybe you should listen to your mother sometimes."

Do you want a gold star? "There was something legitimately off about the psychic. She knew things only Xan would know."

"Did she tell you your story was true?"

"What story?"

"The one you told me when you were five. You came out of your room looking like you were going on a safari. You had a shovel, a sand sifter, one of my makeup brushes, and a huge backpack. When I asked where you were going, you said to dig up your time capsule. I asked when you buried this time capsule. You said in your last life."

"Why did you never tell me this before?"

Ignoring me, she continues with what she wants to say. "If I didn't know that you had a vivid imagination, I would have believed you."

"What was in it?"

"I don't know. You never found it, but you said you'd buried a doll, a book, and a hair thing."

"I'm not making this up, Mom. She knew things. Even you said you didn't understand the connection between Xan and me." I'm doing it again, justifying the bizarreness of our amazing relationship.

I hate it when she laughs at me, belittling my thoughts, my hopes, my dreams. "No, I've never understood how the two of you could be so in love at such a young age, but never once did I think it was because you've lived a thousand lives together."

I don't hesitate to respond to her snarky comment. "Not a thousand. Five." Where did that come from? The numbness in my face and the freezing of time confirm my thoughts; they tie it all together. My dreams. My déjà vu. Are they from past lives? Everything is still. Everything but my thoughts. There are a million different images flying through my head—and somehow I am able to make sense of each and every one of them.

I gasp. "What kind of hair thing did I say it was?"

"One of those hideous comb things Grandma used to wear."

Oh my God. The comb next to Xan's grave. "I gotta go, Mom. Love you." I hang up the phone quickly so she doesn't have a chance to say something that will change my mind.

"Xan! Xan!" I scream, looking for a sign that he's here. "Knock something over! Fly by me . . . I don't care. I know it's you. Please, Xan! Please! I didn't mean what I said; I know you're here!" I beg him to answer.

I don't feel him.

He's not here.

Now that I think about it, I haven't felt his presence since I said I knew he was dead. What have I done? Did I guide him to the light? Was he waiting for me to accept his death? I'm numb with terror and acutely aware that I may be the reason I never see him again.

Xan

FOURTEEN DAYS LEFT

"Think about the night you asked her to marry you." Wes says, trying to help me get back to Lila.

Which time? I asked her twice in the same day. The first was when I gave her my grandmother's ring in my backyard and then we made love for the first time. I asked her the second time afterward because she accused me of asking so she would sleep with me.

I still can't believe she thought I'd do that.

We needed to keep our plans on the down-low. We thought our parents should find out before our friends did. Finding out we'd finally had sex, though, that kind of news our friends wouldn't take quietly. Nobody believed us that we had waited two years, especially since neither of us was a virgin. I wanted her so much—constantly. But I would have waited forever for her. As long as she let me hold her hand and breathe her breath when we kissed, I was happy.

She needed to be ready to let me love her that much. Connecting with her was intense. We got lost in each other's eyes; no words were needed as we became as close as two humans can get. She knew exactly what I was thinking and what I was feeling because she was experiencing the very same thing. It just was. There are no words to describe how intense and beautiful making love to your soul mate is.

It was spectacular.

I had it easy; I had a concert that night and would be on stage with Charlie and Adam. Lila had to hide her hand all night from Hannah and Jason. Taking the ring off wasn't an option—I tried. She refused.

I knew she wasn't going to be able to keep her mouth shut the second I saw her walk into the old barn. She looked so beautiful that night. She could have been wearing a garbage bag and it wouldn't have hidden her excitement. She tried to avoid eye contact with Hannah and Jason, but she was giddy. She wouldn't stop talking, and she had a permanent grin on her face, plus she was trying too hard to keep her left hand in her jeans pocket. They knew something was up, and it was only a matter of time before she lost focus and they caught a glimpse of her hand.

I figured I'd take the pressure off of her and let the cat out of the bag. I leaned into the microphone and said, "I can't wait to spend forever with you, Lila."

She beamed, completely oblivious to the two people bombarding her with questions. She didn't fight Hannah when she grabbed her hand. She was more interested in the two people on stage hugging me. Adam dropped his guitar and nearly knocked one of the speakers off the stage. My friends were ecstatic and wanted to make this the best night ever for me. Hers wanted to make sure she second-guessed how I felt about her.

That was then. This is now. Screaming my name has taken everything out of her. I can only assume her silence means she's finally fallen asleep. "She said she knew I was still here. Why can't I see her?"

"She took one step toward forgetting about you. A step toward moving on."

I'm guilty of saying and doing things I don't mean in a heated moment of anger. In Lila's case, it was a moment of sheer devastation.

Sometime between leaving my house on the day I promised

to love her forever and gave her my grandmother's ring and walking through the barn door of my concert, she found time to call her shrink. She didn't tell me until I dropped her off after the concert that she had called herself in. She was going back to the hospital for a while. I'd never been so proud. I was so in love with her. Until that moment, I didn't realize how far she was willing to go to ensure she didn't push me away again.

"Xan, if you're not going to focus, I can't help."

"You got me. I like thinking about how awful it must be for her." I can't see him walking away, but I know he's almost gone. I throw an imaginary balled-up piece of paper at him. No, scratch that. I'm throwing a rock, a big rock.

"Lila, I know you're in there!" Jason is pounding on the boat door. Why didn't he go to the office and ask for the spare? Marina management wouldn't think twice about giving a key to him. I'm pleasantly surprised he doesn't have one of his own. I have one.

I wish I could see her reacting to his aggressive tirade at the door. The tone in his voice sounds nearly identical to the way it did the night he beat me to a pulp before dropping me into the icy waters of Lake Michigan. Since Wes showed me the pictures of the night he killed me, I remember how it felt to struggle for my last breaths. I can't stop imagining the sadistic joy Jason most definitely had in his voice as he watched me sink to the bottom of the lake.

She doesn't rush to him. She does, however, come out much sooner than I would have liked. She hasn't said anything, so I can't tell what she is thinking. She is obviously not too shaken up; she let him in.

I don't need sight to recognize the glugging of liquid being poured. My guess: Lila is pouring a vodka and diet orange soda, heavy on the vodka.

Jason cracks a can and drains it before speaking. "What the hell, Lila?"

Her glass hitting the counter speaks volumes. Wes was

right. I do know her. I can see the hatred pouring out of the glare she is giving him. The real question is, how is he going to handle that glare?

"So, what, you're just not going to talk to me again?"

Stillness.

"Look, Lila, I'm sorry. I should have kept my mouth shut."

I wish I could see his face. I want to know if he looks as insincere as he sounds.

"Yeah, you should have." She picks the glass back up, and the next thing I hear is the ice crashing into her face. She's finished it already. She is unscrewing the bottle. She is filling her glass back up. No crack of a new can; she's left out the soda this time. "What would be so bad about me thinking the man I love only loved me?"

I think for a moment he might redeem himself. He could have used the long pause for so much more.

"You're seriously asking me what's bad about that?" I can hear him trying to contain his laugh.

Her silence is her answer.

"He's dead. I needed you to see that he wasn't as perfect as you remember."

"You couldn't let me have that, could you?" She's fighting back the tears. Even now, she doesn't want to appear weak.

"No. No, I couldn't." I hear his bare skin peel away from the leather couch. Jason always wears short shorts. What kind of dude wears short shorts? He's moving toward her. "Lila, I'm sorry. I really am. I just wanted you to remember that you used to like me too."

"Jason, of course I like you." Crap, she is buying it. Her flip-flops are flapping; she is going to him. "I even love you. It's just not the same kind of love."

"It could be. If you'd give me a chance, I can make you happy, Lila. I know I can." If I didn't know better, I'd think he actually means what he is saying.

She isn't saying anything. This isn't good.

"Do you remember that time when we watched the movie *Hellraiser* in my boat?"

He's trying to get to her by bringing up the past. Which, from what I understand, was pretty great.

"The storm was awful. I was sure the boat was going to break loose, that we'd float out to open water and get trapped in the dam."

How does he change the subject and get away with it like that?

"The power went out, and right away you grabbed on to me," he so graciously reminds her. His voice is getting closer to hers. "You wanted me to protect you, and I did."

I didn't need to hear that bit of information. I still can't see anything, but I swear I just saw Jason look up at me, smirking.

"And now my life is one big horror film." She thrusts the glass down more violently than before.

His breathing is getting heavier. "Let me in, Lila. I can help. I'm not the enemy. You are." He's getting mad.

She is still holding the glass, I can hear swirling the ice around in her glass.

"You're alone because you choose to be."

Oh no, he did not just go there.

He did and he's not done. "You trust no one. You think everyone is out to get you. That's why you pretend to be obsessed about things you don't even like: that way you can't get hurt when it fails. Is that any way to live?"

Did he just imply that she never liked me? I'm glad I cannot see her face. I don't want to see if she's hiding something.

Who am I kidding? I know what her face looks like. He just reminded her she really has lost everything. It's not me that she didn't truly love. It was her dance. It was Hannah. It was him.

I was the one exception to the rule.

I can't stand hearing how broken she is. Not being able to do anything about it is the worst kind of torture.

I don't know which is louder, her gasp or the whack of his palm against the glass door. "Call me when you decide to stop being such a waste of space!" He is such an ass. He is even stupider than I thought; this is not the way to win her over.

Their breathing mingles: heavy, labored, neither one sure what to do next. I don't like that mixture. Aggression is what he wants from her. She is smarter than that. "I will," she says sweetly. Nothing more.

The door opens slowly and closes more slowly. He's leaving. "Lila." He sounds like a little boy who's just had his favorite soccer ball swiped by the bully at the park. The door stops moving. "Maybe finding out that you slept with Charlie is why he killed himself."

"Fuck you, Jason!" she screams, slamming the door.

She just smashed my heart in the door. It's not that I forgot she slept with my best friend. I just like to pretend it never happened.

I slept with Hannah before I met Lila. Yes, I should have told her. That's why she was so upset, that I didn't tell her about it. She would have gotten over not being my first.

"I can't do this." I collapse onto the invisible floor. It is surprisingly comfortable today—that or I don't have nerve endings to know how it really feels. If thinking about the day I promised to love her forever doesn't bring me close to her, what will?

If I were to disappear, she could move on. She would eventually get over me and learn to let someone else love her. It could be Jason, if he doesn't kill her first.

I've got to get to her. Now. If I don't, I might not be strong enough to keep putting her through this.

Wes told me to think about something that would emotionally connect us. Our chair. Just before her parents split up, we sat on the back of the boat. We watched the sun set into giant waves. It was hypnotic. She sat on my lap while I commented on how absurd it all was, us sitting on the back of a yacht drinking champagne. She said it was normal. I said there is nothing normal about parents giving their teenage daughter and her boyfriend booze, allowing them to sleep in the same bed, and finding the person you want to spend forever with at fifteen.

We kissed.

I close my eyes and visualize myself crawling into bed next to her, pressing my body to hers. I'd give her one single kiss to the magic spot behind her ear; it takes away all her pain. She'd nuzzle into me as she's done a million times, looking for more of me.

"I know. I know you're here, Xan," she says. Before drifting off into a much-needed peaceful sleep, she whispers three magic words: "I love you."

Together we breathe a sigh of relief. She sees me in her dreams, and I get to watch her do it.

Lila

THIRTEEN DAYS LEFT

I used to pride myself on being a person who believed that everything happens for a reason. I preached it. I lived by it. I was one motivational phrase after another. When I couldn't dance anymore, I told myself it had to be true. When my family fell apart, I began to doubt it. When Xan died, I forced myself to at least consider it.

A year ago, I would have taken today's glorious weather as a sign that Xan was here. I wish I could still see it that way. I want to, I do. I need to believe there is a reason for all of this insanity.

I can't.

I can, however, see the big picture. Someone much more powerful than me is making sure I haven't forgotten who is in charge. The unusual string of overly sunny days is to rub it in, to gloat, that he has once again won. God: three; Lila: zero.

Jason is acting like a complete lunatic. At first he was great. I didn't have to ask him to be at the boat the morning of Xan's funeral; he just came. He made sure I was okay when no else cared. But now it feels like he wants to make sure I know all the bad things about Xan. Who does that?

The constant burning in my stomach reminds me that our love was real, not something I dreamed up. My body is ready to move on. It's tired. It's ready to think about something other than when the next round of excruciating pain will attack.

My body might be ready, but my heart and mind are not.

It's too soon to not feel the pain of waking up without him. But will I ever be ready?

I take a sip of my tea and watch a little girl wearing the most adorable pink sundress fight to get her hands free from her daddy's. She can barely walk, but she wants to try so badly. Reluctantly her dad lets go one finger at a time and hunches over her as she takes a few wobbly steps. She's doing well; she's made it off the grass and onto the mossy area under the trees.

I used to love those trees. We loved those trees.

To everyone else walking through the park, it looks as it always has: peaceful, beautiful, and filled with life. I used to see it that way too. Sunny days like today were the best, when the sun reflected off the water and the weeping willow trees danced in the slight breeze coming off the lake.

Now I see the lake angrily roaring, waiting. Waiting for its prey to slip on a rock and fall into its gaping mouth. Where, with one single wave, it wipes the slate clean, washing away the evidence.

Soon it will be completely dark and the downtown skyline will look like the world's biggest Lite-Brite. A million twinkling lights luring the dreamers to its glory, showing them the endless possibilities it has to offer. It deliberately leaves out the bit about going down the wrong street—that you might want to be careful, that you might never get out.

I step into the water and dig my feet deep into the sand, letting the cool water wrap around my ankles. I love the feeling of being planted firmly into the ground. It's a dancer thing, I guess. The waves gently wash away the shield protecting my feet, and once again, they are vulnerable.

I've been sneaking out at night to come to this beach since I was ten. Since Xan died, though, I get an uneasy feeling after sunset—not that I'm in danger, just a feeling like I shouldn't be here, especially around the pier.

I should go. It's going to take me a while to get home. The

house I grew up in on Lake Drive is tainted. That is not my home. Slip 43 is.

As I get closer to the sidewalk, I notice there is no longer anyone on the beach or in the park. It's eerily vacant. The roar of water is the only sound: the harsh spray from the shower hitting the cement as I rinse my feet off, and the waves lapping on the shore. Where did everyone go? I look at my watch. It's only eight forty-five.

I try to walk faster, but I keep stepping on sharp rocks. I can't put my favorite sandals on with wet feet. It will ruin them, stretch them out. A few minutes ago I was dying of heat, and now I wish I had a wool sweater. I will never understand Midwestern weather.

I am relieved to see other people, but I could do without all the love. It's Monday, why are there so many couples walking out walking around town? What did I do that was so bad I don't deserve to have that too? I guess I'm asking God. I don't know who else I would be talking to.

Continuing the debate, I remind myself to keep quiet. From experience, I've learned that the general public thinks it's crazy to have an argument with yourself.

No, you know what? It is my fault. What was I thinking, allowing myself to fall for Xan? Honestly, I don't know how I convinced myself that getting into a relationship with him would end well. To open up my soul and love someone was risky, maybe even irresponsible. To allow that person to love me back was dangerous, if not just plain stupid.

I should have known better than to think I could have a happily ever after. Happily-ever-after endings don't happen to people like me. They do to people like Xan. So why is he dead?

"Don't even think about it." A familiar voice distracts me, preventing me from playing devil's advocate.

A million places to be in the Milwaukee metro area, and Jason has to be walking down the same street at the same time as me. Of course he does. 'Cause that's how the cards in my deck seem to fall.

I must have been more caught up in my thoughts than I realized. I wasn't aware I'd left the lake, let alone made it all the way to Madame Tula's front steps. When did I put my sandals back on?

"I was just looking," I say when he catches me standing outside the psychic's. I figure that's better than the truth, which is "I have no idea how I got here." I wonder how long I've been standing feet away from her door. How long has he been watching me? Oh God, I hope I really did have that conversation in my head. Sometimes I get carried away and end up talking out loud.

I pull my eyes away from the flickering neon sign, which once again calls to me, and I walk away. I keep my head down and make a conscious effort to keep enough distance between Jason and me so we don't touch. I focus on trying not to step on any cracks in the sidewalk. It's bad luck.

He tells me I'm the one who is crazy. I may be, but he is the one who has some kind of personality disorder. In the last week he's replaced his obnoxious nonstop attempts to make me smile with snarky comments meant to ensure I remember that Xan is dead and was an awful person. Did Jason ever care, or did I need someone so badly that I created this good version of him, the Jason I used to know, or that I thought I knew?

"Will you wait up?" His steps are getting closer together. I move quicker too. "I'm sorry, Lila."

Is that the only thing he knows how to say? I come to a screeching halt. I am done. I am done being treated like I am overreacting. "My boyfriend just died." I turn around. I don't shy away from getting into his personal space. I drive my unmanicured finger into his chest as hard as I can, over and over again. "He may not have been perfect, but neither am I. We both made mistakes. You can try to make him look like the bad guy every day for the rest of your life. But even if you live to be one hundred, you will never be the person he became in seventeen years. Never."

I stare at him with intense hatred, exhilarated by what I've just done. He looks at me unchanged, with the same possessed need to say something that he always has.

"What's your problem, anyway?" I take my finger away from his hot, firm chest.

He watches me bend my finger back and forth, trying to revive it. He tries to grab my hand. I pull it away, even if the warmth of his hand does feel good.

"*My* problem?" He's not happy that I'm refusing to let him touch me.

I wait for him to say more. He doesn't. Oh my God, the look on his face is defensive. He thinks the way he has been acting is fine, that I am the one with the problem. It's like dealing with my parents. Why is the entire world so convinced that what they believe is right and everyone else is wrong?

A logical person might start to think everyone is right. But I've never claimed to be logical. I won't allow myself to believe I'm crazy. I can't.

I don't get more than a few sidewalk squares away before my momentum is stopped. He doesn't say anything. He grabs me. His fingers dig deep into my arm, separating my muscles and tendons from the bone. It hurts. Why isn't he saying anything to explain the vengeful look on his face?

"Ouch, Jason! Let go!" I try to break free. It's pointless. All I'm doing is giving myself a snakebite.

The hatred he is looking at me with is more intense than the look I gave my father when I told him I never wanted to see him again. I don't know what he's going to do next. I don't know if he knows.

"For years, I've loved you. And now, even after he's dead, you'd rather have a relationship with him." He is speaking through clenched teeth, his grip becoming even stronger.

"You think trying to hurt me is going to make me fall in love with you?" I'm still fighting to pull free from his grasp. He is clenching tighter and moving in closer. The warmth of him is no longer comforting. I knew he was jealous, but this is insane. He is insane.

My hand is purple and it hurts. The blood pooling beneath my elbow is throbbing. I try to get the people across the street to notice me. They are oblivious. Jason is so discreet, not one of them would think twice about looking in our direction. If I got killed right now, there would be at least twenty witnesses who wouldn't have a clue what they just saw.

Now I understand how all those people get murdered and raped in broad daylight without anyone seeing.

"You've been such a bitch lately. I keep thinking it's PMS, but it never ends."

"Hey! Is everything okay?" an officer asks as he crosses the street.

I send thanks to the God I just cursed. I've never been happy to see a cop. "We're fine," I lie. I finally wriggle my arm free. I try to pump the life back into it and rub away the handprint embedded on my sensitive skin.

Jason sees the mark my hands aren't big enough to hide. He wraps his arm around me, like we are on a date. "I wanted ice cream." He laughs. Holding me tight, he points across the street. "The one time she doesn't want any, I guess!"

Amazing. His personality has flipped one hundred and eighty degrees. He is once again the jovial friend I have to believe is the real Jason. If this is the Jason I know, what causes him to turn into the monster more and more? No way is it just because he can't have me.

"Lila?" The officer moves into the light so he can see my face more clearly.

Once he confirms that it's me, he hugs me. Officer James used to be one of my dad's golfing buddies. He used to come to dinner on Saturday nights with his wife, before they got divorced. My parents followed his lead soon after.

Officer James is also the one who told me when they found Xan.

Stepping back, I tell him, "It's good to see you, Officer James." I bet he can see how relieved I am to see him.

"I was on my way over to your place."

"Really?" I question. "That's kind of a coincidence."

He looks at me, then to Jason, and back to me. I hope he can see the terror I am trying to hide.

"I wanted to check in, you know. See how you're doing." He is lying. If he wanted to check in, he would have stopped by during the day. Cop or no cop, you don't randomly show up at night on the doorstep of a girl who lives alone. Come to think of it, he would have called.

To be honest, I don't care why he's here. He is and it's given me an excuse to get away from Jason. "Walk with me." I don't ask. I link my arm through his and begin walking toward the marina.

This isn't going to fix things with Jason. It will probably make it worse. What if Jason comes back tonight after Officer James leaves? Maybe I can convince Office James to stay. How do I get him to stay?

"I'd be delighted."

Jason looks furious. What is he going to do? Grab the cop?

"I'll see you later!" I try my best to sound friendly but secretly hope he can understand my underlying tone, which says, *Stay the hell away from me.*

Officer James doesn't ask any questions until I look back to see if Jason is following; he holds my arm tighter and walks faster. Jason no longer looks furious; he looks terrified. He is probably worried that I'm going to tell Officer James what he just did. Maybe he is back on drugs? That would explain everything. Oh my god, I've been a complete bitch. I've been so wrapped up in missing Xan that I didn't even notice the signs.

I took a joint from him the other day. How did I not put two and two together? I'll call him tomorrow. No, I'll stop by.

The dock rocks as we walk by the pontoons, then the fishing boats, and finally the Jet Skis, which all look like bath toys compared to the yacht tied to the end of the dock. My home is the largest in the marina. It's one of the largest boats in Milwaukee.

"There have been some new developments in Xan's death," says Officer James abruptly.

"What do you mean?" I take the hand he has offered to help me board the rocking boat. I unlatch the door attached to the platform and hold it open so he can follow.

He stays put on the dock. "We don't think it was a suicide."

My stomach drops. "What?" I'm nervous. I don't know if it's because this is confirmation of what I've known all along, or if it's because I don't know what else he knows.

"We came across a pile of rocks that didn't fit in with the rest of the pier. They were not in a natural pattern; they had been rearranged," he begins to explain.

"What does that even mean?"

"Forensics is still looking into it, but they found some blood, and pieces of rope and plastic stuck underneath of one of the rocks," he tells me. "I'm going to have one of my officers keep an eye on you," he continues. "Nothing invasive, just watching." He isn't asking for my permission. "If you notice anything or think of anything, call me." He hands me a business card. "You should get inside. You look freezing."

"I'm not cold," I insist, shaking uncontrollably.

Xan

TWELVE DAYS LEFT

Lila doesn't bite her nails unless she is contemplating something. She is pacing.

I need to show her I'm here before she does something stupid.

I don't think she noticed me rubbing her arm after Jason grabbed her yesterday. I must not have been in the right frame of mind to comfort her. The darkness around me has faded away, so I can stand next to her again.

I feel close to her. Actually, it's the closest I've felt to her since I died. Or, does it seem that way because she was taken away from me for a short period of time? It doesn't matter. It's nice to run my fingers through her hair and smell the coconut shampoo she just used. To feel her blood flowing as I pass my hand through hers is something I will never get used to and something that I never want to be without again.

She needs to know it's me moving things and pulling the hair out of her lip gloss, not a force of nature. I look around the living area of the boat. Something is different.

It's brighter. The black tarps have been removed. Her mom had covers made for the windows to prevent the interior of the boat from fading. I'm glad she took them off. Lila needed a little sunlight in her life.

She is on the move. Once Lila has a mission, there is no stopping her. It's nice to see that hasn't changed about her. She's headed toward her car and is showing no signs of slowing down. Where is she going?

How is it that she can go seventy miles per hour in a forty-five-mile-per-hour zone and not get pulled over? Yet when my taillight burns out, I get a ticket? Where is Officer James? I thought his people were going to be watching out for her.

I lose focus again, looking for cop cars when I should be following her. She has stopped the car and is parked three blocks away from Jason's house.

Is she trying to get herself killed? She might've been able to fool Officer James, but I saw the terror in her face last night. She is afraid of him. She got the confirmation that I didn't kill myself. Why would she run toward a person who has been threatening her?

My no-longer-beating heart stops. What if she figured it out?

What if she is here to confront him? She can't.

He will kill her.

She snaps herself out of her meditative state. Putting the car in drive, she slowly turns the corner, pulling up to the gate. She doesn't need to be buzzed in. She knows the code.

The steel gates at the base of the driveway slowly open. They are the kind of gates designed to keep those who don't fit into their world out. Slowly, cautiously, she drives in. After stepping out of her car, she walks up to a house so large it eats entire blocks of houses like the one I grew up in.

"Jason!" she calls, tapping the brass *M* against the door. She's not using the angry pound she should be. It's more of a sorry-to-disturb-you knock. He doesn't answer. She doesn't leave. She keeps knocking, persistently but ever so gently, until he opens the door. By the look on his face, I don't think he answered because he wants to see her. He answered because he knew it was the only way to get her to stop.

His newly built body fills the door frame. I bet he took his shirt off once he knew it was her at the door. "What?"

That was the worst attempt at pretending to sound annoyed I've ever heard.

Any smart person—let me rephrase that, any non-psychopath—would be on his knees begging for her forgiveness. Not Jason. He's not concerned with how his Dr. Jekyll/Mr. Hyde persona may be affecting Lila.

Her face is speckled, like one of those malted Easter egg candies. I saw her entire body get that way once. It was right before her audition for the ballet school in New York. She was terrified. I guess that's how her body reacts to being extremely nervous. It was horrible. She started to scratch, which made huge red welts. I never told her this, but she must have blown them away with her talent, because she looked awful.

Lila is not just pretty; she is stunning. It took a bit of getting used to, the heads turning from across the street to look at the girl I was with. This didn't just happen in the middle of the summer when she was wearing a sundress. No, it happened even in the dead of winter, when all you could see were her little pug nose and red cheeks peeking out from between her hat and scarf. Her hypnotic blue eyes can draw in even the shyest stranger.

That day, the day of her audition, she was not pretty. Her talent is what got those people to come to Wisconsin so they could watch her perform on her own stage.

I miss watching her dance. I miss the fiery shade of red her cheeks would get when she'd catch me watching her. I miss standing in the wings. She would always lock eyes with mine when her partner would step away for a moment or two. I gave her the seductive vengeance she needed to give the crowd chills. I miss how happy dancing made her.

I miss how happy I made her.

Her sweet voice breaks my concentration. "I came to say I'm sorry."

Is she on the verge of tears? No, she is closer than that; she's holding them back.

"What?" Jason and I ask simultaneously. The chunky protein shake he is drinking nearly comes out his nose.

Did I miss something when I was stuck in the darkness? He threatened her. She was scared. What is she doing?

"I know." She takes a step forward, trying to push her way into the house. If he tilts his head down, his lips will be on hers. It feels like an ice pick in my chest as she places her tiny hand on his chest. She is supposed to touch my heart, not his.

"Know what?" He looks as clueless as I feel. I can't help but notice the dynamic between them. He looks like a wounded animal, and she wants to nurse him back to life.

"I'm not going to tell your parents," she assures him.

"You're not?" He is clearly still oblivious to what she is talking about. He plays the victim well, pretending to be the poor little puppy that needs to be rescued. He's no puppy; he's the pit bull you feel sorry for because he's been raised to fight. You tell yourself it's not his fault, that all he needs is love, and he too can be good.

Wrong. You can't teach something to be good when it's in its blood to be bad. When you let your guard down, nature takes over.

I want to swat her hand off his chest. "Not if you let me help you," she continues. "I've been so focused on me that I haven't noticed what's going on with you." Her voice is pathetic, begging for forgiveness.

How can she beg for forgiveness when she hasn't done anything wrong?

"You have been pretty preoccupied lately." His shoulders drop as he opens the door just enough so that she can squeeze through.

Dude.

"Lila, wake up!" I shout. I push through her and smack into

him as she stops in front of his bare chest. I keep forgetting I can't go through anyone other than Lila. Is she really buying this?

"I know. I'm sorry." Her nails claw into his bare chest. "I'm working on it, I promise." Pulling her shivering body in to him, she hugs him like she used to hug me.

Not what I was going for. The chill of my body pushed her into his arms.

I was wrong. Jason isn't an idiot. He is taking full advantage of this, wrapping her in his arms. The two of them stand in the foyer of a fortress. With me dead, Lila has no reason not to walk in. With him, she'll be taken care of for the rest of her life. She won't have to worry if her dad is going to replace her name with Hannah's on his will. It won't matter what she does when she grows up. She can work at the mall if she wants. If she stays with Jason, she can be anything she wants to be.

He brushes her long hair away from her neck, and a devious grin appears on his face. "I want your help," he says, just enough so she will continue. He needs her to say more so he can figure out what he did that needs fixing.

I'd like to know as well.

She pulls away. I like that. What I don't like are the dopey happy eyes she is giving him. "Good."

"What?"

She throws herself back into his chest. "I was checking to see if you were high right now."

I wish I could put a mirror in front of Jason so Lila could see what a fraud he is. Holding her tight, he composes himself. As long as her head is buried into his chest, he doesn't have to worry about her finding out that drugs aren't what he's hiding.

"You're a different person when you're high. This Jason I like." She hugs him tighter before pulling back. "You were high last night, weren't you?"

He takes a moment. Wisely, he is thinking before opening his mouth. He is much quicker than I gave him credit for. "Yes.

Yes, I was." He invites her into the house.

The rest of the day I watch them act as if they are twelve, as if nothing has changed. As if I never existed. She is laughing. She's not doing it because she has to; she wants to. He is making her laugh. He is making her happy.

"Do you have any licorice?" She is sprawled across his king-size bed. He is on the floor. For now. I sit next to her, ready to act if he tries anything.

He plays a royal flush and takes all the candies in the center. I've never met anyone who hates losing more than Lila, not even Hannah. "Licorice?"

"Yeah, we always used to eat licorice when we played cards." She tries to swipe a Tootsie Roll he missed on the rug. He is quicker than she is. She reached the candy, but he reached her first. They fight over the disgusting chocolate taffy much longer than necessary. He could have ripped it out of her hand in an instant if he'd wanted to.

That's not what he wanted. Touching her hand is more important than a piece of candy.

Finally he gets it. He holds it up to make sure she knows who the winner is and tosses it to her.

"You remember the weirdest things," he responds as he takes the cards out of her hands. He touches her again unnecessarily.

She does. Lila remembers everything; she is like a frickin' elephant. She may tell you she forgives you. And she might, but she will never forget. Most likely she is keeping it locked up to use against you in the future. Don't mess with Lila.

"Do you have any or not?" Sitting up, she unconsciously places her left hand on my thigh. Her hand retracts from my leg as if she touched hot coals. Holding her hands together, she looks at me.

Right at me.

"I'm here, babe. Why can't you see me?" I whisper, kissing her hand, which appears to be hurting.

"No. I have Hot Tamales, though."

"No way! I haven't had those in ages!" Her excited smile turns skeptic. "You hate Hot Tamales."

Getting up, he heads down the immensely long hallway. Once out of sight, he shouts, "You like them!" He knows her better than I thought, using fat-free candy to win her over. Brilliant.

Score one for Jason.

She is bouncing up and down like he is about to bring her a contract to the ballet company of her choice. I don't know if she was this excited when I gave her the ring she still wears on her left hand. I've never seen her so excited about food. Ever.

This is how she used to be. This is the Lila I never met. This is the Lila Jason knows. She has somehow managed to push the last two years out of her mind. She is light. Carefree. She is happy.

I don't interfere. I watch her not crumple over in pain every five minutes and talk to someone other than the dead. I want to tell her I'm here and remind her of what a jerk Jason has been. But I can't. I'm not going to be the one who takes away that smile.

They spend the rest of the day reminiscing, reliving stories I've only heard about. Before I know it, the only light is coming from the TV. Like old times, she curls up next to him as they watch a psychopath chase a beautiful girl through the woods.

Little does Lila know, she is starring in her own horror film. She is the beautiful, oblivious blonde fighting for her life. As in all great horror flicks, you must never trust the one closest to you.

Death is calling. It's an unidentifiable tugging from within. Tonight, the same intense force that draws me to Lila is pulling me away from her. It's not the harsh, punishing energy that took me away from her a couple of days ago. This one is calm. It wants me to find peace.

The movie finishes, and I watch Lila close her eyes. She isn't twitchy or anxious. She is peacefully falling asleep in the arms of another man.

ELEVEN DAYS LEFT

If I move, I might wake him up. As long as he's asleep with his head buried under the pillow, I can pretend it's Xan's heart I feel beating underneath my hand. I wonder if I could go through life with my eyes closed, pretending Jason is Xan.

The last time I woke up content was the day Xan went missing. The only difference from that day and this is that I didn't try to let him sleep. I woke Xan with a million kisses. He happily responded. I nuzzle my head under Jason's chin. We don't fit. Xan and I fit together like a puzzle, in every way. It was very strange.

Where is that music coming from?

We fell asleep on the couch last night. Jason's couch is more comfortable than most beds anyway. I call it the chofa. It's bigger than an EasyChair and smaller than a sofa. I love how the cushions suck me into its velvety goodness. It's French. Jason's parents got it last time they summered in Nice.

I hold my breath so I can hear the faint noise better. It doesn't sound like it's coming from upstairs. Where else would there be a radio?

Very slowly, I lift my arm. The cool air instantly gives me chills as I pull away from his warm body. My leg is going to be harder. Still holding my breath (for some reason I think it helps make me stealthy), I unlock my foot, which is hooked around his calf. I freeze when he moves. Rolling toward me, he adjusts.

Like a Band-Aid, I pull away, the quicker the better.

I wait until the deep breathing starts before moving again. The cushion wheezes, filling itself with air as I stand up. In hopes he will think I'm still lying there, I wedge pillows next to him.

I tiptoe out of the room, trying to remember where the creaky spots are. I make it out of the living room and halfway up the stairs before I hit a loose board. Frozen, I wait to see if he heard me. He snorts.

The closest thing to music upstairs is the noise machine Mrs. Montgomery uses to drown out Mr. Montgomery's snoring. When I shut it off, I hear nothing: silence.

Knowing Mrs. Montgomery isn't going to be home anytime soon, Jason wanted to make it clear that we would have the house to ourselves for the next several days. I use her bathroom. She has amazing beauty products. I squirt a small amount of facial scrub infused with eighteen-carat gold flecks onto a washcloth. This I've used before. My face gets soooooo soft after using it. Who knew gold was a good exfoliant! She would have a heart attack if she knew I was in here using her caviar eye cream or algae-and-kelp face lotion.

I contemplate taking a shower in the marble sanctuary with twelve heads. Twelve. This one takes the cake, and I have seen my fair share of fancy bathrooms. I shudder when I think about how many girls Jason has probably brought in here and decide against using it. Plus, she would notice water spots if I didn't wipe it down perfectly. I brush my teeth with my finger and erase any trace of myself before leaving the room.

The weak sound of music reappears when I step into the hallway. It's not coming from upstairs. Following the sound, I head back down the stairs and check every nook and cranny on the main floor. I even look inside the washer and dryer.

It has to be coming from the basement. The game room, theater, electrical room, pool, showers, and exercise room are all silent. So are the garages, all four. Nothing.

I sit down on the floor next to the chofa. I'm going crazy. I really am. The large puddle of drool under Jason's face tells me he isn't waking up anytime soon.

Yesterday was a good day. I touch my hand to his. How is he going to react with me being here? I've never been around him when he is detoxing.

He looks sweet when he's asleep.

There it is again, the music. It's classical. I can spot an overture from a mile away. Who would be playing music so loudly at—I look at the TV—oh, it's noon. This is going to drive me nuts until I find out where it's coming from.

I already checked the basement, but the fibers of the carpet vibrate between my fingers, taunting me, daring me to prove that there is no music playing anywhere in this house. I triple check to make sure Jason is sound asleep. He doesn't need another reason to think I'm nuts.

Once I'm certain he is still out cold, I press my ear to the floor. I hear it clear as day: Vivaldi's *Four Seasons*. "Autumn," to be specific. The familiar sound takes over my emotions; any sense of logic is gone. Instinctually, my mind does what I was born to do. It dances. I could perform this routine blindfolded, but still I visualize the steps, just in case.

I lift my head off the floor. The sound is soft. I put it back down. Loud. Up, quiet, down, loud. I repeat this more times than I'd like to admit before going back downstairs to find the source I obviously missed.

Silent.

I go back upstairs and put my ear to the kitchen floor. Vivaldi. The laundry-room floor, Vivaldi. The bathroom, Vivaldi. *That's impossible.*

It has to be coming from outside. Why did I not think of that before! That's why it's so subtle.

Lawn mowers, yes; laughing children running through sprinklers, yes; electric hedge trimmer, yes; music, no. Not even from a passing car with ridiculously obnoxious bass.

"Miss Walker!"

Shocked to hear someone other than Jason calling my name, I jump. I didn't think to put clothes on before going outside. But my panic is short lived; I have on the jeans and tank top I wore yesterday. Embarrassed to be wearing the same thing as yesterday? Yes. Relieved not to be caught at someone other than my boyfriend's house wearing only my underwear? Yes.

"Mr. Cummings!" I call, walking toward the mailman.

Mr. Cummings has been my mailman, well, my only mailman. He is the one who delivered my letters each spring telling me which summer dance programs I got accepted into. He learned quickly that thick envelopes were good news, and the thin ones not so good. Once I caught him stuffing a letter back into his pack when he saw me come out of the house crying.

He eagerly waited for me to come home the Saturday he delivered the extra-thick envelope from New York School of Performing Arts.

I completely forgot he is the Montgomerys' mailman too.

"I haven't seen you in a while." He sounds concerned. He probably thought I went off to New York early. No, he knew I was injured.

"Yeah," I say awkwardly, trying to figure out how I can begin to explain.

"It's really nice to see you." He saves me from myself.

"You too." It is good to see him. I've always liked Mr. Cummings. I used to put an envelope of money in the mailbox at Christmas time when my mother would give him a box of chocolates. Neither of them ever knew I did it.

"Oh, I have something for you." He reaches into his giant duffel bag full of mail. He refuses to use a car because he says walking keeps him young. He pulls out a letter that looks like it has been sitting on the bottom of his bag for months and hands it to me.

Confused, I take the letter. My hands go numb when I see who it's from, and I can't find the words to thank him. How long has he been holding on to this?

He seems to understand my implied gratitude. "You're welcome. I thought this might be one you'd want me to hand you directly. I knew I'd see you sooner or later. Please don't tell anyone, or I could lose my job!" He smiles, giving my hand a loving squeeze. Not a creepy squeeze, but a good-to-see-that-you-are-okay squeeze. "Take care of yourself, Lila," he says, stuffing the Montgomerys' mailbox and moving on.

My blood has turned ice cold and my heart is going to explode. The letter-sized envelope in my hands is from the New York School of Performing Arts. Small and thin. What do they want? They gave my spot to the first person on the waiting list. To them I am just another has-been, another girl who could have had it all.

I tear it open. I read and reread and reread.

"Lila?"

I gasp and spin when I hear Jason. Stunned, shocked, and confused, I hand him the letter. All he is wearing is boxers, very tight boxers.

"What's this?" He sounds nervous.

What does he think it is? *It's a letter, stupid.* Does he think I took something out of his mailbox? "Where did you get this?" His face drops with each line he reads.

He should be smiling. He should be happy for me. Why is he not smiling? "Mr. Cummings." The high noon sun beats down, burning my shoulders, and the red bricks that make up the driveway are starting to burn my feet. I don't move.

He hands the letter back to me. "He delivered a letter to you, at my house?"

Why would I lie about this? "He's been holding on to it. He wanted to give it to me personally." I am so glad he did. I never would have gotten it if he put it in the box at my dad's house.

Tracy would have thrown it in the trash. If Hannah had found it, she would have shredded it.

The déjà vu is back. Since I drank Madame Tula's potion, I've started paying attention to what's going on when it hits, trying to make sense of it. What if I have them to slow me down, to make me aware of something? "They still want me." I'm unable to believe the words coming out of my mouth.

It's been months since I've danced. In the dance world—especially the ballet world—months is equivalent to years. I am not getting any younger, and I am most definitely not in shape. I put my hand over my abdomen, which is still bloated. I wish my period would just come so it would go away.

Is this why Xan was taken from me, so I would be free to go to New York without hurting him? Was he taken away so I wouldn't have to make the choice?

"Lila, you can't be serious. You can't go."

"Why not?" I can't stop myself from thinking that maybe I am supposed to be a ballet dancer. It can't be. It has to be a coincidence that Xan was taken from me and now I receive an invite to dance again. A broken brick on the driveway becomes my point of focus. What kind of master plan is this for someone? I am starting to hyperventilate.

"You're hurt," he reminds me.

I was hurt. I haven't hobbled in weeks. Come to think of it, I never called in my last pain medication refill. "I've been injured before; I always come back." I always come back.

"You have an artificial hip!" This must be why my mother likes him so much; he is a pessimistic bastard like her.

"Dancers get hip replacements all the time," I say defensively. They do. I can use this to my advantage. Turnout was always my weakness. Now, with a man-made hip, I can do things I've only dreamed of. Things human bodies aren't meant to do. I'll be the Iron Man of ballet, indestructible.

I get carried away and envision myself dancing in New

York, San Francisco, Paris, Russia, and London; the stages that were once my destiny call out to me. I can see my face on the cover of a program. I could once again be the one little girls dream of becoming.

"Lila." Jason shakes me out of my daydream. Based on previous experience, Jason grabbing me is never a good thing. He lets go when I tense up. "Maybe that car hit you for a reason."

What the hell kind of comment is that? I can't even respond. What is his problem? Why would he say such a thing?

That night was awful. I will remember it as long as I live. It was dark, rainy, and icy. I was waiting for my mom to pick me up from ballet class so I could go to my weekly shrink appointment when I saw the car coming toward me. I was tired and had pulled a muscle in rehearsal, so my reaction time was slow.

It looked like the car was heading right for me. There wasn't another car in sight. He had the entire road to himself, yet he hit me on the sidewalk. I told Xan I thought he hit me on purpose. I never told Jason. How does he know that? My parents must have told him; they can't keep anything to themselves once the cocktails start flowing.

"I didn't mean it like that." Will he ever learn that you can't take back what you say?

I know I should go before he gets angry. Things aren't going his way. I don't see this ending well.

"Lila, stop!" he begs when I push past him on my way to my car. I stop because he sounds tortured. "Just listen, then you can go."

I listen. I don't turn.

"Lila, you are the one thing I've always wanted."

That's not true. He had his chance with me before I met Xan, but he blew it. He seems to conveniently forget that all the time.

"We had a good time yesterday, right?"

We did.

"We're good together, Lila. Picture it. I can make you happy." The loose bricks wobble with each step he takes toward me.

I can picture it, the two of us living in a house like this, going through the motions of life. I would put on the image of a perfect wife when in public, and then when the doors closed, the truth would come out. I can picture me surviving. "You deserve better than a life with someone who wishes they were with someone else."

As I turn to say good-bye, his stiff lips meet mine. I used to dream about kissing Jason. I prayed he would notice me.

"It's *my* turn to have you," he growls as he throws me aside and walks away.

ELEVEN DAYS LEFT

She is going to need more than the back of her hand to wipe off the poison he's left on her lips.

There is pain in her voice. It could be because he's rejected her in his messed-up way or because she doesn't want to admit to herself that she needs him. She won't ask him to; she wants him to want to come back.

"You're running." He says dismissing what she has to say. He is headed to the back of the house.

"Excuse me? Who is the one literally running from me right now?" She stands up a little taller.

That got his attention.

"Great," I say. Nothing makes Lila happier than a debate. Her despair or confusion or whatever she was feeling has been replaced by determination to prove him wrong.

"It's what you do!" he yells as he comes back for her. The only thing preventing his face from touching hers is a thick layer of tension. "You run when things get good." He is trying to break through her invisible barrier.

Stepping in to him, she laughs at his stupid comment. "Good? You think my life is good?" I used to love it when she gave him this look of utter disappointment and disgust. It reassured me that I was still number one. Today, it's not making me happy. It makes me sad.

"You won't risk it," he pushes.

He is as stubborn as she is. She won't take it from him; at least, I don't think she will. Lila let me call her out when she was being ridiculous. I only did it when nothing else was working. If anyone else tries to put her in her place, she becomes very defensive.

Lila knows he's right, she is a runner, but she needs to find the right words to convince him otherwise.

The two of them stand face-to-face, each waiting for the other to make the next move. The way I see it, either one of them will throw a punch or they'll devour each other. I'd rather see him hit her than kiss her again.

I did not just think that.

Lila waves the letter in his face. "It's not running when they invite you." She thinks she has played the winning card.

She'd better not let him see that smirk. I love that she is looking on the bright side of things, but she is going to need a lot more ammunition than that to take him down.

He doesn't try to stop her from leaving.

I deflate when she hesitates. She needs him. She needs him to want her to stay. Jason is the only thing preventing her from running away to New York City. I can see it in her sad, tired eyes. She doesn't want to go back to who she used to be. She wants to live.

He waits until she has one hand on the car door handle before speaking up. Typical. I should have known he'd make a dramatic comeback. "Going to New York where nobody knows you, choosing a lonely career where you don't have to let anyone in. You're right. You're not running."

Uhhh, he is just like her. He wants the upper hand as badly as she does. He is good. He knows how to get to her.

She stands next to her black convertible, watching, motionless, as Jason storms into his house having a temper tantrum like a two-year-old.

I saw it. It was subtle, but I saw it. She stopped herself

from taking a step toward the house. What is it about him that she can't walk away from? Why does she not see that this is exactly what he wants her to do, follow him and apologize for something she hasn't done?

"Don't do it, Lila. Don't do it!"

She is contemplating it.

Angrily, I smack the letter, and to my amazement, it flies out of her hand. We both watch as it floats into her car and lands face up on the passenger seat. My seat. "Cool."

She flings the car door open and dives in to catch it before another random gust of wind takes it away. That letter is much more valuable than her pride. "Don't touch my letter, Xan." She grabs it, holding it close to her chest before carefully folding it back up and putting it into the envelope. She slips it in the middle of the owner's manual to flatten it out, and then tucks it in the back of the glove box, where it will be safe.

"I've been replaced by a letter."

"It's a chance at happiness,"Wes says. I didn't feel him approach.

She is trying not to fall apart. The poor steering wheel is the victim of her death grip. Her knuckles are white and her face is the shade of a cherry. I think she quit breathing a few minutes ago.

It's not the life I wanted for her when I was alive—being a ballet dancer, I mean. But what kind of life is this? Sitting frozen in her car, unable to move or breathe because she knows if she does the tears will start. Lila will suffer for the rest of eternity before showing any sign of weakness.

What kind of life is worth living when you are afraid of your own tears?

I won't blame her if she accepts their invitation. But if she goes and gets wrapped up in that world again, she's never coming back. "It will kill her," I inform Wes.

"She's dying anyway."

She pulls out of Jason's driveway, and I prepare to follow

her. I need to make sure she is okay, that she doesn't do anything stupid. How did this happen? I don't know much about the ballet world, but from what Lila said, ballet schools like that don't give second chances.

Wes's energy is sharpened. I try to see what Lila is doing that's upsetting him.

He isn't looking at her. He's looking at Jason.

Lila has calmed down and is driving safely. I go and see what Wes is looking at. "Where's he going?"

Jason waited until he was sure Lila wasn't coming back before pulling out of the driveway.

"I don't know. I don't like it."

Lila drives in one direction and Jason takes off in the other. Wes and I follow his black BMW down the side streets. Mothers walking with their children and dogs shout as he drives by at a ridiculous speed.

"I know where he is going."

Wes keeps following. "Where?"

Talking is wasting time. I need to catch up to him. I want to get there before he does.

Wes stops me with his barricade of an arm before I can get ahead of Jason. "No, you can't go in."

"I'm going in." I'm as successful at trying to push past his arm as I would be attempting to move a hundred cement blocks. "Let me through," I grunt.

"I'll go. Madame Tula doesn't know I exist," Wes willingly volunteers.

Like hell I'm going to let Wes be the mediator here. "No." I duck under his arm, only to have him clench a fistful of the skin on the back of my neck. I'm not going anywhere. "Xan, don't. You could lose days. Or worse." Then he drops me.

The bell on the door dings and Jason storms in.

"Why did he come here?"

"Be still and listen. Don't think about Lila, and you will be able to hear everything." Wes is following Jason, keeping one eye on me to ensure I'm not trailing.

"Why not?"

"If you think of her, you will be rushed to her side."

Every time I think about Lila, I am at her side. I just assumed it was because I was trying to get to her. I am almost always by Lila. Then again, I am always thinking about her.

"You said it would all work out!" I hear Jason yelling. "All you've done is given her hope that she can be with him again!"

"Stay," Wes orders me like a dog.

Her bone-chilling cackle fills the room. "You didn't tell me who she was." Madame Tula doesn't seem fazed by his abrupt entry or the amount of anger he is filled with. The clanking of glass is making it hard to focus. I try harder. The gas and flame of the stove hum so gently a human would never notice. She is making another concoction. Is that all she does—make magic potions?

"Who is she?" The ignorance in Jason's voice almost makes me feel bad for him. Almost. He takes five steps. He has stepped off the carpet in the entryway and is now in her lab. Even designer tennis shoes squeak on vinyl floors.

She puts her spoon down, and I hear her shoes pivot. "My dear boy, there is nothing more I can do for you."

"You said if he was gone, she would fall in love with me." It sounds like he is trying to figure something out. He sounds confused. Defeated, but confused.

The spoon is back in the beaker. "I said no such thing."

I can't see her, but the look I imagine she is giving him is one of *I told you so.*

Jason's been here before. He was lying when he came with Lila. It was an act. He already knew Madame Tula.

Why is Wes still in there? Is he asking for a death warrant? He obviously doesn't know what she is capable of. "You told me there was an obstacle preventing Lila from being with me," Jason says with guilt pouring out.

The sweet Russian accent she had the first time I met her has returned. "That I did. I never said what that obstacle was." She shuts the stove off and approaches him. The clacking of her heels pushes his squeaky sneakers closer to the wall. "What did you do, boy?"

Nice Russian lady is gone. Scary lady from the Bronx is back.

He has no idea what she knows.

She has no idea what he did.

She really isn't a very good psychic.

Panic. Sheer panic. He's just realized he misunderstood her reading completely. I don't know what else would make someone's heart rate skyrocket that quickly.

Jason met with Madame Tula. He thought she told him to kill me. Talk about reading the right cards to the wrong person. No wonder he's been less than stable.

"Stay away from the girl."

"There is nobody else I want." There is no fight in him. I think I hear devastation in his voice, but I can't be sure; I've never heard Jason sound sincere before. Maybe it finally sank in: his killing me is the reason Lila is dying. He is the reason she is suffering.

"She is not yours," Madame Tula repeats.

"What does that mean? Whose is she?" His heart is pounding so hard I half expect to see him standing next to me any minute.

"Stay away from the girl," she warns again, escorting him out the front door.

He doesn't ask any more questions. He doesn't try to go back inside. He doesn't even get into his car. He walks in the opposite direction of his house. He could be on his way to the marina to see Lila. But for some reason I get the feeling he is actually going to the rocky pier.

NINE DAYS LEFT

I hold my belief that it is not breaking and entering if you have a key. I didn't break in the first time and I didn't break in tonight.

It feels like an eternity since I've been in the ballet studio. Ninety-seven days, to be exact, the last time I waited until the last person had turned off the lights, locked the doors, and gone home. I've tried over a dozen times in the last twenty-four hours to enter the studio. I'd reach the door and I'd back down. I'd walk away. Rejection is a feeling all too familiar to me. I wasn't sure I was ready for it. To voluntarily walk into the place that spit me out.

Rosin-coated dust particles fill my lungs. Like I'm a superhero, the stale sweat lingering in the air gives me incredible strength. I take another breath to gain optimum power. "I've missed you."

I have missed it here. I spent a lifetime fighting to become the best so I could get out of Wisconsin. I've forgotten what it feels like to want to be in the studio because I *want* to dance. What if this is what I am meant to do? What if its not? What if I can't find my place here again or if I can't remember why I started dancing in the first place? What if I can't feel that?

Everybody describes their home differently. To most, it is the house they grew up in. To some, it's the town. For others, it's anywhere their family is. For me, before I met Xan, home was in a pair of pointe shoes. With a pair of custom-made

Freed of London shoes on my feet—size 5, width XX, deep vamp, three-quarter shanks, V Maker—I was invincible. I could handle anything.

I pull out the well worn pair of shoes I still carry with me in my purse and slide my foot into the shoe, and like a blob of silly putty it melts into place. The molded plaster inside the shiny box remembers my foot. No need to fidget; everything automatically goes where it belongs. I could run a mile in a pair of broken-in pointe shoes. Good thing I don't run.

I flick on one set of lights—enough so I don't run into anything, not enough for me to have a clear vision of myself in the mirrors.

Lightly I place my left hand at my unofficial place at the barre: in front, where I can faintly see my silhouette in two different mirrors. I could be away from this delicate piece of round wood for a million years and I would still know where to go and what to do when I returned. It's in my DNA.

Remembering not to clutch, I loosen my grip on the wooden rail. Standing up straight, I close my eyes: head up, chin down, relax the shoulders, tighten the abs, pelvis tucked under, tailbone to the floor, ribs relaxed, lengthen the spine, and legs cemented to the ground like tree roots.

My body fights me as I try to find the correct position.

Like a machine, I am ready. Stiff, but ready. Bach plays loudly in my head, preparing me to begin the routine I've been programmed to do. Carefully, controlled, beautifully, I start.

The microchip imbedded within me reminds my arms and legs that they are connected by an invisible string; they need to work together. Another invisible string tests my arms. Are they being held strong or do they look like wet noodles? Legs are next. The fronts of my thighs need to wrap around to the back, my butt should be tucked down and under (no clenching), and my entire foot is connected to the floor, toes flat and relaxed.

Turn out. Turn out. Turn out.

Abs flat, hips tucked, ribs calm. I am ready for pliés. The voice of Marina, my ballet teacher, echoes in my head. Don't bend, wrap. If you wrap the thighs enough, the knees will begin to bend on their own. Wrap, wrap, wrap as I go down. Squeeze, squeeze, and squeeze the inside of the thighs toward the front of the room as I come up. No sharp movements. Readjust: hips under, legs engaged, abs tight, head up.

This feels good.

Crap. My arms are floppy and I am looking at the floor.

I start over.

Forty-five minutes later I have successfully completed three exercises.

It's two a.m.

Someone will be here by seven. I don't have much time.

Keeping my thighs glued together and the sole of my foot on the floor as long as possible, I seductively scrape the dust off the floor with my foot as I extend it into a beautifully arched masterpiece. I worked so hard for these feet. I look at myself in the mirror. My second position *en l'air* is precise; you could slide me between two walls.

I try a *rond de jambe en l'air*. Just as beautiful: even my arms are in sync. My long arms are always flailing around uncontrolled. I release my grip on the barre to test my balance before walking to the center of the room in front of the wall of mirrors. Maybe I can do this.

I don't think; I feel. Effortlessly, I dance. My lines are fluid, my turns unwavering. My jumps have silent landings.

I feel no pain. Faster and faster I throw myself into the movements oozing out of me until a spot of rosin on the otherwise slick wooden floor brings me to a screeching halt.

I am not a superhero.

I am not worthy of love.

I am an imposter.

I am stupid.

I am ugly.

I am fat.

I am alone.

My bloated belly catches my eye. I look like one of those malnourished babies you see on TV, the ones covered with flies searching for clean water to drink, waiting for you to send them money. My beautiful ribs proudly show through my sky-blue leotard, only to be downplayed by the ghastly bulge between my hip bones.

We had a deal, I remind God. You keep my abdomen flat and I'll keep my stomach empty. Oh, that's right—you don't honor deals. No, I never made a deal with him regarding Xan. I didn't know I needed to.

The photos that flank the walls of students who have made it into professional companies catch my eye—they taunt me. I remember the first day I came to this ballet school. I was so intimidated by the older girls, those on their way to greater things. I wanted so badly to be one of them, the ones with their photos on the wall, the ones who made it. I couldn't imagine my picture on the wall, and I could never see which ballet company I would join. I guess I couldn't imagine it because it was never going to happen.

I wanted girls to dream of becoming me. Nobody is ever going to want to be me. Not now. I'm normal. Average. The only person who wanted to love me is dead.

Self-doubt is what happened. I know exactly when the seed was planted. Fourth-grade music class. Mr. Crasby, who looked like an egg on stilts, mind you, announced to the class, "It seems Lila would rather sit and look pretty than actually sing." To his credit, he was right.

Then, in fifth grade, I was especially proud of a report I had done on giraffes. Not a doubt in my mind I was going to get an A. I got a C. The Rolaids-popping teacher told me it was nothing special. From there, the roots of destruction grew.

Have you ever tried to uproot a tree? Even when you think you've gotten all the roots, little pieces remain, fragments that continue to grow, reminding you of what you can't be. Roots buried so deep, it is impossible to get rid of them. They take on a life of their own. They always grow back.

I hate nature.

I deceived the world. I made them think I was perfect when really I couldn't stand myself. I stopped living so I could appear perfect, so someone—everyone—would want me. I made it my mission to prove anyone wrong who said I couldn't.

Xan saw through my façade.

Xan is gone.

My eyes have adjusted to the dim light, and the racks of glittering tutus can no longer hide. The stiff satin of the white beckons for me; she wants me to put her on. She has missed me as much as I have missed her. I go to her. Slipping the heavy garment on instantly makes me feel twenty pounds lighter.

I am no longer a sad, fat, pathetic loser who is alone. I am a delicate and extraordinary swan.

On my toes, I go to the record player that has been playing the same albums since I was eight. It only gets used for the little kids now. A few years ago we finally became a real ballet studio and hired a piano player. Dancing to recorded music after having it live is like downhill skiing on icy Wisconsin hills when you've tasted the fresh powder on the mountains of Colorado. It gets the job done, but all you can think about is what you are missing.

I leaf through until I find the album with cartoon swans on the front. I slide it out of the protective sleeve and set it on the record player, which is eager to sing. The telltale scratching begins, and I scurry to take my place center stage. My hip throbs. I'm not sure I am going to make it past the first eight counts.

I need to try.

I take a deep breath and let the music take me to the world I so desperately miss. The world I would have sacrificed everything for, the world I was so close to being a part of. The world I would have abandoned for Xan.

With my weight lifted and centered, I rise up onto my toes and carry myself around the studio as if it were the Metropolitan Opera House. Every muscle in my body works to ensure I stick each movement with precise strength.

I am powerfully in control, landing with authority and elegance.

I've made it to the final turn sequence, thirty-two fouetté turns. I find my own eyes in the mirror and vow to come back to them each and every time I come around. Go! Up, down, up, down, three, four, five, six, seven, eight, nine, ten, spot, spot, spot, bam, bam, bam, up, down, up, down, turn, turn, turn, bam, bam, twenty-four, twenty-five, twenty-six, twenty-seven, twenty-eight, twenty-nine, thirty, thirty-one, up, up, up, land.

"Impressive." A male voice emerges from the darkness.

I fall out of my perfectly executed routine. *Oh shit.* No one, under any circumstances, is supposed to touch the costumes without the help of a seamstress.

"Can I ask what you are doing here?" he asks, coming closer.

I don't leave my spot in the center of the room.

"That was pretty cool. You should have turned the lights on. Easier to see yourself." His badge catches the light. A cop.

"About time. Aren't you supposed to be keeping an eye on me or something?" I didn't hear him come in. How did he get in here without making the floor creak? I thought I locked the door.

"You haven't noticed me?" His voice is beautifully endearing. He sounds familiar. Mocking me the way people have done for years, Officer No Name twirls and prances across the studio. I can't read his name tag; it's too dark. "You a dancer?" He looks at me as he is taking a bow.

Damn tattoo guys downstairs must have called me in.

"I was." *Please don't make me leave.* Trapping the emotions that are trying to escape, I focus on the boning in the bodice; it feels so good wrapped around my body. I love being shoved into something so tight I can hardly breathe.

I haven't noticed him—or any other cops for that matter—since Officer James told me he was going to keep an eye on me. I figured they had better things to worry about—you know, murders and drug dealers. He steps into the light. I definitely would have noticed him. He is cute. And young. Is he old enough to be a cop?

I need to stretch. I plunk my right leg up onto the top barre. This makes me cringe. Not because it hurts, which it does. But it's worse than that. If I can't even fold my body over my legs, how am I going to make it at the New York School of Performing Arts? Who am I kidding?

The officer watches me and asks, "A little creepy in here, don't you think?"

"No."

He walks around looking at the pictures on the wall. "Your picture up here?"

Who is this guy? *No, my picture is not up there. I suck. I wasn't good enough. I failed.* "Injuries." I point to every part of my body.

The ballet studio used to be where I'd come when everything else was falling apart. This was where I came to feel normal. Now it's like the rest of the world: a place of torment. "Dance was the only home I ever knew." Why did I just tell him that?

"And Xan."

"And Xan." I smile. I feel compelled to talk to this guy. I don't even know his name. And I don't like how he said that: And Xan. Like he knows what I'm going through. Wait, how does he know about Xan? I decide Officer James must have told my babysitter my saga.

"You wanted to be a professional?"

Obviously. Why else would I have pushed away the only person I loved to spend more hours than I can count in class? Why else would I have starved myself, danced through torn muscles, broken toes, and bruised ribs? For fun?

"Why break in? Why not take a class?"

I can't. I can't not be the best. "I didn't break in; I have a key."

"Maybe someday you'll do it because you love it."

The last time I broke in, Marina caught me. She wasn't mad. She gave me a mini class at midnight. It was hard. I could barely lift my leg. She wanted me to dance too. She told me that just because I wasn't going to be a professional didn't mean I couldn't dance. Easy for a world-renowned dancer to say. Then, out of nowhere, she scampered into a version of the Black Swan she learned when she was twelve. She was showing me that I would never forget the things I love. They are part of me.

"Maybe."

"Let's go. I'll buy you a cup of coffee on the way home," he offers.

Okay. "Tea."

"You might want to change before we go." He points to my wardrobe.

Even at three a.m., a tutu, pointe shoes, and leg warmers might look strange. People would think I'm some insane homeless girl the nice police officer is helping back to the crazy house. I've spent enough nights there; I'm not going back. Not tonight.

I unzip my destiny and watch as my protective gear falls to the ground. Batman would be helpless without his disguise. Wolverine would not survive without his claws. Spider-Man needs his spidey senses and webs to save the innocent. Without my tutu, I am unarmed. I am exposed. I am vulnerable.

Carefully I put the skirt on a hanger. I want to take it with me. I don't care how much trouble I get in. This skirt, this nasty old room, it's who I am, who I was. Without Xan or a ballet to rehearse, who am I?

I turn the lights off in the dressing room and return the

costume to its rightful place on the rack. I go back to the barre. How can such a simple piece of wood from Home Depot have such power over me? It's my crack cocaine. It lures me to it. I need it. It tells me I can be the ridiculous thing I've dreamed I can be. I crave it.

I forget about Officer Do Good and get lost in another set of pliés. A comforting blanket of ice wraps around me. I want it to be enough to support me. It's not. The pointe shoes in my hand drop first, and then I follow. I've fallen on this hardwood floor many times, but it's never hurt as badly as this fall.

Like a stealth ninja, the cop is at my side, offering to help me up, luring me with a promise to make me feel better if I go with him. "Let's go get that tea." He doesn't ask any questions about why I'm suddenly a blubbering mess.

"What's your name, anyway?" I allow him to help me, to guide me out of the studio.

Keeping one hand firmly planted on my lower back so I can't turn, he introduces himself. "Conner."

"Nice to meet you, Conner."

NINE DAYS LEFT

Other than Jason, I think I am the only person who has seen Lila cry. Until her parents broke up, I think I'd only seen her cry once, and that was by accident. I never told her I saw her.

Feeling the intensity of her emotions is just that: intense. I haven't gotten used to it yet, and today they are strong. This is the most I've felt her struggle. She is having a hard time fighting them. She is losing.

The overwhelming urge she has to cry as she takes off the outfit that she feels sets her apart is becoming unbearable for her. She hangs the unraveling skirt up like it's a priceless gown. She may leave the skirt behind, but I wouldn't count on the school getting back the the key she is clutching in her hand.

I follow her back into the studio.

I've always thought of myself as a sensitive guy, in tune with my emotions. Getting a taste of how Lila feels about me is a whole different ball game. I feel guilty. I knew the moment I laid eyes on her that she was the one for me, and that I could never live another day without her. But she doesn't seem to understand the depth of my love for her. She thinks her love for me is ten times deeper than mine for her. She is wrong. Very wrong. She needs to know the love I have for her burns as it flows through my frozen veins and gives me a painful adrenaline rush.

I wrap my arms around her. She used to spend hours at the barre. "Because without your center, you cannot dance," she would say. She liked to poke me in the stomach to make me stand up straight. Lila needs to dance in order to feel, but she can't dance when she doesn't feel anything. It's an awful catch-22.

I think she found that love again tonight. Tonight she danced. She felt. She was spectacular.

I stand behind her, my left hand on top of hers. She's back at the barre. My right hand holds hers, following it as she brings it above her head. Together, in sync, we move to the same inaudible song playing in our heads. For a few counts of eight, we move. And for twenty-four counts, to be exact, she is pain-free.

I pull my hands away from hers, and as if I've sucked every last bit of life out of her, she collapses to the floor in tears. But before she fell, she leaned in to me, hugging me with no arms. She always gave me one last lingering lean when it wasn't appropriate to grope me. The lean was her way of telling me she couldn't wait to be alone with me.

I miss that.

The harder she cries, the more I realize how much is at stake and that the odds are against me.

I'm torn. I need her. I need her badly. But I don't want to be the cause of her pain anymore. If she goes to New York, she can be happy. Lila is a fighter. She can do anything she puts her mind to. If I leave her alone, could she learn to live without me?

I watch helplessly as another dude who is not me comes to her rescue. This time it's a cop. "Let's go get that tea," he suggests, helping her to her feet.

She lets him help and she doesn't let go of his hand. "I wanted to be close to Xan," she tells him.

I cringe as he takes her into his arms. Who is this guy? At least it's not Jason.

Where is Jason? I expected to see him lurking around the corner like the sneaky little cockroach he is. He's been waiting in the wings, waiting for me to be out of the picture so he could be the hero. I should be thankful that she has someone who will take care of her. Someone who can help her get through this.

I should be thankful.

I'm not.

This new guy moving in on my turf isn't asking questions. He isn't prying. Lila will respond to this. For that reason, I should be worried. I'm not. But I am worried about how Jason is going to react when he finds out Lila has shown someone other than him affection. He will find out. He always finds out.

They are alive. I'm dead.

Where is Wes? He never seems to be around when I need him. He needs a phone.

I've got a choice to make. I can hang around and see what Lila and Officer of the Year do next, or I can check in on Jason. His creepy aura isn't here, which means he's up to no good somewhere else. If Wes were around, he'd be able to confirm my concern. He seems to be awfully in tune with Jason.

Lila isn't going to do anything with this guy, is she? Something isn't right. I can feel it. I stand in front of her so she can pass through me before I go. I need to feel her blood flowing through me. She does, and for the slightest flash, we are whole. The heartbeat she loses isn't wasted; it beats inside me. She passes through me without so much as a flinch. If we are supposedly connected like we are, why can't she see me? Isn't that how it goes in horror movies? One person can always see the dead?

"Why can't you see me!" I jump in front of her again.

This time she reacts to the electricity we create. She has to be trying to figure out why she keeps getting momentarily zinged. What does she think the cool pockets of air are? Does she notice that they only happen when she is thinking about me? "C'mon, Lila! You're smarter than this!" Her hypnotic eyes stare directly into the empty space in front of her. She should know she is looking right at me. She doesn't. Or does she?

A partially deflated Mylar balloon bops around the corner of the now-dark ballet studio. I doubt she even saw it hidden behind the costume racks. I zoom across the room and grab the purple ribbon attached to the star-shaped balloon. I get back to her as quickly as I can.

She leaves the studio. So do I. So does the balloon.

The cop—now known as Conner—holds the main door open, then follows her, making sure she doesn't turn back. I shove the balloon in the door frame as they head down the stairs. The balloon prevents the ballet school door from slamming shut.

There is no bang.

Lila pulls away from Conner and comes back. She takes the balloon from my hand. Looking around, she tries to logically to come up with an explanation. "I'll meet you downstairs," she tells him, without even looking in his direction.

"Are you okay?" He is hesitant to leave her alone.

I don't blame him. After her recent breakdown, clearly she is not okay. Is that why he wants to stay by her side? Everyone seems to have deep dark secrets these days. Is he really just watching out for her, or is he after something else?

"I forgot something," she lies. Lila takes the balloon and goes back into the ballet school.

"I'll be right outside if you need me."

She doesn't acknowledge him. Not even a wave of the hand to show she heard him. Looking around the dark, empty halls, she waits until the door at the bottom of the stairs slams shut before speaking. "Xan?"

I gasp. She turns in my direction the minute I suck the air away from her face. As she lets go of the balloon, I catch it. I don't move. Neither does the balloon.

Face-to-face. Holding her hand up, she searches for me. I grant her wish. This time, she is the one gasping. She keeps looking, waiting to see something. Waiting to see me again so she believe it. "It was you at the graveyard." Her heart isn't racing like she's just seen a ghost; it's racing like we've just kissed.

I had completely forgotten about that. I used a balloon that day too. I never would have guessed balloons were the answer.

Why hasn't it happened yet? She is right here; she knows it's me. She is talking to me. So why can't she hear or see me? I thought all I had to do was convince her I am here.

"Wes!"

Lila takes a step back. She felt the negative energy and looks a little freaked out. I try to calm her down. I don't want her to leave. At least not before giving me some sort of indication that she really thinks it's me.

I touch her promise ring, and she yanks it away. "Ouch."

I was wrong. I thought she looked scared before, but this is her terrified face. She is waving her left hand around like she touched a hot stove.

I've always sent cool chills her way. Did I just make her ring hot? I touch it again. This time I don't even get a full grasp of her hand before she pulls away.

"Xan," she whispers, looking toward the door. "If this is you, tell me." Her breathing is what gives her fear away. She tries to control the shaking. She can't. I'd be scared too.

I'm two centimeters from her face. If she can't sense me now, I don't know when she will. I try running past her a few times, making a draft. Walking through her doesn't seem to be fazing her. Five minutes ago, all of these things got her attention. Now, after I touched her ring, the rules are different?

Conner pokes his head around the door. "Lila, did you find it?"

"Find what?" She's startled. I don't think she heard him come up the stairs. Neither did I. Weird.

He doesn't ask again. He knew she was lying. "Ready?"

Taking another hopeful look around, she tries to see me.

When she doesn't find me, her heart breaks all over again. The fear I felt in her wasn't because she was afraid of me. It was because she was afraid it wasn't me.

She follows Conner's lead. If she walks out that door with him, I may not have another chance. I can't drop the ball. *Think, Xan, think.*

I made music play at Jason's house. I was thinking about her dancing. I'm in a ballet studio. It shouldn't be too hard to picture her taking class. The piano. There is always a pianist. It's the same music every time, a bit repetitive if you ask me.

She stops. "Do you hear that?"

"Hear what?" I think he is starting to think she's a little nutso.

He takes her hand. I think about her spinning around and around in the center of the room. Lila loves turns, and she's really good at them. For her, spinning around three times on her tippy toes is like giving candy to a baby.

She stops again. "I hear music." She goes into the vacant studio and listens intently.

She heard it, and she is starting to believe.

This time, when she turns to go back to him, she can't, at least not without passing the balloon. She pushes the balloon to the side so she can get by. I won't let her. She pushes it left, I push it right. Left, right, left, right, left, right.

She tries to be tricky and grab the ribbon. As her hand is about to clasp it tight, I pull it just out of her reach. Together we smile. "Thank you," she says.

This time I'm positive she saw me.

NINE DAYS LEFT

Is this really happening? I know it is, but, like fairy-tale endings, things like that don't happen to people like me.

But if it wasn't real, if it wasn't Xan who brought me the balloon, why do I feel giddy and content, like I don't have to live without him anymore? Let's say he was there with me in the ballet studio last night. Where did he go? If Xan came to me, he would never leave. That I know for sure.

I nearly fall overboard when I step outside and see a man sleeping on my boat. I grab the metal pole we use to keep the boat away from the rough walls of the lock and dams or fish a towel out of the lake. I tiptoe behind him to get a closer look. What if this is the guy who killed Xan? That's ridiculous. A murderer wouldn't wait for me to come outside. No, he would have slaughtered me in my sleep.

It's not a murderer. "Conner?" Why is he still here?

"After you went inside"—he begins to justify why he himself has turned into a creep—"I noticed a guy lurking around."

I can feel the furrow in my brow increasing. I put the pole down and wiggle my forehead, trying to release the tension. I don't want to be rude, in case he really was looking out for me.

"I didn't like the way he watched me, waiting for me to leave." He stretches as he stands up.

Oh my God, you could bounce a penny off his abs, at least the ones peeking out from under his shirt as he stretches. When he pulls his shirt down, I look away and hope I am not as red as I feel.

"It was like we were having a Mexican standoff. I got a bad vibe, so I stayed. I'm sorry if I scared you." Conner looks genuinely concerned. Was the same person who killed Xan coming for me last night?

"You slept here all night?" I ask. Impressive. I've fallen asleep while lying in the sun in one of the chairs on the back of the boat, and I couldn't move when I woke up.

"I stayed. I didn't sleep." But he clears his throat as he says it.

I made him feel embarrassed for falling asleep on the job, or for the small pool of drool in the corner of his mouth. He meant well, I think. "Thank you. Next time, knock. You can sleep on the couch." I wipe the smile off my face the moment I notice I am doing it. I feel unfaithful to Xan.

"Just doing my job." He folds the beach towel he used as a blanket.

No he wasn't. He was off duty when he found me in the ballet studio. "Don't you have to be at work or something?" I don't want him to get in trouble because of me and my unwanted visitor. But I do like it that he was watching out for me.

"It's all good. Officer James gave me free rein when it comes to you. He said if you don't order me away, I am to stay." Awkwardly, he plays with his belt loops. I think he's blushing.

Well, if he is going to be hanging around, the least I can do is offer him breakfast. "Can I get you something to eat?" He must be starving. I hope there is something other than rice cakes and frozen grapes in the kitchen.

"I know this is going to sound forward," he says as he is rubbing the back of his neck, "but would it be too much trouble if I took a shower?"

It is slightly strange. A naked man in my boat. I don't mind, but I'm blushing. "No, not at all." I lead the way in. "Close the door behind you. Don't want to let the cool air out." Oh my

God, I sound like my mother.

He closes the heavy door with ease and looks like he has just found himself in Oz. "Dishwasher." I pat the counter.

He looks like he could use a joke. It's not a joke; there is a dishwasher. I just know how ridiculous it sounds to most people that we have a dishwasher in our boat.

He doesn't laugh. He follows me through the kitchen, up the stairs to the helm, through the galley, and down the stairs to the bedrooms. I show him the first room on the left, the master bedroom.

I don't think he has ever seen anything like this before. It never stops amazing me how people gawk as they walk through my boat. To me, it's normal. Maybe I am the abnormal one.

"Gross, right?" He's looking at the mirror above the bed.

"I don't even want to think about it," he says with a shudder.

We laugh and I show him where the towels are. "This is my dad's." I open one of the walk-in closets. "Take whatever you want."

"He won't care?"

Valid concern. "Nope." Dad would kill him if he saw Conner walking around in his one-of-a-kind silk swim trunks.

I show him how to use the shower. "I know this sounds stupid, but really, showering in a boat is a learned skill. First of all, the water tank is really small, so there is only so much hot water. In order to make sure you have enough to get you through the shower, you must shut the water off after you get yourself wet, lather your hair with shampoo, then turn the water back on to rinse it out. Repeat with conditioner and again with soap. Try shaving your legs in there. Not fun."

"Throw your clothes in the washer!" I call as I leave.

He laughs. "Seriously?"

I was about to tell him it's no problem. But he isn't surprised that I'd do his laundry for him. It's the fact there's a washer and dryer in the master bedroom.

I hear Jason's voice and feel the boat rock as I slide the tracked door shut for Conner.

I put both hands flat on the door that leads back to Conner and prepare to face Jason again. It wasn't a stalker last night. It was Jason. What was Jason going to do? Wait for Conner to leave and waltz in at three in the morning? Wait, how did Jason know I'd be alone at this very moment?

"Have you been spying on me?" I have to pass him to get to the kitchen. I need to get Conner something to eat. I wonder if he likes eggs. Who doesn't? I decide on a bacon, egg, and cheese bagel sandwich. Sounds like a manly breakfast. I look at the clock. It's two o'clock. Should I be making lunch?

"You're taking in strays now?" Jason asks. Not nicely.

I turn on the stove and pretend I don't hear him over the clicking of the gas igniting.

"Did you sleep with him?"

I slam the block of cheese down and glare at him. "What, because I'm making him something to eat automatically means I slept with him?"

Conner would never be interested in me.

"You never make me anything to eat."

Huh, true. That's because I don't cook. "Relax, he's a cop."

I thought that would have calmed his nerves, knowing someone was watching out for me. But it seems to have made him more agitated. "Why are you hanging around cops now?"

I watch him clutch the back of his neck. He isn't trying to rub out a knot like Conner was. He is actually clawing at himself. "He caught me in the ballet studio last night." Pointing my knife at Jason, I try to lighten the mood. "You should be thanking him. If he had put me in jail, you'd be the one bailing me out."

"Why is he still here?" His fingers massage the marble countertop as he closes in on me.

Is this all because he is jealous? I need to change the subject before he gets too worked up. "I assume you were the guy he saw lurking around last night?"

He sits on one of the bar stools behind the counter. A faint wheeze comes out as he plops onto it. I can't help but giggle.

"I wanted to talk to you." He playfully hits me in the arm.

He's back. I thought I'd lost Fun Jason. "At three in the morning?"

"I felt bad how things ended the other day." He is working on tearing a paper napkin to shreds.

In my shrill baby voice, I mock him and ask if he wants breakfast. "I can make Jason a sandwich too." I offer him my hand, a gesture of peace.

He shakes his head no and doesn't take my hand. Jason becomes still when we hear the water shut off.

"Are you okay?" I pry my hand into his. Gross, it's all clammy.

"Come with me."

I want to. I do. It would be great to disappear on the Jet Skis for a few hours. The way he is looking at me, those baby blues dancing, this is the Jason I love being with. "I can't." I gesture down below. I can't abandon Conner, not after what he did for me last night.

Taking his hand away from mine, he switches gears. "So you'll run away to a place where nobody knows you. But you won't spend an afternoon with me?"

"I want to, Jason. I just can't right now. How about tomorrow?" I offer.

He has started pacing the room. "I don't get it, Lila. You fight so hard to get what you want. You nearly killed yourself trying to make it as a dancer. Then, when you made it, when there was nothing left to fight for, to prove, you lost your sparkle. You quit." Lowering his head like a little boy, he looks tormented. I want to run up and hug him, take away his pain. "You did the same thing to me."

He is reminding me that I was once desperate for him to

want me. I was. That was a long time ago. Before Xan. Before ballet. I was twelve; I didn't know any better. "I didn't quit. I got hurt," I clarify.

"Now, you've recovered. It's all about the chase with you. That's why you want to go to New York City. You like to prove people wrong. You only want what you can't have. You don't love to dance."

"I do love to dance." I'm not sure who I'm trying to convince more.

"I gotta give it to him. Xan beat your system."

I am getting defensive. "What are you talking about?"

"Your parents didn't like Xan at first. He was everything they didn't want for you. He came from a poor family. He was a musician. He wasn't a star athlete and he wasn't planning on running a Fortune 500 company after college, if he went to college at all. That's why you fell for him."

I slap him across the face and fight the burning tears. He doesn't deserve my tears.

He gets in my face and says, "You think you're so brave. You're not." Driving his finger into my chest, he continues. "You might be one of the weakest, most terrified people I've ever met. You are afraid to be happy. Afraid that life might somehow not be horrible. That's why you won't let Xan go. It's your excuse not to live. What are you so afraid of, Lila? What are you really running from?"

His hand has become soft on my chest, the warmth trying to heal the damage he's just done to my sternum. I should be angry. Furious. The words coming out of his mouth are harsh. His voice is crackling, but in his sick and twisted way he is trying to help.

He is right: I do run away when things get tough. However, he is wrong about one thing. Very wrong. "You may have figured me out, Jason. But don't ever doubt my love for Xan. He is the reason I am still alive." I remove his hand from my chest.

The door from the master bedroom room unlatches. Jason kisses me on the cheek before flying out of the boat like a bat out of hell. He wants to fix whatever is wrong between us, but I don't think he knows how.

His kiss was different today. It was soft. It spoke. It said he was sorry. What is he sorry for?

"Are you sure your dad won't mind if I borrow a couple things?" Conner asks. He emerges from the lower cabin area drying his hair with a towel. I don't need a mirror to know I am once again the color of an apple. I should look away; it's rude, and I have a boyfriend. I had a boyfriend. I didn't know bodies like his really existed. I thought all the photos in the magazines were Photoshopped.

His smooth voice is even more appealing when he doesn't have any clothes on. I shake my head no. I don't know what will come out of my mouth if I speak. After getting my approval, he pulls a lime-green polo over his head. I've always hated that shirt; it is hideous on my dad. But on him it looks great.

Grabbing the sandwich off the counter and shoving it into his hands, I say, "I made this for you. I hope it doesn't taste awful."

"Thanks."

I watch nervously as he takes a bite. When he doesn't keel over, we both let out a sigh of relief.

"Who was that?" He points outside with a mouthful of cheesy egg goodness. He can't seem to get the food into his mouth fast enough. I wonder if I should make him another?

I offer him a bottle of water. "Jason?" Idiot, who else would he be talking about? He must have heard us.

Conner answers my unspoken question. "I saw him through the window in the bathroom."

Ah, forgot about those. "That would be Jason."

"Your boyfriend?"

"Hell no!"

"I was just wondering who he was, how you knew him."

Taking his empty plate, I go into the kitchen. "We've been friends for years. Why?"

"That's the guy who was hanging around last night."

"We had a fight the other day and he wanted to talk about it."

"At three in the morning?" he asks suspiciously.

I wondered the same thing.

"Aren't you going to eat?" He offers me the rest of his sandwich.

"Already did," I lie. I let him finish and offer to make him another.

He declines.

Does he not want more because he is full or because it was disgusting? I let it go. "Want to go for a walk?" I ask, feeling the need to get off the yacht. On my way to the shoe basket, I accidently bump into him.

"I should be getting back."

Great, he is probably leaving because I keep raping him with my eyes. "Okay." I hope that didn't sound as disappointed out loud as it did in my head.

Reaching out to me, he insists, "I'd like to stay, but I should go into the office for a couple hours. If I'm going to be keeping an extra eye on you, I need to get my paperwork done during the day."

Whether it's true or not, it's nice of him to try. "Thanks for not turning me in last night." All I need is to add convicted felon to my rap sheet. My personal ad is going to read: Single white female, widowed, crippled, anorexic, felon, and hates cats. I'm a real catch.

His hand is on mine. I'd forgotten how good it feels to have a strong hand touching me that isn't angry. My eyes go to Conner's chest. I can see his heart beating underneath his shirt and I find myself imagining what it would feel like to rest my head on it. I've missed hearing Xan's heart beating against my cheek.

He takes a business card out of his wallet and writes a number on it. "My cell. Don't hesitate to call if you see anyone strange hanging around."

I take the card. I am going to keep this one. What if Jason is right? Is it time for me to stop running? If I can't have what I love, what I want, is it time I start trying to love what I can have?

I grab his hand before he has a chance to get away. Throwing myself into him, I wrap my arms around his neck. He kind of smells like Xan. The stubble on his face that has grown overnight scratches me. His lips are soft. Really soft. He tastes like wintergreen, just like Xan. Our tongues try to find a rhythm. We've only just met, but he doesn't seem to mind my abrupt initiative.

His strong arms follow my lead and hug my waist, protecting me from everything. I run my hands through the short hair on the back of his head and he pulls me closer. We should stop. We don't.

I want more of him. I shouldn't want him. I do. Is this what Jason is talking about? Jason is good for me. He loves me. He would take care of me. He's good-looking. He's rich. He is everything I should want, yet I have chosen to have my first post-Xan kiss with a complete stranger.

"Would you like to have dinner with me tomorrow?" He gives my ear a kiss before stepping back.

"I shouldn't." I shouldn't, but I want to.

"Let me know if you change your mind." He looks back at me as he walks down the dock.

Xan

SEVEN DAYS LEFT

From the looks of it, she can't believe it happened either. How did a dinner of fish tacos turn into a sleepover? How did he get her to eat fish tacos? She hates fish.

I wish I could read her mind right now. To know if she looks like she's going to cry because she regrets what she has done or because she liked it.

Lila always cried tears of joy after we had sex. The morning of the day I died, it was as if she knew it would be the last time. That's impossible, right?

Where is Wes? He's been MIA for days. What kind of mentor leaves when things get complicated?

I remember one night in particular, right after her first hospitalization. We hadn't had sex yet; all we did was hold each other. She'd missed me so much, and I'd been so worried about her. She clutched onto me so tightly that my arms and legs kept falling asleep. We talked until we couldn't keep our eyes open anymore. We lived for nights like that. So close. So in love.

I want to be mad at her. I want my jealousy to get the best of me, to make me walk away and never think of her again after what she did. I am standing behind her, and the two of us stare at her reflection in the mirror. I love her more than ever.

I rest my chin on her shoulder so she can release the tears. I kiss her neck. She needs to know I'm not going anywhere.

"I am so sorry, Xan." She can't look at herself anymore.

I won't make her.

She needs a hot shower.

I turn the water on. I look behind the curtain and stick my hand in, a little chilly. Lila likes it borderline scalding. Slowly the water warms up.

Shocked to hear the water running, she looks around for an explanation. Like always, there isn't one. Sure, it could be a plumbing issue. One problem: boat water doesn't travel through pipes, at least not regular ones. The shower is connected to a tank. You have to manually flip a switch to turn the pump on. It doesn't just turn on by itself. Ever.

She feels the water and decides not to turn it off. It's perfect. "I don't know what I was thinking." She takes off his T-shirt and boxers.

I don't either.

She isn't worried about saving hot water today. She stands under the steaming water, letting it wash away all of her sins. She is going to need a lot more than that to erase the memory of what happened last night. "Please make it hotter." She doesn't take her face out of the stream of water.

How can I deny her?

"Thank you."

We shower together like we've done a million times in the past. It is very strange feeling the heat of the water and not getting wet. I try to step away from her a couple times. She feels it and asks me not to go. I think she's afraid that if I go, I'm not coming back.

I know how self-conscious Lila is about her body. She hates the way she looks. Everyone else sees the truth: she could gain a hundred pounds and still turn heads. I begin to leave when she shuts the water off. "Xan?"

I stop; half my body is already through the door.

"I love you. Please stay."

I go back to her side and kiss the top of her head. She is so scared. I stay long enough for her to know I'm not leaving. She is freezing and needs to get dressed.

I step away and watch the room fill back up with steam. "Thank you," she says.

While she gets dressed, I'll check on her guest. He's up. Is he the kind of guy who is going to hang around pretending to be interested in her, or will he run before she gets out of the bathroom?

He is making a pot of coffee. "She drinks tea, dumbass." Even Jason knows that.

"Right, thanks."

Did he just answer me? Can't be. He must be on one of those nearly invisible headphone sets. I walk toward him. He hasn't moved since he spoke. Either he just got some really bad news on the phone, or he heard me.

I get closer than any man should ever be to another man. Holy shit. He's looking at me—not like Lila, who looks in my general direction. He's looking directly at me, like I'm a long-lost friend he hasn't seen in years. I've never seen him before in my life.

"Do you have to stand so close?"

In shock, I back up.

"Where is the tea she likes?" We are now face-to-face, and any thoughts about him not being able to see me have just been thrown out the window. He can see me. He can hear me.

I stick my hand through the closed microwave door to show him where the tea is hidden.

He opens it and finds a box filled with herbal teas. Laughing to himself, he says, "Thanks. I never would have looked in there."

"You can see me?"

"Clear as day."

"And you can hear me?"

"Who else do you think I am talking to?"

I know that tone. "It's not possible," I say to myself.

"When is the last time you saw me?" he asks. He pours boiling water over a mint tea bag in a large cup. She will be thrilled; it's her favorite.

No. How is this happening? I haven't seen him since we followed Jason to the psychic. "Is that why you wouldn't let me go in?"

"No." He puts the tea down and looks at me in true Wes fashion. No doubt, it's him.

Unable to ignore his ridiculous number of muscles, I ask, "Is this what you looked like when you were alive?"

His face isn't bad either. I'm drawn to him. I have to touch him. He feels human. My hand squeezes his bicep. It doesn't sink in.

Giving me a dirty look he answers, "Yes."

"What the hell is going on?" I can't stop touching him. I know it's wrong—creepy, even. He looks normal, but he is as rock solid as he was when he was where I am.

"Madame Tula saw me. I didn't think she could see anyone other than you."

"So?" Does he feel this hard to Lila?

"So, she made me a deal I couldn't resist."

Are you kidding me? "You told me she was bad, that I should stay away from her. That she could hurt Lila and me."

"She has no interest in you anymore. I gave her what she wanted."

"That would be . . . ?" Why is he making toast? I have a huge problem, and he is playing master chef?

"My eternal life."

"I thought Lila and I were the only ones who had that right now."

"So did I. Apparently the light fades, but it never disappears. She saw me, and I couldn't resist her offer."

"You couldn't resist? What about me? What am I supposed to do? How am I supposed to make things right with Lila if I don't have you showing me what I am supposed to do?"

"She knows you're here."

"So why can't she see me?"

"I don't know."

"Maybe you messing with things had something to do with it." I knock the peanut butter–covered knife out of his hand.

"Xan, there is nothing standing in the way of you getting to her now. I did this for you," Wes explains.

"For me." I can't control my laughter at this point. "You slept with her for me?"

"I didn't mean for that to happen."

"You're right, screwing someone just happens by accident."

"You've never made a mistake before?" he asks, rubbing my own mistakes in my face. "I traded my immortality for life. Xan, I get to die."

"Why would you do that?"

His expression changes as he answers softly, "My soul mate died last month."

"Why didn't you say anything?" I remember him telling me his mate would go back to the sky when she died, that he wouldn't ever see her again.

"I didn't want to discourage you. When I couldn't get to her in time, I lost her. She was given one last life to live, while I was made to help others be reunited with the loves of their lives. For eighty-seven years I watched her as I made pointless attempts to reunite souls. I couldn't figure out why it never worked. Now I think it's because they were all imposters: whole souls that happened to merge on their descent to Earth. That's what I assumed you were; there are dozens if not hundreds of them walking around at once. But there was something different about you and the way you looked at Lila: Your pain was different. The pain of a true half of a soul is a feeling like nothing else. It's the emptiest and most hallow feeling. A yearning, a need to be with the part of you that is missing. A need to be with that part.

I finally found someone I could help."

Knowing he would never lay eyes on his soul mate again, Wes no longer had a reason to be alive—if that's what I am.

"Why do the rules keep changing?"

"I don't know. That's why I took the deal. I don't want to live forever if I can't be with her. I thought if I came to Earth, I could keep Lila away from Jason. He is stronger than I thought. Something isn't right about him."

"How did you mess up? What did you do?"

"I was scared I wouldn't make it in time, and I killed someone. I crossed the line—and that took away what little time I had left." He sounds full of shame and regret. "I know you want to hurt Jason. Don't. If you do, it's over. Think about it, Xan—is there anything worse than killing a man?"

"Sleeping with his girlfriend is pretty high up on the list." I want to tear Jason to shreds, but not at the risk of losing Lila forever. "I'm down to seven days. How am I supposed to do it alone?" I ask.

He pats my back. "You're not alone. I told you, I'm here to help."

"How do you know it was killing someone that got the two of you separated? How do you know it wasn't just because you didn't make it in time?"

"Who are you talking to?" Lila has come up the stairs. I don't know how neither of us heard her coming. By the look on her face, I think she's been listening to Conner's one-way conversation for a while.

Now he is the one who looks white as a ghost. "Bet you didn't prepare for this," I say. He looks at me, then Lila.

"Who are you *looking* at?" A normal person would be telling this dude who obviously has serious psychological issues to leave. Not Lila.

"I was talking to myself. Bad habit."

She isn't buying it.

He tries again. "When you live alone and sit in a cop car all day by yourself, you find someone to listen."

"That's the best you can come up with?" I laugh at his pathetic attempt to lie to her.

"There, you just did it again." Lila is pointing in my direction. She crosses her arms and settles into her left hip. She isn't going anywhere until she gets an explanation.

I should help the poor guy out. Or not. He did just sleep with her. But if he is telling the truth and he did give up his life to help us out, it's the least I can do. He didn't sign up for this. I've made mistakes too. I'm lucky enough to be getting another chance to rectify them. At least for now.

I walk away from him, stand next to Lila, and touch her promise ring. If it gets hot like it did in the ballet studio, she will react.

Bingo. She pulls her hand away from mine and holds on to it with her other hand. She watches Conner/Wes watch me. "You can see him?" She isn't scared. She is upset. She is jealous.

He nods. He doesn't know what to do.

"Who are you?" she asks him. Releasing her grip on her ring, she searches for me. I take her right hand into mine. I don't want to burn her anymore.

"You wouldn't believe it."

"You can't chicken out now, dude," I insist.

She snaps at him, "Are you even a cop?"

"No," he confesses.

Amazing, the man made of rock doesn't know how to handle a few prying questions from a seventeen-year-old girl. He can't look at her. I think he is starting to sweat.

"She isn't going to bite," I tell him. Bad choice of words. Sometimes she does like to bite when she gets overly turned on. I just got goose bumps. Not good ones.

"What the hell is going on?" With every step she takes toward him, he takes two back. She has an advantage, and it isn't long before she has him cornered in the kitchen. He has nowhere to go. He's going to have to look at her sooner or later, because she is not stopping until she hears what she wants to.

"Who are you?"

"My name is Wes." He is still looking toward the ground, at her cute pink toes.

"Why did you lie about your name?"

"Because I didn't want him to know who I was."

"Say it."

He doesn't.

"Say his name," she demands.

"Xan. I couldn't tell Xan I was here."

He looks into her sweet face just in time to see her turn white. She is wondering if she's really losing her mind or if there is more to this world than she thought. She stumbles to the couch.

He follows and sits next to her. It's probably wise for her to be sitting for the next part.

"Lila, listen. I didn't mean for things to happen." He awkwardly tries to justify last night.

"Is he here?" she chokes out. She isn't interested in anything he has to say if it doesn't pertain to me. She has miraculously collected herself and is ready to deal with what she has been given. This is what Lila does best: pushing her feelings away so she can get what she wants.

"Let me get this straight. You're not questioning any of this?" Wes asks.

"I'm still sitting here, aren't I?"

"Good point."

She follows his finger when he points to where I am standing. The disappointment on her face is unbearable. "How come you can see him and I can't?"

He stalls, twiddling his thumbs.

"Just tell her," I encourage him. She isn't going to buy his bullshit.

"I used to be like him. Until a couple days ago, I was where he is," he begins.

"Where is that?" She is still looking for me, unaware that she keeps sticking her entire arm through my face.

"What the psychic told you, that you and Xan have already lived lives together, it's true."

I haven't seen her face light up like this since the day I told her I loved her.

"He only has so much time for you to realize he isn't dead," he continues.

"I know he's here!" she shouts. She is starting to panic. Her shoulders are beginning to speckle.

Looking at me, Wes says, "I know. I'm not sure what is going on." Reaching into his pocket, he pulls out a small vial of black liquid and gives it to her.

She takes it and asks, "What is it?"

"I don't know. I took it from the psychic when I was there. I found it sitting next to the bottle with the jumping twigs."

"You've been to Madame Tula's place?" She opens the bottle and winces at the smell before putting the cap back on.

"She is the reason I am here," Wes says.

Lila is still examining the bottle. "Is this the bottle she wanted me to take and drink when I was there? She said it would bring me to Xan. I didn't take it, not because I didn't want to be with Xan, but because there is something off about her. It didn't feel right."

"You were right not to drink it in front of her. She wanted you to drink it so Xan would materialize and she could kill the two of you."

"I'm not afraid of dying," Lila tells Wes, in case he didn't know.

"Madame Tula wanted your eternal life. She has been waiting for the two of you for decades."

"Wanted?"

"Wes, what are you doing?" I shout, trying to knock the bottle out of her hand.

He is looking at her but speaking to me: "Madame Tula has what she wants, Xan. She has no interest in hurting the two of you anymore. It might help."

Not much gets past Lila. "You did this for us?"

He doesn't answer.

"Why?"

"It doesn't matter," he answers with the threatening authority I've grown to love.

I smile and thank him. She doesn't need to know the gritty details.

"Where are you going?" she asks as he slides open the door.

"You have my number if you need me." He points to the little bottle she holds in her hand. "I think you need some time to yourselves."

"Conner—I mean Wes," she says, "do you know what happened to Xan?"

He nods and closes the door before he has to lie to her anymore.

SEVEN DAYS LEFT

The tiny vial filled with liquid tar taunts me. How can such a small amount of liquid hold such power? What's in it? Did it just bubble? I blink and take another look with fresh eyes. It looks the same, eerily alive.

What if I drink it and nothing happens? What if something does? I'm crazy for allowing myself to think Conner is who he says he is. I'm crazy for having this dialogue with myself.

"Crap." I accidently drop the vial and quickly snatch it out of the sink, which is filled with soapy water, before water can leak under the cork. Too late—the cork is soaked. It's now or never. I don't want the purity of water ruining the effectiveness of the darkness lurking inside.

I wiggle the Tic Tac–size cork out of the bottle and drink. It's less liquid than you'd give a baby. It doesn't matter; it's potent, and it's not coating the back of my throat like a soothing cough syrup. No, it's alive. Like a demonic serpent, it weaves its way around my insides looking for the first point of entry into my bloodstream.

The creature finds my heart, binding the still-beating organ into a tight ball of twine. I drop the glass. It shatters into a million pieces when it hits the marble countertop. I don't pick the mess up. I don't even push it into a nice little pile to pick up later. I don't care about the broken glass.

Xan is standing behind me. I can feel him.

"Turn around."

Bracing myself on the counter, I shake my head no.

"Why not?"

This cannot be happening. I am hallucinating. People do not come back from the dead. Xan just took a step closer to me. His hands are on my hips. His entire body is touching mine, especially his pelvis.

"I won't be able to handle it if you're not real."

Kissing the back of my neck, above my shoulder blades, he tries to convince me. "Turn around, Lila. I'm here."

As he continues to kiss me, I believe him. Even when he is dead, I can't resist his touch. His wintergreen breath awakens me from my trance as I turn. I cup his face; he leans into my hands. My stomach drops. He takes my wrists tightly, and I brace myself to look into the eyes that have never judged me.

I expected to find him full of death: Xan in the flesh with a soul sold to the devil for one last moment with me. I was wrong.

The more he touches me, the more I remember. I feel everything he's been going through. Everything. "How is this possible?" I ask him as I watch the story of us play in his eyes.

"I don't know," he answers honestly.

He tries to look away. I stop him. I want to see it all. I want to know. "How many—"

He finishes for me: "Lives have we lived together?"

I nod.

"Five."

He takes me into his arms and hugs me tighter than I've ever felt him hold me. I clutch him just as tight, if not tighter. Together we cry. Because we are happy. Because we are scared. Because we are confused. Because we don't want this moment to end.

But every moment, even the best ones, must end.

I take him by the hand, leading him down below.

He doesn't resist.

I shut and lock the bedroom door. Habit. My parents might have known we were having sex, but I didn't want them walking in on us doing the deed. The only person who might walk in on us now would be Jason, though that might be worse than my parents. I climb onto the bed. He stays close behind, our bodies never separating more than an inch or two, our fingers never unlocking.

I have never wanted him more than I do right now. I grab the gray Army T-shirt he was buried in and pull him toward me. We stare at each other as he hovers over me. Our clothes are still on, yet I've never felt more a part of him. Our individual breaths become one constant flow of air. Our hearts listen to each other, playing ping-pong with their beats.

I haven't seen him in a month. I'd swear it's been a lifetime. I don't know how much time we have before he disappears into oblivion. I reach up and kiss the lips I have missed so much.

He responds tenderly, running his hands through my hair, bringing our heads together. We have always felt connected on an otherworldly level; it is starting to make sense now. My heart leaps out of my throat into his, where it belongs. We don't think. We just feel. The electricity flowing between us is out of control. Terrified to separate, I cling to him like a leech. Afraid he will vanish if I blink, I keep my eyes open until they burn with dryness. I've never been happier.

He backs up onto his knees. I stop breathing when his hands separate from mine. He doesn't evaporate, so I relax. He isn't going anywhere, at least for this moment. Good, now I can focus on him being shirtless.

I sit up and allow him to take off my shirt. I always make sure the lights are dim before my clothes come off. Today I want to see everything, even my imperfect body next to his godlike structure.

"Oh my God, Lila! Your boobs are huge!"

I look down. They are. I must be gaining weight. But I

haven't really been eating much. I look at my gut and second-guess the daylight sex thing.

Lifting my chin, he forces me to look at him. The tears welling in his eyes break my heart. I close his eyelids and wipe the tears away so he can see. A single teardrop wobbles on my fingertip. Are his tears the same as mine? I kiss his sadness away from my finger. Salty.

Xan brings my wet finger to his lips. He holds my hands tightly into his, placing them against his chest. "You are beautiful." When he lets go of my hands, I keep them firmly planted on him, trying to touch the heart underneath that is no doubt in as much pain as mine. "When will you ever realize that?" He is cupping my swollen breast in one hand and caressing the insides of my gigantic thighs with the other.

Xan is the only person in the world who could get away with touching me when I feel fat. I tell myself to stop. This isn't the time to be thinking about how much I hate my body. I unhook my bra and toss it aside. The warmth of his torso on mine makes me forget all of my insecurities.

Piece by piece the rest of our clothes come off. We take our time, feeling every inch of each other. From the tips of our fingers to the ends of our toes, we go over every single curve, remembering what was never forgotten, just temporarily out of reach.

The morning turns to afternoon and the afternoon turns to evening. "What happens now?" I'm safely tucked under the pit of his arm, where I fit perfectly.

"I don't know." He pulls me closer, if that were humanly possible. It's as if he's trying to pull my body into his, trying to make us one. "You should sleep."

I should. I'm exhausted. But I won't. I will not fall asleep in his arms to have him gone when I wake up. How long will this potion last? Will he fade away, or will he be here one minute and not the next?

I need to do something to wake myself up. "Want to take a shower?" I ask. I prop myself up so I can see him. I can't stop touching him. I'm not entirely convinced this isn't a dream. And if it is a dream, I am going to be very upset when I wake up.

He can't keep his hands off me, either. It's not a sexual touch. Even when we were making love, it was different than before he died. It wasn't sexual desire that kept us going all day; it was something much more. There is a fundamental need to be near each other, as if we need to be together in order to exist.

I thought when I finally did see him we would talk more. I thought I would want all my questions answered. The overwhelming passion for him is making it hard to do anything other than just be with him. Death hasn't changed the softness of his skin, and it didn't take away the perfect rosiness to his cheeks. Maybe he really isn't dead. But if he isn't dead, who did I bury?

The scalding-hot water seals us in our own personal time capsule. Kissing and hugging, we only come up for air when the water running down our faces drowns us. We shower until the hot water is long gone and I can no longer control my shivering. The steam is so thick when we step out of the shower it swaddles us like a blanket. If he is dead, why is he warm? Why can I feel his pulse beating inside me?

We race to the bed and crawl under the covers. We continue where we left off in the shower, becoming one in every way imaginable. Barely moving, we connect. I exhale; he takes my breath as his, and I lose it.

I didn't want to waste time crying. That's what crying is: a waste of time. It doesn't fix anything. I can't control myself.

"Are you okay?" he asks, concerned.

I nod yes. I am. I am okay. I am better than okay. Biting his bottom lip through my staccato breathing, I compose myself.

He backs away, and I panic. He never pulls away. Sensing my fear, he kisses my forehead and wipes my eyes so I can see into his. Like always, he knows what I need. It wasn't his voice I needed to hear. I needed to see the irrational, the unimaginable, and the impossible. I needed to see for myself that this is our reality.

As if it's been put on pause, I look into his eyes and watch the story of us continue. My body fills with goose bumps when I see what happened to the baby we lost.

That is why I had the déjà vu at the church when I went to see Pastor Gary. It was our baby being baptized.

My hands go numb as I watch us live life after life together. The rest of me follows my hands when I remember it all. Not déjà vu. Remember, actually remember. So many times in life we see something and can relate to it and say we've been in a situation like that before. This is different. I have actually been in every single situation playing in this movie.

I look away only after I see what happened to Xan. When I see how he died, I wish I hadn't watched.

"I'm sorry," he says. He didn't mean for me to see that either.

"Who did it?"

"You didn't see?"

I shake my head ever so slightly. I was able to see everything else: how we died in previous lives, how in other lives he suffered as I have in this one. Why didn't I see who killed him this time?

The strongest feeling of déjà vu is happening right this minute. I hold on to Xan. Maybe the drug is wearing off and he is going to leave soon. I am not ready for him to leave just yet.

"Who did it?" I ask again. I could recognize this move of his a million miles away.

He's pretending he didn't hear me. He tries again to get me to go to sleep. "Close your eyes," he whispers in my ear.

I don't want to, but the beating of his heart is lulling me

to sleep. Lying on his chest and listening to his heart is one of my favorite things to do. No matter how upset I am, how distracted, how angry, like the hypnotic swirl of his eyes, his heart has the ability to take away everything bad.

Xan

SIX DAYS LEFT

"You've got to be kidding me!" I fell asleep with Lila, flesh to flesh. I felt her heartbeat pounding into my rib cage. And now I am back where I started.

She is going to wake up and think it was the best dream she ever had. What if it was it a dream? No. I'm stronger than I was yesterday. I feel her flowing through my veins. I've never gotten this kind of power from passing through her. Lila is the only person who could give me strength like this. The strength I feel now, could only come from flesh to flesh contact.

The sheets are still warm on my side of the bed. I touch her, and she rolls over onto my pillow, destroying the only evidence that I was there.

"Wes! Conner! Whoever the hell you are!" Please hear me. The only other person I know where I am is Irene. I am down to six days. I can't lose one.

"I'm right here," he says.

Without another thought I am sucked in his direction. He has the same power over me that Lila does. He isn't far from Lila's boat. By the looks of it, he's been there all night. He looks like crap.

"Dude, when you are human, you need to eat and sleep," I remind him.

He thanks me for the much-needed reminder and tells me he isn't on Earth to survive. "I told her I'd keep her safe. I'm going to honor that promise."

He doesn't say it, but I think it's his way of making up for what he's done. He looks really guilty. He won't look at me. I should tell him it's okay. It's not okay, but I get it. I can't resist her either. I don't have to. "She drank it."

"What happened?"

Is he for real? "Do you want the details?"

He stops acting as if he's truly interested in the reeds of grass he has made into the world's longest grass rope. "What did it do?" he spells out. He looks like he is about to cry.

"I came back."

He didn't know what it would do. He sits up a little straighter, then stands up. "No shit, heartbeat and all?" he asks, clearing his throat.

Recalling the feel of her skin on my lips automatically brings a smile to my face. Tingles fill me up, and I find myself biting my lip like a twelve-year-old girl seeing her favorite movie star in real life.

"I'll take that as a yes," he says, patting me on the back.

We take a step back from each other. "Did you feel that?" I ask. Wes examines his hand like he has just touched an alien. "I'll take that as a yes."

"Why are you still . . ." After clearing his throat, he continues, "You connected with her, right?" He's not asking. He's trying to figure it out himself.

"Shit, you don't know?"

"This doesn't make any sense." He is still looking at his hand. I've never seen a man think so hard. I think it's painful for him, trying to come up with an impossible explanation. "Xan," he begins.

I don't let him finish. "I still have six days." What choice do I have but to look on the bright side?

He isn't paying attention to me anymore. He's looking at the boat. "She's up."

Does he have other supernatural abilities, or did he see the boat rock? Lila weighs less than most dogs. Her jumping off the bed wouldn't make that mini ship move an inch.

"She's sick."

"What do you mean she's sick? She was fine a few hours ago." Simultaneously we race to her. I go through the fiberglass walls. Wes uses the door.

We arrive in time to see her violently throwing up. I rush to her side, but I back up just as quickly. Making her shiver isn't going to help. Wes gives me an honest-to-God look of sympathy. In return, I give him the okay to move in on my territory.

Helpless, I do nothing as he holds her hair back and dabs her head with a cool washcloth. He gets the shower ready for her. I tell him to make it hotter. He only leaves the room once she is stable enough to stand on her own. He makes her promise to sit on the bench in the shower and assures her that he will be waiting right outside the door if she needs anything.

I don't leave the room, but I do stay far enough away so I don't make her colder.

She looks awful. What did we do? Is that potion going to kill her? The only time I've seen Lila throw up was right after she found her dad with Hannah's mom. This is bad.

Letting the water beat down on the back of her neck, she drops her head between her knees and vomits more. Together we watch the bright orange bile spiral down the drain.

"Are you okay?" Wes asks. He cracks the door a few inches and tosses in a pair of sweatpants and a sweatshirt. I shoo him out; he's letting cold air in.

"I'm fine," she lies between barfing.

She sits hunched over for a few more minutes, letting the water warm her body up as much as possible before shutting it off. Once I know she's not going to fall over, I leave so the steam can keep her warm.

Wes and I wait on the other side of the door, petrified of

what could be happening to her.

"Oh my God." Lila exhales.

Neither Wes nor I move.

We wait for more. More puke. More tears. More signs that she is in pain and needs us. All she does is shut the fan off and open the door. An aggressive cloud of fog makes it hard to see at first. Once it clears, we see it. In the mirror, the words *I love you* are written as clear as day. In my handwriting.

Lila is sitting on the toilet, whimpering. I've seen those tears before. They are happy tears. I wrote that on the mirror last night after our shower together.

The color is starting to come back into her cheeks a little. She should go to the doctor in case she needs to get that stuff she drank out of her system.

Wes gets my message. He offers to take her.

Lila wouldn't be Lila if she welcomed help with open arms.

"Listen, I'm sure you're fine. Please." He is giving her his best attempt at a guilt trip. It's pathetic. She isn't buying it. "I'll be very happy when the doctor tells me you have the flu. You can even say I told you so," he offers. "I hope it wasn't that sandwich you made me yesterday."

He's good. He got a smile out of her. Even better, she's grabbing her purse.

The urgent care center is busy, unusually busy. We wait and wait and wait. Four people go before Lila is called. Don't get me wrong, I want Lila to be seen ASAP, but really, they can't take the baby who's been screaming, trying to rip his ears off his head for the past two hours, in first?

Hanging on to her stomach as she hobbles after the nurse, Lila quite resembles the Hunchback of Notre Dame. I'm with Wes; I'll be glad to hear she has a bad case of the stomach flu. I'm going to be in that room to hear it for myself.

Wes stays in his seat in the waiting room, where, like a good friend, he will wait until she is done. But just as Lila reaches the examination room, she realizes she is alone and looks back to Wes. Wes looks at me. Lila follows his gaze in an attempt to find me. Brokenhearted, I agree. She shouldn't have to be alone just because I'm jealous.

Lila takes off her sweatshirt and shoes before stepping on the scale. The nurse tells her it's unnecessary. Barely able to stand up straight, she's still worried about adding an extra few pounds. The nurse doesn't reveal a number. However, she does give her a concerned look before recording the number in her chart. I peek at her file while the nurse takes Lila's blood pressure and temperature: ninety-five pounds. The nurse may be skeptical of a weight below one hundred. But I smile. For Lila, this is actually pretty good. She is doing well.

"The doctor will be in shortly." The nurse says after guiding Lila and Wes into an open room.

Lila looks around the room, searching for me. When she realizes she has no idea where I am, she turns to Wes for help. He points her in my direction. The thin paper covering the bed crackles as she sits down. Wes sits in the chair next to the desk. He picks up a model of the female reproductive system. It's enough to break the uncomfortable silence. The two of them talk about this and that until the doctor comes in.

"Miss Walker?" he says, extending his hand to her. "I'm Dr. Mixon. What brings you in today?" He's reading her chart. It is obvious when he gets to her weight, because he looks her up and down with concern.

"I've been really tired, and this morning I was pretty sick," Lila tells him. "I haven't been thinking clearly lately, making a lot of bad decisions." She looks at Wes, embarrassed.

"You did just lose your boyfriend," Wes says.

"Yeah, I'm sure it's just stress," she says as the doctor looks into her throat.

"Could be. Deep breaths," the doctor instructs. She takes three deep breaths before he pulls his hand out from under her shirt. He removes his stethoscope from his ears, holds her wrist, and takes her pulse. "I want to run a few tests." Dr. Mixon gives her hands a professional yet comforting squeeze.

"Okay."

I saw that. The plea she just flashed Wes.

The doctor leaves. Wes and Lila are alone. They sit in silence until the nurse comes to take Lila away. Wes stays, and I go with her.

First the nurse draws her blood, three test tubes worth. What if they find traces of the potion in her system? I have to imagine there was some kind of illegal drug in it.

After drinking a small cup of apple juice, Lila is sent into the bathroom. She has to pee in a tiny cup. I'll stay outside for this one. A few minutes later Lila produces a cup full of very yellow pee. I'm sure they're not going to like seeing that, either.

After what seems like hours, the doctor returns. Lila and Wes are nervous. I'm sure Wes is for the same reasons as me. Neither of us wants Lila taken away for doing some sort of illegal drug she didn't even know she was taking.

"I've got an answer for you, why you are so sick," the doctor says. He looks first to Lila, then to Wes, like he's waiting for one of them to say it first. Aren't there some kinds of laws that require a parent to be with a minor? Why are they including Wes in on these results?

I guess they assume he is her boyfriend or something. No, wait—Wes just told the doctor she recently lost her boyfriend.

"You're fine. But you will probably be sick for a few more weeks," Dr. Mixon says.

We stare at him blankly while he looks at us like the answer is obvious.

When nobody says anything, he fills us in. "You're pregnant."

Lila has gone white.

Wes looks at me. He is green.

I am dizzy.

"I didn't know a test could come back positive that quickly," Lila says.

Flipping the chart closed and putting it down, the doctor chuckles. "Quick? Seven weeks isn't quick! That little bugger already has a heartbeat."

Wes looks at me. Lila follows his gaze, looking for mine. The energy of our emotional cocktail fills the room. Relief, fear, and happiness make the room silent. The doctor doesn't have a choice but to notice.

Lila's eyes are glassed over. Wes appears beyond relieved. What the good doctor doesn't know is why Wes is suddenly comforted. He's just realized he's not the father. I am.

"Here are some prenatal vitamins. You need to start taking them immediately. And you need to start taking better care of yourself: you are eating for two now."

In unison, they nod.

"Good. Do you have an OB/GYN?" he asks Lila.

She shakes her head. Possibly for the first time in her life, Lila is speechless. He hands her several pamphlets on pregnancy and a list of doctors who are accepting new patients. She hands them to Wes.

Why hasn't the doctor asked about her parents? She is only seventeen.

"Seven weeks?" she asks. She needs another verbal confirmation that the baby is mine.

Handing her a prescription and another large bottle of vitamins, he gives her the verification she asked for. "Seven weeks. Your ultrasound will tell you the exact date of conception."

She doesn't need an ultrasound to know the day. She knows exactly what day this baby was conceived.

SIX DAYS LEFT

Wes and I sit in the parking lot of the marina. We've been here for the last twenty minutes. All I can think about is what could have been. What should have been. Our wedding day. The birth of this child.

Xan and I have had children. We have lost children. I place my hand over my stomach and silently tell our baby that this time it will be different. We will be a family. Somehow.

I unbuckle my seat belt and open the car door. "Are you sure you don't want me to stay?" Wes asks.

He means well. He does. And I'm thankful he was with me today. Wes has to be who or what he says he claims to be. A mere mortal wouldn't have understood my reaction. No human would have known what I was thinking without me saying a word.

"I'll call you," I promise. I intend to. He hands me the bottle of vitamins I left in the cup holder. How do people swallow these horse pills without puking? They smell like crap. I have to take them. It's not just my body anymore.

"Call me," he instructs.

"You are leaving with my car. I'll call you," I say with a smile.

Hesitantly, he drives away. Did Xan stay in the car with him, or is he with me? The life I'd been planning with Xan was taken away from me. Just. Like. That. I've been thrown another curveball. A few words and one single moment turned my entire world upside down. Losing a few pounds, Jason acting psychotic, wondering what I'm going to do with the rest of my life. It doesn't matter. Everything that seemed important a few hours ago is now trivial.

"Where have you been?" Jason asks. I didn't see him. I might have turned around and tried to catch up to Wes if I had known he was waiting for me.

I don't want to deal with him. Not now.

I inspect him intensely. His question doesn't sound threatening, but lately with Jason, I never know. Taking my chances, I climb aboard.

"Why haven't you returned any of my calls?"

Robotically I answer his questions, taking extreme caution not to divulge any more information than necessary. I haven't had enough time to completely wrap my head around the fact that I am going to have a baby. I'm not ready to battle with Jason about it. "I forgot my phone." Avoiding eye contact as I unlock the door, I attempt to get inside without him noticing the massive pill bottle I'm trying to hide.

I am unsuccessful. He removes the bottle from the refrigerator the second I let go of the door. Dr. Mixon told me the pills don't smell as bad if they are kept cold.

"You slept with him?" he asks, sounding heartbroken.

"You really thought we hadn't slept together?" I snatch the bottle out of his hand. The dumbfounded look on his face makes me feel like a slut. He doesn't know I slept with Wes.

Does he? Oh God, he thinks it's Wes's baby.

"It's Xan's." I clarify any confusion.

I expected him to be mad. That seems to be Jason's preferred emotion lately. I keep a safe distance from him, in case he decides to come at me.

He doesn't.

He takes the vitamin bottle back and opens it up. The stench makes both of us gag. He sets a single vitamin the size of a massive jellybean on the counter. Handing me a bottle of water, he points to the pill. "Take it."

I do as I'm told.

He hasn't had a real reaction yet. Maybe this is it. He's looking down at the floor. I duck under so I can see his face. After I force myself under him so he has no choice but to look at me, he stands up, lifts me, and sets me on the icy countertop.

Jason is the first one to start talking. "Do you remember the time we went to Sea World, when we got to go behind the scenes and see where the dolphins were kept?"

I try to forget that day.

"You started yelling at the trainers about how cruel it was to keep them in such small spaces." He laughs.

I cringe, thinking about it. I didn't care what people thought of me at the time, but now, each time I relive it in my head, I grow more and more mortified. The trainers asked me politely to shut up. I didn't. I made a bigger scene, calling them out on their hypocrisy. I only said things that were true, but apparently they didn't want the rest of the world knowing their secrets. After being escorted out kicking and screaming, I had to wait in the bus alone for the rest of the group to finish the tour.

"What happened to that girl?"

He can look all he wants for that girl. She is long gone. I shrug and twist the bottom of my sweatshirt around my fingers. That day, when I got kicked out of Sea World, I realized that it doesn't matter what you believe in or what you know. Someone bigger and more powerful is in control of your life.

He tries again. "What happened, Lila? That girl left long before you met Xan. I've been blaming him, hating him for stealing you away from me, when I should have been thanking him."

"Excuse me?"

"Lila, Xan saved you."

Why is he being so nice, acting as if Xan is the BFF he

missed out on because he was jealous? "I stopped being deluded that I could actually make a difference," I say.

"Is that the problem?"

"What?"

"That girl, the one who didn't care what others thought, she had a voice that demanded to be heard. That girl, the one I fell in love with, is still there," he says, touching my heart. "She's in there, I know she is."

I tell him she is dead.

"Not dead. Lost. It's the perfect time to find her, Lila."

Here he comes, the Mr. Hyde to Jason's Dr. Jekyll. I hop down off the counter.

"You're hiding behind him."

I stop walking.

He doesn't approach me, and his voice is soft. "Lila, he isn't coming back."

Placing my hand on my belly, I know he is wrong.

"Open your heart to me, Lila. See that there is still beauty in the world. Go outside and look at the trees. Look at the lake. Stop torturing yourself."

I wish I knew how to explain all of this to him without sounding like a crazy person. I want to tell him that I am not delusional. That I'm not holding on to hope that isn't there. I want to tell him that last night I looked into Xan's eyes and saw the impossible. I want to be able to tell him how wonderful it was to fall asleep in Xan's arms again. How the echoing of his heart is what got me out of bed this morning.

"Let me do this with you, Lila."

I can't tell him. I can't tell him, because he doesn't want Xan to exist. Jason wants to be the one who replaces him, not the one who brings him back from the dead.

I should say something, but what? Why is he not freaking out, telling me I need to "take care of it"? I've seen Jason's way of dealing with unexpected pregnancies. He's had several. I can only assume that he would see this as an unwanted pregnancy.

"I'm supposed to believe that you are ready to help me raise a baby?"

"Yes."

"In high school?"

"Yes."

"What about college?" I ask.

"We'll figure it out."

"You're going to be faithful to me for the rest of your life?"

Swallowing the painful thought of having sex with one person for the rest of his life, he answers, "I will." He tries to cover up the awkward pause, but I heard it. I am making him uncomfortable.

I can have multiple personalities too. I pull him even closer and reach for his hands. They are clammy. I smile. "Love the baby as your own when you'll never be able to forget that he is the child of the man you hated?" I ask. I place his left hand on my stomach, which I now know is swollen with the life inside me, not period bloating.

Taking his hand off me, he lies, "I can do this, Lila."

I stop torturing him. "No, you can't, and you don't want to."

"How do you know what I want?"

"Jason, you've slept with more girls than I can count. Drugs and alcohol are your go-to vices when things get tough."

"I'm not that guy anymore and you know it. You're trying to put this on me, make me look like the bad guy so you don't have to feel guilty when your child doesn't have a father and you don't have a husband."

A few days ago, maybe even this morning, this might have bothered me. "Jason, I'm not good for you. The sooner you realize this, the sooner you can stop painfully trying to force something that isn't meant to happen."

"Lila." He has to take a moment to compose himself. "You don't even know the amount of agony I'm in."

Is he serious? Did he just compare the embarrassment of me refusing to be with him to me losing Xan? Why is he laughing like that? It's creepy.

"You should go. I'm tired." I am. But that's not why I want him to leave. I'm dying to tell Xan the mind-blowing, extraordinary news, though I'm sure he was in the room when Dr. Mixon said I was pregnant. I know he was. I caught Wes looking at him.

I tune out Jason's ramblings when I realize things are the same as they were yesterday. I can't see Xan. I've been so preoccupied with throwing up and finding out I'm having Xan's baby I didn't notice. After last night, we were supposed to be together. I don't care if it's here or there. I need to be with him. Why are we not together?

Jason isn't leaving, and I am starting to freak out. I grab my cell phone and head for the door. If I can't see Xan, I need to talk to someone who can. "I'll see you later, Jason." I slam the door behind me before he has a chance to stop me.

My parents told me never to run on the dock. It isn't safe. They are right; it is rickety. Today I ignore everything they have ever told me. The fear of never seeing Xan again pushes me to run faster.

I don't stop when I hear Jason calling for me. When I hear him jump off the boat, I run faster. Passing the cars in the parking lot, I hide behind the Dumpsters and stay frozen while he looks around for me. Wes has my car; maybe Jason will forget that, and go chasing after me, thinking I drove away. I can see he wants to look under every car and behind every shed, but Jason is smart. He knows that everyone knows who he is here. If he looks suspicious, people are going to start asking questions. The screech of his tires as his car peels out of his parking spot isn't enough to convince me he is gone. I wait to come out until I'm sure he's left the marina.

My stomach rumbles. I'm sure it's gas or hunger, but I

imagine it's the baby moving. Warming her up, I hug her with my palms. The gas bubble moves again. This time it tickles the underside of my hands. "Xan, are you there?"

He doesn't answer. There isn't a cool breeze, my ring isn't on fire, and I can't feel him hovering behind me.

I slam my back into the empty Dumpster. The crash travels through the marina and back. What am I doing? What kind of mother am I going to be if I keep holding on to the unrealistic fantasy that my baby's daddy is coming back from the dead? I can't do that to her. Or him. Or me.

I don't want to let Xan go, and I don't want to admit that Jason might be right. I need to start thinking about what is best for my child, not what's best for me. I try one more time. "Xan, please, if you're here, please give me a sign." Please, please, please. I rock myself back and forth waiting for his answer.

I wait. Not for a few minutes, not for a few hours, but until it turns dark. He isn't coming.

TWO DAYS LEFT

It's been four days. It's worse than usual. It's like it was the day I was buried, the day this all started, before I made the choice to contact her. I can see her, so I know how much pain she is in. I can even sense it. What I can't do is hear anything, and I can't get close enough to her for her to feel me. I am once again on display at the museum, and I think my exhibit is about to expire. Where did I mess up?

Wes killed a man. It makes sense why he lost. I didn't touch Jason. I did everything I was told, and look what it's gotten me. Will I ever get to hear my baby cry or hold Lila's hand as the baby is being born? Am I going to be able to lie next to Lila as she falls asleep, or do I have to watch from a tightly sealed glass box as she moves on with her life?

Lila has been playing with her phone all morning. She hasn't taken any calls since she found out she was pregnant. I saw her try to dial my mom's number a couple of times, but she can't bring herself to hit the send button. Jason goes to voice mail. So does Wes, which surprises me. She likes him. I know she does.

"Who is she afraid to call?" I am talking to myself. I place my hands on the glass and try to break through. It's pointless.

"You can find out," a female voice says. Unless there are others in this realm who I don't know about, it's Irene.

Her icy finger tracing the back of my neck confirms my assumption.

"What do you want?" I ask, pulling away from her.

"It's not what I want; it's what you want," she teases.

"Time is up." I have one more day after today before Lila is gone forever. "I messed up."

"Giving up so soon? I thought you were a fighter, Xan."

If this is her way of trying to make me feel better, it's not working.

"You have until the end of tomorrow; that is a very long time."

Spending two days camping is a very long time. When it's all the time you've got left with the woman you are destined to be with, it's no time at all. "I only have one day to offer you, and that's not even enough to get to punch Jason in the face."

"I'll make you a deal," she offers.

"I'm listening."

"I will give you one last chance with Lila for your one remaining day."

"Alive?"

Irene laughs. "No. Not for one day. For one day I will let you out of your glass prison so you can hear her, smell her, feel her."

"If?" There has to be more.

"If by midnight you figure out why the two of you are not yet together, you win," she says.

"If we don't?"

"If you don't, I get the complete, indestructible soul."

She'd have to kill Lila to get her half. "No way." I want to walk away from her, but I have nowhere to go. I'm a caged animal.

"Have it your way. I hope she is able to love your baby."

Why would she say something so awful? Lila will be a great mother. She will love that baby more than life itself. She will love it because it's her child, it's our child, and every time she looks at it she will think of me. But this could make the baby a constant reminder of what should have been, what can never be. She won't be able to forget me even if she wants to.

"I'll do it. Irene?" I call.

She is nowhere.

But I can hear Lila. I didn't see who she called. My guess is Wes. I don't think she would have called Jason to meet her at Madame Tula's. I sit next to Lila on the front steps. I sit very, very close. She rubs her left arm and hugs herself tightly. She can feel me.

She bounces up when she see Wes coming around the corner. Reaching up on her tippy toes, she hugs him, trying to contain how excited she is to see him. I think she is a little relieved that he actually showed up.

"How are you feeling?" He touches her belly, which is actually beginning to look pregnant—she is so skinny that any added weight is obvious. Or it could be that I see her as pregnant now that I know she is.

It is so good to hear her voice.

"Good," she lies.

He doesn't believe her.

"I'm fine, just trying to take it all in." She sits back down on the steps. "She isn't here."

Wes looks leery. Should he be here? Should she be here? Should I be here? "You scared?"

I'm not sure if he's asking about the baby or Madame Tula.

"I can't keep living like this, waiting for him to show up, hoping for a cool breeze to sweep across my face. It's not good for me and it's not good for the baby."

Ouch.

He looks at me for help; he doesn't know what he should tell her. Wes doesn't know I made a deal with Irene. If he tells Lila what she needs to hear, that she needs to let me go, I will be thrust into exile, game over. If he tells her what she wants to hear, that I'm here, she will continue to hope. By midnight this will all be over. *Bad place to be, my friend.*

"What if you raise the baby?" I say to Wes.

"Stop it." He could be talking to her, but I'm pretty sure it was directed at me. He isn't going to stop fighting for me until he watches me get sucked into whatever world I'll be going to if this doesn't work.

Wes is going to be so pissed when he finds out we've only got today to figure this out. "It's the last day," I say under my breath, half hoping he doesn't hear me.

Exploding off the step, he gets in my face. I've never been so happy to be in a different realm from Wes. He is so angry he doesn't know what to do. The rage is flowing out of him anywhere it can. He looks like a cartoon character just before smoke is about to come out of its ears. He is ready to kick my ass right now. "Did you not learn anything from my mistakes?"

No.

Lila watches as Wes silently faces off with the boy she can't see but knows is there.

"I know I shouldn't have done it," I start. "After we were together, I couldn't hear her. I was put behind the thick wall I was behind the day you found me. Four days!" I know it doesn't justify what I did. He has every right to be pissed.

"That doesn't make any sense."

"I don't know what I did wrong. I had to be close to her. Wes, two days. I'd rather choose one last day of being close to her over two last days completely out of reach. If these were the last moments I was going to be near her, I had to be as close as possible," I explain.

He doesn't want to understand, but he does. "Tonight?"

"Tonight what?" Lila asks. "What is Xan saying?"

Wes and I try to find the right way to tell Lila. But is there a good way to tell her that if we don't figure out what went wrong by midnight tonight, she is never going to see me again and that we will not have another chance at life together? I don't think there is any good way to deliver that message.

"What is going on?" She is so jealous that he can see me and she can't. She should be upset. She should be able to see me.

The two of them have stepped a few feet away from Madame Tula's shop and have fallen into the rhythm of my pacing. Madame Tula didn't say hello. I think she was trying to sneak by them. But the loud click of the key turning in the old door makes her presence known.

"You could put a sign out that says when you'll be back!" Lila fires at her. She doesn't wait to be invited in.

Wes is less eager to enter. He knows what this woman is capable of. But the very same fear that keeps him standing outside the door is what makes him enter. He doesn't want Lila to get hurt.

Madame Tula ignores them, going about her business as if they are not there. She takes the scarf off her head and turns the stove on. She is always at that stove.

"You stole something from me," Madame Tula says. She pours three cups of tea; Lila and Wes look at them skeptically when she offers it to them. "Relax. I no longer have any reason to hurt either of you. Or you," she says, toasting her glass to me.

Lila glances in my direction and misses me by a few feet. Double kick in the stomach. It's really not fair that Madame Tula can see me too and she can't.

"Did you drink it?"

Lila nods.

"What happened?"

Like an insecure child, she seeks Wes's approval. Since when does Lila need permission to speak? "He was here," she stammers.

"Interesting."

"Why is that so interesting?" Wes snaps, breaking his silence. "That's why you created it. So Xan would materialize and you could kill him."

Her demonic cackle fills the room as she climbs a ladder. Hidden on the top shelf, behind dozens of jugs, is a tiny box that resembles a casket. After pulling a skeleton key out from under her shirt, she unlocks the box.

We watch to see what could be so valuable that it requires not only being hidden and unreachable, but locked with a key safely tied around her neck.

What she pulls out shocks us all. A jar filled with things that have belonged to Lila and me over the years. Globs of hair that look like she scooped them off the floor at a barbershop. A golden heart necklace I gave Lila. Are those fingernail clippings? Gross. Photos of us from each life we've lived.

"What is that?" Lila asks, taking a closer look.

"You think I would leave the key to eternal life sitting on a shelf for the world to see?"

She has a point.

"So what did I steal?" Wes asks.

Lila doesn't let her answer him. "You told me you had something that would bring me to Xan."

Madame Tula smirks as she holds the box up and shakes it.

"What did I drink?" Lila asks, holding her stomach. She has to be wondering what she put in her system. What she gave our baby.

"Vinegar, salt, molasses, and habanero peppers," Madame Tula says, locking the box and putting it back up on the top shelf.

Lila is on her way to a full-fledged panic attack.

"Wes, you gotta tell her it was real. I know it was," I insist.

Wes agrees and tries to comfort her.

She shoves him away. "Then how?" Lila asks. She looks like her brain is going to explode.

Coming down off the ladder, Madame Tula cautiously approaches Lila. For the first time, she looks kind. "My dear, you came to me looking for someone to tell you what you wanted to be real."

"It wasn't real?" Lila asks, heartbroken.

"I didn't say that. I got what I needed, thanks to this fellow." She grabs Wes's arm. "If Xan was in your arms, it was because of the two of you. You made magic," she insists as she shakes Lila.

Lila can barely breathe.

"I told you the very first time I met you that the two of you together are extremely powerful. You didn't need me. You came to me because you needed someone to tell you that you are not in fact crazy."

"Am I crazy?"

"No, you're not," Wes says.

ONE DAY LEFT

"What the hell are you doing, Jason?" I ask, hiding behind Wes like a coward. I may be brave, but I am not an idiot. Don't piss off the guy with the gun.

If Wes hadn't suggested turning around and heading back to the boat, Jason probably would have shot us in the back of our heads.

Why does Jason have a gun?

His focus is terrifying. A bizarre series of twitches has taken over his head. He looks possessed, like he's trying to shake a demon out of himself. "I got rid of Xan so we could be together, Lila. She told me that if I got rid of the obstacle, we could be together. Why am I not good enough for you? Why?"

He is rapidly approaching us, gun shaking in his hands, still pointed at us. I know this park like my own backyard. Wes and I are going to hit sand if he backs us up about four more feet. After that: water. Wes tries to stop me when I pry his hands off my arm. This isn't his battle. It's me Jason wants.

"You didn't know!" Jason laughs. The way he is flailing the gun around, I'm not sure he knows which direction he wants to aim or who he wants to shoot.

"Lila, come back here!" Wes commands.

I ignore Wes and take two steps closer to Jason. He isn't going to kill me. Jason wasn't afraid Madame Tula was going to tell me something about Xan; he was afraid she was going to tell me something about *him*. It also explains his nervousness when he thought a cop was near. "Why?" I ask.

It all adds up. He said he did it. Jason has been in his fair share of trouble, but murder, that's a whole different ball game.

"Jason, put the gun down." Wes tries talking some sense into him.

Aiming the gun at Wes, Jason takes his focus off me, giving me a chance to get closer without him blowing my head off. Where did he get that gun? "You don't get to talk here," he tells Wes. "This is between Lila and me."

He sees that I've moved. He doesn't like it. Grabbing me by the arm with the strength I've become too familiar with, he slams my body into his. With me securely at his side and a gun pointed at Wes, he hisses through clenched teeth, "We are supposed to be together."

I know this isn't the time to be a control freak. I know that, but I can't help myself. "No. We're not."

I haven't been able to sense Xan much these past few days. It could be my imagination, but I'm pretty sure I just heard him scream at me.

It's not my imagination. Wes is arguing with him as I try to defuse Jason, who is too focused on keeping me glued to him to notice the apparently insane person talking to himself three feet away.

His strength is miraculously increasing, constricting me tighter by the minute. "We could have had it all, Lila, if you would have just loved me." He shifts his noose-like grip from my arm to around my neck.

"Loosen your grip, man. She can't breathe!" Wes yells, pointing at my face, which, if I could see it, would probably look gray by now. The pressure behind my eyes is intense. I wouldn't be surprised if they popped out of my head.

My vision is blurred, so I don't know exactly how Wes got Jason to realize he was killing me. He loosens his grip, and I squirm free, collapsing to the ground.

In slow motion, like in the movies, it happens. Somewhere between Wes lunging to catch me and me reaching up for him, Jason gets in the middle.

Two shots are fired.

The black pistol drops out of Jason's hand, landing with a gentle thud in the sand.

It's late. There isn't anyone around to see what happened. There isn't anyone to help.

"Wes!" I scream! What do I do? I didn't think I needed to know what to do when someone has been shot. Being involved in a shooting? Not on my to-do list. "Call the police, Jason!" I have to use all of my strength to grab hold of Wes's limp body as it falls toward the sand.

He can't die.

I prop Wes up in my lap. "I lied," he whispers. "There can only be one complete soul."

Holding him, I ask, "What?" Now is when he wants to confess his sins?

"Now, there is only one," Wes utters, barely audible.

He is trying to say something else, but I can't make it out. He's starting to gurgle. I don't know much, but in the movies this seems to be the beginning of the end. I put the phone down and focus on him.

"Three," Wes barely spits out.

"You're going to be okay." I rock him, trying to believe my own words. He is covered in blood. "I don't know what you're saying."

"You're shot," Jason says.

"Shut up, Jason!" If I have any blood on me, it's from Wes. I hate Jason. I've never hated anyone or anything more in my life. I thought my dad was the lowest piece of scum on this Earth. I was sorely mistaken. My dad is a saint compared to this asshole. Someone needs to pistol-whip the crap out of him. He's ruined my life.

Wes clings onto my waist as I stand. My legs must have fallen asleep from having his head in my lap.

Jason looks like a wax-museum figure. He doesn't move as I come within reach of him. I wish he were wax; all I'd have to do is stick him under a heat lamp to get rid of him.

"Lila, you're hit." His voice is shaking. Slowly he points the hand that moments ago held a gun at me.

I rip off my shirt to prove him wrong. I can use it to help slow down Wes's bleeding. Once it's under control, I will give Jason a piece of my mind.

I dramatically flaunt my half-naked body to show him that the only thing wrong with me is the ghastly white color of my skin. As much as I need to be right, I am not. I can't prove him wrong, not tonight. Below my ribs, above my left hipbone, is a bullet.

I wipe away a pool of blood surrounding the object lodged in my side. Immediately the bullet is hidden behind a flow of blood gushing from inside me. It doesn't hurt. I feel no pain. There has to be a mistake.

No mistake. I drop to my knees. I may not be able to feel the pain of having a hole in my side, but I can't feel my legs, either. Like a piercing only the craziest punks request, my stomach is adorned with antique gold. It's wedged three-fourths of the way in.

Digging my left hand in the sand for leverage, I use my right to burrow my fingernails in my flesh. Once I've got a good grip under the ridges of the bullet, I pull. "Ahhhhh!" I shriek.

A tiny piece of metal sealed my fate. Covered in blood, it doesn't even glisten in the moonlight. I throw it at Jason. It hits him in the forehead before sinking into the sand leaving a bloody mark between his eyes.

I laugh. First, a small giggle, wishing I were a superhero so I could fix this messed-up situation. Now, it's a deep belly laugh I can't control. With each contraction, blood spurts out. It looks ridiculous and makes me laugh even harder.

How did this happen? How did I go from having it all—the career and love of my life—to dying alone on the beach? I should be scared; death is most likely minutes away. I'm sad—not for me, but for the baby. She didn't deserve to die. She never even got a chance at life. That isn't fair.

But I'm happy. "Thank you."

I can barely move my legs, and I'm losing a lot of blood. I am getting weak. Dragging myself with my arms, I make my way to Wes. He isn't very far away, but I'm not sure I can make it in time.

I'm too late. Wes is gone. I kiss his cheek, it is still warm.

"This is your fault, Jason." It takes a lot, but I find it, the strength I need to get up before it's too late. He can't get away with this. He took everything from me. I want him to watch me die knowing what I really think of him. In my effort to stand, I end up toppling over on Wes. His left shoulder is supporting all my weight. I start to apologize, and then I remember he's dead. Struggling, I brace myself on his arm until I am sure I can do stand up fully without falling. I am almost upright when I see Wes's finger. He is clearly pointing at something, and his head is looking in the same direction. It could be the moon. It could be Jason. I follow it to see.

It's neither.

I find a focal point. I've lost a lot of blood, and I just saw a man die. I could be dying myself. The moon is barely a crescent. He is here. He isn't far away. He is next to me, holding my hand.

"Lila?" Xan asks. Trusting he is really here, I disintegrate into his arms so he can cradle me as I did Wes moments ago.

"What the hell is going on?" Jason screams.

I wish I could see Jason. I want to see the terror on his face. I want to see him get what's coming to him. I don't want him to die. I want him to suffer.

Of course I can see Xan; I'm dead.

Xan's touch is warm on my stomach. The heat quickly turns

to fire. His hand sinks into me, turning my insides into lava. He is saying something, but the only thing I can hear is the scream of agony in my head.

The world turns to a blacked-out blur. The outline of the moon is the only thing I see through my half-closed lids. It hurts. A lot. I try not to yell or cry. Xan strokes my face. I must not be doing a very good job of pretending I'm fine.

The inferno never spreads. My arms, legs, and head, and the rest of my torso, remain cool. I focus on the chilly sand under my fingertips and imagine it putting the flames out.

It seems to be working. The pain has dulled, and I can hear his voice again. I hear the water lapping against the shore. I am swaddled tightly in Xan's arms. He is shaking. I've never felt him tremble like this.

He is devastated. I can't allow him to think I'm dead. I can't hide any longer behind my fear of what will be when I open my eyes. Wait. "Am I dead?"

"I don't know," he says with a huge sigh of relief.

"Are you?" I ask.

"I don't know."

When he lets me out of his death grip, we examine each other, looking for an explanation as to what is going on. I peel his hand away from my stomach. "It's gone," I say. The bullet, the blood. There is no evidence that I was ever shot.

Xan turns me over and searches the rest of my body. Nothing. We both look, over and over again. Nothing. My torso is as flawless as a porcelain doll.

Looking at Wes's still-lifeless body, I question his words. "Wes said something about there being only one soul, and that there were three. Oh, and he said he lied." I'm trying to make sense of the pieces Wes told me moments before he died, saying them out loud, hoping Xan can help.

"He didn't lie," Xan says, turning back to me. Caressing my cheek, looking at me with the eyes I've missed so much. The face that can't find the words to tell me how much he loves me, but I can feel them. "He chose to not tell us everything."

And then it hits me. Placing my hand on his cheek, I return his intensely powerful gaze. "He knew we would never let him go through with all of it."

Xan nods, pulling me close again. "A complete soul is *two* people. Wes realized he was the third wheel—that with him still in existence, we couldn't succeed in being together. He knew his chances were gone, but that if he died, we could live forever together, as intended."

Jason stands over the two of us and Wes, unable to comprehend anything that has happened tonight. Seeing the person he beat, killed, and pushed to the bottom of Lake Michigan standing in front of him has to be a pretty terrifying sight.

"So Wes died and you came alive," I say slowly, understanding.

"He died so we could have a chance. But I don't think we are alive," Xan says.

That's fine and dandy. I'd believe him with my astonishing healing and all, but if we are dead, how can Jason still see us?

Xan shrugs and shakes his head in disbelief. He is thinking the same thing I am. Wherever, whatever we are, we are together. Like the day I met Xan, we are able to read each other's minds.

After standing up, I help Xan to his feet. I lead us away from Jason, from this beach, from this world. It doesn't matter if we are dead or alive, because we're together.

ACKNOWLEDGMENTS

Shawn Stevens—Hi, Baby . . . Your confidence in my ability to create something from nothing and your unwavering support continue to leave me speechless. Thank you for always knowing when I need to be reminded I must write. You see me, baby—all of me. Because of you, I know what it feels like to love, what it feels like to be loved— Because of you, I've found peace. I'm happy . . . I'm home . . . You are my other half. Against all odds—we found each other . . . and now, we are an iceberg. Thank you. Thank you for celebrating my wins with me, and for always believing in me, especially when I didn't believe in myself. I love you—infinity.

Matthew, Keegan, and Cady—I have accomplished the greatest thing: I have proven to you that if you really believe in something, work hard, have patience, and trust that your dreams will come true . . . they will. Dreams do come true.

My parents, Nancy and Randy Stevens, thank you for your endless unconditional support. For never giving up on me. For always believing that one day, my dreams would come true—espsecially when I didn't. Thank you for allowing me to find myself, not in the easiest of ways, but my way. Thank you.

Melissa Stevens and Steve Schelkopf, thank you for believing I could actually write and sell books! Your generosity—being willing to help with anything I need—has never gone unnoticed or unappreciated. I will be forever grateful for your very insightful suggestion as to which name I should use. And your reminders to just "Do it! Do it! Do it!" are always appreciated!

My writers' group: Sheryl Davis-Troller, Cathy Walters, and Emily Norris. Who would have thought all those nights at Panera would have resulted in this! Without your input and guidance, this book would still be sitting on my zip drive. Thank you doesn't begin to describe my gratitude.

The entire team at SparkPress and BookSparks— Crystal Patriarche, Lauren Wise, Hannah Sichting, Brooke Warner, Robert Soares, Krissa Lagos, Kristin Bustamante—and anyone I forgot—I sincerely apologize!!! Having someone excited to publish my book is one thing. Having an entire team of incredible human beings committed to bringing my story to as many readers as possible is more than I could have ever hoped for. THANK YOU! THANK YOU! THANK YOU!

Karen Sherman, my editor. Thank you for believing in my writing—for looking at my story with as much love and care as I have. Thank you for seeing things I never would have considered, for helping me make this book better than I ever could have imagined. THANK YOU! Thank you from the bottom of my heart.

Thank you to the artist/musician who so graciously allowed me to use his lyrics in my debut novel.

No one has been a bigger supporter of my writing process than Emily Norris. Never once did she doubt that I would one day be able to call myself an author. With every manuscript request that came in, she felt the joy, hope, and excitement—through the almost-theres, complete rejections, and moments of wondering if I should stop altogether, she allowed me to feel the disappointment before pushing me to send out another query. She reminds me that I can't stop writing, not because I have a story to tell, but because it's who I am and what I am. Em, thank you for believing in me, supporting me—having complete faith in me.

ABOUT THE AUTHOR

CHEEKY MONKEY STUDIO

Jessica Stevens grew up knowing without a doubt that she would become a professional ballet dancer. When life told her otherwise, she went to college like the rest of the world and earned a degree in psychology. Shortly after, while raising her two boys, she found herself glued to her computer all hours of the night while everyone else slept. Today she lives in the suburbs of Milwaukee, spending her free time on lakes and rivers, in the air, and traveling as much as possible. Learn more about Jessica at www.jessicastevensbooks.com

SELECTED TITLES FROM SPARKPRESS

SparkPress is an independent boutique publisher delivering high-quality, entertaining, and engaging content that enhances readers' lives. Visit us at www.gosparkpress.com

Running for Water and Sky, by Sandra Kring. $17, 978-1-940716-93-0. Seventeen-year-old Bless Adler has only known betrayal—but then she falls in love with Liam. After a visit to a local psychic and a glimpse of Liam lying in a pool of blood, Bless now has 14 blocks to reach Liam and either beg him to fight for his life, or say good-bye to the first person who made her want to fight for her own.

Serenade, by Emily Kiebel. $15, 978-1-94071-604-6. After moving to Cape Cod after her father's death, Lorelei discovers her great-aunt and nieces are sirens, terrifying mythical creatures responsible for singing doomed sailors to their deaths. When she rescues a handsome sailor who was supposed to die at sea, the sirens vow that she must finish the job or faced grave consequences.

Beautiful Girl, by Fleur Philips. $15, 978-1-94071-647-3. When a freak car accident leaves the seventeen-year-old model, Melanie, with facial lacerations, her mother whisks her away to live in Montana for the summer until she makes a full recovery.

Blonde Eskimo, by Kristen Hunt. $17, 978-1-940716-62-6. In Spirit, Alaska on the night of her seventeenth birthday, the Eskimos rite of passage, Neiva is thrown into another world full of mystical creatures, old traditions, and a masked stranger. When Eskimo traditions and legends become real as two worlds merge together, she must fight a force so ancient and evil it could destroy not only Spirit, but the rest of humanity.

The Alienation of Courtney Hoffman, by Brady Stefani. $17, 978-1-940716-34-3. Fifteen-year-old Courtney Hoffman is determined not to go insane like her grandfather did—right before he tried to drown her when she was seven. But now she's being visited by aliens who claim to have shared an alliance with her now-dead grandfather. Now Courtney must put her fears aside, embrace her true identity, and risk everything in order to save herself—and the world.

Bear Witness, by Melissa Clark. $15, 978-1-94071-675-6. What if you witnessed the kidnapping of your best friend? This is when life changed for 12-year-old Paige Bellen. This book explores the aftermath of a crime in a small community, and what it means when tragedy colors the experience of being a young adult.

ABOUT SPARKPRESS

SparkPress is an independent, hybrid imprint focused on merging the best of the traditional publishing model with new and innovative strategies. We deliver high-quality, entertaining, and engaging content that enhances readers' lives. We are proud to bring to market a list of *New York Times* bestselling, award-winning, and debut authors who represent a wide array of genres, as well as our established, industry-wide reputation for innovative, creative, results-driven success in working with authors. SparkPress, a BookSparks imprint, is a division of SparkPoint Studio, LLC.

Learn more at GoSparkPress.com